ENTER THE RAVEN

A TANNER YORK THRILLER

ANDREW KENNING

ENTER THE RAVEN

A TANNER YORK THRILLER

ANDREW KENNING

DYK PUBLISHING, LLC

OTHER BOOKS BY
ANDREW KENNING

THE TANNER YORK THRILLER SERIES:

DEVIL DON'T GO

Published by
DYK Publishing, LLC
Raleigh, NC

Enter The Raven
Copyright © 2026 by Andrew Kenning.

All rights reserved. No part of this book may be used or reproduced or transmitted in any form or by any electronic or mechanical means, including photocopying, recording or by any information storage and retrieval system, without the written permission of the publisher, except where permitted by law.

This book is a work of fiction. Names, characters, places, businesses, organizations, and incidents either are the products of the author's imagination or are used fictitiously, and any resemblance to actual events or persons, living or dead, is entirely coincidental.

This work of fiction contains graphic sexual content and is for mature audiences only. It is intended only for those eighteen years of age or older. All sexually active characters portrayed in this book are consenting adults eighteen years of age or older. As a work of fiction, any similarities to any situations or persons living or dead are entirely coincidental. See trigger warnings in front of book.

Library of Congress Control Number: 2025922240
ISBN paperback: 979-8-9914197-2-7
ISBN ebook: 979-8-9914197-3-4

For information contact: DYKpub.com

Some cover images are licensed from shutterstock.com

Edited by: Scribendi.com
Cover and interior design by: Miblart.com

First Edition: 2026
1 3 5 7 9 10 8 6 4 2

DYK
PUBLISHING, LLC

For my Father August Kenning
A Hero

POSSIBLE TRIGGER / CONTENT WARNINGS

Spoiler Notice: Some items may reveal key plot points or outcomes in the story. Reader discretion is advised.

✦ Please take care of yourself while reading. Your mental health matters—to me and to you. If at any point these themes feel overwhelming, it's always okay to pause, step away, or return when you feel ready. ✦

- Violence and physical assault – including fistfights, beatings, and references to physical harm.
- Murder and death – including loss of loved ones and references to violent deaths.
- Medical experimentation – non-consensual trials and unethical pharmaceutical practices.
- Abuse of power – government secrecy, surveillance, manipulation.
- Psychological distress – trauma, anxiety, grief, and PTSD-like reactions.
- Language – strong profanity used in dialogue.
- Sexual content – consensual adult relationships, including heterosexual and same-sex intimacy.
- Substance use – alcohol consumption; possible references to drugs/medication.

- Loss of a child/young adult – references to the death of a character and others.
- Themes of betrayal and mistrust – among friends, allies, and authority figures.

For those who press on, welcome to the dark corners and bright sparks of this story. I hope it grips you, unsettles you, and most of all—I hope you enjoy the journey.

Andrew Kenning

CHAPTER ONE

The club was alive with the pulsating rhythm of the music, the bass thumping through the crowded room like a heartbeat. The smell of sweat and perfume hung heavy over the dance floor. With a confident stride, she stepped onto the stage with a fierce intensity, daring anyone to look away. A kaleidoscope of colors danced across her skin like fireflies on a summer night, casting a spell of seduction over the audience. With unwavering composure and undeniable authority, she held the spectators spellbound.

Most of the girls who worked at the Kinky Kitten Gentleman's Club, on the north side of Chicago, saw it as an opportunity for economic empowerment. The flexible hours and high earnings allowed them to support themselves and their families, pursue education, or save for a better future. The club provided a sense of community and support, where women looked out for each other and built lasting friendships. For many, it was more than just a job; it was a pathway to independence and personal growth. But that night, this dancer was there to save a life and stop a killer. The seriousness of the situation reflected in her eyes just as the lights reflected off the mirrored ball that hung above.

Topless, she strode to the chrome-plated pole at center stage as the spotlight highlighted the curves of her 5'6" frame. She pressed her bare back against the pole, and a cool wave swept through her. She gave her beach-blonde hair, with hints of caramel and gold, a playful tussle that sent the strands tumbling around her heart-shaped face. Her bow-shaped lips, painted into a perpetual pout, curled into a mischievous grin.

As she danced, they watched with desire etched deep on their faces. "Whoa, baby!" someone yelled as she shimmied down the pole. The crowd erupted in cheers and applause, their voices hoarse from shouting. "You're hot!" someone barked, as she bent and twisted, her movements fluid and seductive. The silver pole blurred around her, every movement sharp, fluid, and fully in control.

She dropped to all fours and prowled toward the edge of the stage, her focus narrowing to a woman seated near the front. Each movement was slow and deliberate, laced with intent. The room buzzed with tension, crackling with anticipation as something unspoken passed between them—an instant connection that needed no words.

As the dancer crept, a flurry of bills erupted—a rainbow of denominations fluttering above the sea of heads as they vied for her attention. One man, with a bent nose from an old break and deep-set eyes that gave him a hard, watchful look, flicked a ten-dollar bill toward the stage with practiced ease. Then he whistled—sharp and cutting. "Hey baby, marry me!" She passed on without answering.

The next man let out a loud whoop, waving a wad of cash. His eyes gleamed with excitement as he high-fived his buddies, the slap of their palms thundered through the room. "Woohoo, yeah!" he bellowed, his voice like a freight train crashing through the night.

Her feline-like advance continued as she passed a man who looked like he'd been plucked straight from a bygone era. His faded, ill-fitting suit seemed to be held together by threads of nostalgia, and the worn straw fedora perched atop his graying hair gave him a comical appearance amid the luxurious surroundings. He waved a limp five-dollar bill, staring intently at the dancer, a wide grin pulling at his mouth, sharp and joyless, like a wolf baring its fangs.

As her measured pace came to a standstill at the edge of the stage, the woman leaned forward, her face inches away, breath hot against the performer's skin.

"Come on, baby," the woman huffed, her voice husky with desire as she reached out to claim her prize. But the dancer was too quick, dodging the woman's grasp with a subtle twist of her body. She wagged her finger in a playful rebuke.

"No, no. No touch," she teased, a seductive edge in her voice.

"*Tu es un vilain petit chaton*, Sammy," the woman scolded.

"*Oui*, Jill, and it's Kylie in here, remember?" Sammy replied.

Jill dipped her head, her cheeks flushing a deep pink as she fumbled with her drink. "Oh, right, sorry Kylie," she muttered, her voice barely audible over the thumping music. The cacophony of the club swallowed their conversation whole, leaving only the faintest hint of her embarrassment. Jill reached out to place a hundred-dollar bill into Sammy's thong. "You're a naughty girl," she mumbled, as she slid the bill between Sammy's hip and the outstretched thong strap. Sammy released the strap, and with a snap, the benjamin was hers. Her hips wheeled, her body undulating like a river as she moved, her eyes never leaving Jill's face. The crowd exploded into cheers and applause, the roar surging over the stage like a tidal wave.

On the very first night of her dancing career, Samantha Rhodes became an undeniable force, her stage name flowing through the mob like a whispered legend. She was a sensation, effortlessly parting patrons from their money with a smile and a sway, and they surrendered it without a second thought.

Sammy's provocative pace continued. She shook her head, her long hair swishing behind her like a golden curtain. A scruffy bearded guy waved a ten-dollar bill, pleading for her attention. He bellowed like a bear. "Hey, Kylie, what will this buy me?"

"Your lunch tomorrow, from the dollar menu." Sammy gave the man a cheeky grin.

The man's buddies slapped him on the back, their faces red with amusement. As she continued her slink, a male rule breaker jumped on the stage, following her with hungry intent. Without missing a beat, she kept up her sensuous glide. Tiny, the club's massive bouncer, intercepted the intruder, tackling him with ease and ushering him off stage. The show must go on.

As the last of the heavy bass beats faded, Sammy gathered up her bra and made her leisurely stage exit, blowing a kiss to the audience as she disappeared behind the curtains. Now backstage, it took Sammy a moment to adjust to the dimly lit stairs leading into the hallway that connected to the dancers' changing room. Sammy's bare feet pattered against the steps as she descended, the damp coolness backstage, a welcome respite from the heat of her performance. She hit the bottom stair and launched into Tanner York's arms, her lips crashing against his in a searing kiss.

"Hi Tiger, so was my performance great?" she purred, her thigh wedging between his legs as she pressed against him.

Tanner York's face softened into a slow, easy smile as he lost himself in the depths of her cognac eyes. "You were fantastic."

Sammy spun around, pressing her back to Tanner's chest as she leaned into him. "Tell me, who's that tall, handsome, delicious black man over there?" she asked, her serpentine smile sliding across her face like a whispered secret. Still topless from her performance, she began a sensual walk toward the man. Her hips swayed with each step, a hypnotic rhythm that caught every glance. The man looked up, held onto her briefly before turning away with a cool, indifferent expression. But Sammy wasn't deterred; her gaze sparkled with mischief as she closed the distance. "Oh, I think he's trying to play hard to get," she called to Tanner, her voice bubbling with amusement.

"Sammy, not now." Frank's voice was a low growl, his stare flashing with warning.

But Sammy was undeterred. She moved closer, her gaze connected with Frank's in a way that felt electric, a spark passing between them. "Ty, come on, control your woman, man," Frank said, his voice rising in frustration.

Sammy took another step closer, her body inches from his, her breath tickling against his skin.

"I wish I could, Frank." Tanner's tone dry.

Frank's head darted around the room, as he shifted uncomfortably. "Damn it, Sammy," he muttered, his voice barely audible over the pounding of his heart.

Sammy's fingers danced across Frank's chest, tracing the contours of his muscles like a skilled artist. "Mmm, I just love a man with a well-chiseled chest," she said. "I hope you could see my performance from way back here. Did you like the part when I spread my legs open...?"

Frank's face went dark with embarrassment. "Ty, please, we're on a case. This is supposed to be undercover surveillance."

Tanner tossed her a robe, the fabric fluttering through the air like a lifeline. "Okay, Samantha, enough. You're making the big, strong, ex-military guy uncomfortable. Put this on and cover up. I'm about done seeing you exposed to all these guys anyway," he said, his voice firm.

Sammy pouted, her lips curling into a sulky frown as she covered up. "You guys are no fun," she said, her voice tinged with playful annoyance. "I have to go settle up for the night." She spun around and sashayed down the hall to the office.

Frank ambled over to Tanner, "If you weren't my buddy, and I didn't love you so much, I'd be on her like white on rice," he said, his voice low.

Tanner chuckled, "I get it, Frank. She's a hellcat if there ever was one. But I think she knows you wouldn't act on her advances. I know you wouldn't either. She just loves to tease you though, pushing your buttons like a pro."

Frank's brow furrowed, his look darkening with worry. "Makes life interesting, I guess. That's a wrap for tonight. I'll find out if Hammett has got anything new, and you debrief Sammy. I hope she found something."

Tanner nodded. "I know this is night one. To be honest, I was willing to go along with this, but I'm at my limit."

Frank's expression turned grim. "Ty, this kidnapping ring is very good. They know what to do and how to do it. I'm not crazy about using Sammy as bait, but we have no choice. We're running out of time."

Tanner understood Frank's concern, his gut twisting with anxiety. He didn't enjoy using the woman he loved as a lure to trap a kidnapping ring that targeted women for drug trafficking. But Frank was right; time was running out. They needed to find the person who was doing this.

Sammy emerged from the office, a wad of bills clutched in her hand. "A little over two grand tonight," she said, triumph shining on her face. "This girl's working hard for her money. And a nice sum for the women's abuse center this is going to." She waved the bills overhead.

Tanner swept Sammy into his arms, like a possessive claim.

"Come on, Tiger, take me home to bed," she said. Now dressed in jeans, a sweater, and a black leather jacket, she looped her arm around Tanner's and nestled close.

As they headed out the backstage door, Frank called out, "Where's Jill?"

Tanner scanned the dimly lit parking lot, his eyes narrowing. "Frank, look up front. Last I saw her, she was in front of the stage. I'll take Samantha to the car. We'll wait in the parking lot for ya."

The velvety blackness of the night enveloped them like a shroud, the Chicago autumn air crisp and cool. Sammy shivered, her grip on her jacket tightening.

"I see Jill's car is still here," Tanner said, his voice low and thoughtful. "I'll check it out."

Tanner jogged over to Jill's vehicle. The parking lot was a vast, empty expanse of asphalt, the few remaining cars scattered like lonely sentinels in the darkness. Most belonged to employees wrapping up for the night—a mix of sedans, SUVs, and a beat-up old white Chevy paneled minivan parked awkwardly near the back, its rusty body seeming to sag under the weight of years.

Reaching Jill's car, Tanner leaned down and peered through the windows, his gaze scanning the interior with a growing sense of unease. The darkness within seemed to swallow all light and leave only an oppressive sense of emptiness. He tried the doors, but they wouldn't open. Tanner's jaw clenched in frustration.

Frank came running up, his face set in a grim mask. "I checked the entire club, no sign of Jill," he said, his voice low and urgent. "Angie said she saw her leave with a young Asian woman and that Jill looked groggy. Like she was drunk. But I know Jill wasn't drinking alcohol tonight."

The news hit Tanner like a punch to the gut, leaving him breathless and reeling. Had they miscalculated? They were operating on the assumption they'd be looking for a man all this time. Was a woman the go-between to the kidnapping ring?

Sammy walked up to the men, her expression wide with concern. "Tiger, what's wrong? You don't look well," she asked, her voice trembling.

Tanner's face twisted in a grimace. "Oh baby, we think they may have taken Jill."

Frank's stare drilled into Tanner's, his expression a mixture of anger and fear. "Ty, what do you want to do?"

"I'll fucking tell you what we're going to do," Sammy huffed, her eyes welling up with tears. "We're gonna get her back. They don't know who they're fucking with. Do you still have that Uzi?"

PART ONE

CHAPTER TWO

ONE WEEK EARLIER

The dying breath of summer rolled in on a cooler wind, the kind that made the city feel like it was exhaling after weeks of sweating under its own grime. I pushed through the front door of York Investigations, my footsteps echoing in the hollow ribs of the converted warehouse on Chicago's South Side. The place was half office, half construction site. Saws whined. Hammers beat out a rhythm only a contractor could love. The air was thick with fresh paint and sawdust—smelled like money being spent and time being wasted.

I passed my office door—"Tanner York" in simple block letters—and felt a strange kind of calm. I hadn't planned on owning a detective agency at fifty-one, but life has a habit of blindsiding you. Now I was running the joint with my closest friends. Jillian Sinclair, a thirty-five-year-old single mother of two, who had a knack for keeping her kids—and our paperwork—in line, and she was as dependable as they come. Samantha Rhodes—twenty-nine, a beautiful, sharp-eyed blonde, and just as skilled at picking locks as she was at picking apart my excuses—was my partner in the business and in life. Jill and Sammy shared their own brand of closeness, the kind that made late nights in the office a little more interesting. And Frank Brannon—he's been with me since we were kids, two orphans who stuck together when the world had other plans. An ex-military tech wizard, he made sure our gadgets and intel stayed two steps ahead of trouble.

Dropping into my chair, I thought about the early-morning haul from our Lake Point Tower condo. Weekdays belonged to Chicago, the renovations, and whatever cases crawled in through the door. Weekends were for our cabin in Kickapoo, a place so quiet you could hear your own thoughts—if you wanted to.

Frank drifted in like a man still negotiating terms with consciousness. He dropped into the chair across from me.

"Hey, man, how was your night?" I said, watching him over the edge of my grin.

"Good," he muttered. "Catch the game, or did Sammy keep you busy?"

"A gentleman never tells."

"Yeah, but you're no gentleman."

"I'll put it this way—she let me watch the first half."

The laugh we shared bounced off the half-finished walls. That's the thing about Frank—we could go from ball-busting to business without missing a beat.

"Any dates of late?" I asked.

His jaw tightened. "Saw someone a few times. Thought it was casual—she didn't. Things went sideways fast. Little too much drama for my taste. After Addison..." He let the name hang there like a storm cloud. "...just haven't felt like signing up for another mess. I'm good focusing on work."

"I hear you. If you need anything—"

"Yeah, I know. Thanks." He glanced out at the half-built skeleton of our operation. "Think we overshot on this place? Don't exactly need a warehouse for an investigation business."

"The plan was an all-in-one setup," I said. "Living quarters, space for your cars. Batcave without the rubber suit."

He smirked. "I might just come up with that secret entrance."

Jill leaned against the doorway, relaxed, a quiet confidence rolling off her. "Morning, boys. You're in early."

"Trying to get a head start," I said. "They're laying the front entryway floor today."

"Coming along nicely," she said. "Where's our girl?"

"Sleeping in. She's been busting her tail painting offices. She earned a little down time."

The morning dragged like a busted tailpipe. I was hammering out a report on an infidelity case for the ROC law firm—Randolph liked his papers early, and I enjoyed keeping a client happy. Between the high-pitched saws chewing wood and the nail guns cracking like popcorn, it felt as if I were trying to type in the middle of a prize fight.

Somewhere between the racket, I heard laughter from the kitchen. Not just any laugh—hers. Samantha's laugh had a way of sliding under my ribs and planting itself there, warm and impossible to ignore. It wasn't the polite, careful kind you bring to Sunday dinner; it was untamed, alive, the same sound that knocked me off my feet the day we met. Still floored me now.

I stepped in and caught her smile—a flash of warmth that curled quick into that sly, serpentine grin she wore like perfume.

"Hello, Tiger," she said. "Frank was just telling me how bad I was for not letting you watch the rest of the game last night. I didn't tell him how bad you were when you weren't watching. My tushy's still a little sore from the paddle."

I cleared my throat, playing it cooler than I felt. "Funny," I said, and kissed her. "I need you to proof my report before I send it to Randolph."

"Sure, but it's hard to concentrate with all this banging." Her brows pinched together.

"We could work from home," I said, "but there'd be just as much banging there."

That got a spark in her eyes. I liked catching her off guard—it reminded me I could still be quick on my feet when she wasn't running the floor. Samantha had a way of loosening the screws on my straight-laced life. Maybe I liked it too much.

"Well now, Mr. York," she purred, "with the quick wit and the dirty mind. Bravo."

We spent the next hour trading edits and small talk until the noise wore us down. I suggested a break, and she agreed.

That's when Jill showed in the doorway.

"Ty, there's someone I think you'll want to meet."

She stepped aside, and a woman in a dark coat entered like bad weather.

"This is Mrs. Capone," Jill said. "She says you knew her husband, Craig—back when he was on the force."

Craig's name hit like a sucker punch. The air went heavy.

Samantha touched my arm. "I'll let you take care of this, Ty." The smile she gave me had an apology in it. We all knew what Craig had done for us—and what it cost him.

I turned to the widow. "Let's go to my office. Can I get you anything?"

"Coffee. Light cream, sugar."

"Jill—"

"I'm on it," she said, gone before the words cooled.

I offered her a chair. Memories pressed in—Craig and I first crossed paths in the intricate dance of investigative work, with him serving the Chicago PD while I navigated the complex legal landscape at the WAR law firm. From that initial encounter on one case, our friendship flourished. He taught me tricks the police academy didn't. He kept me alive more than once.

"How are you holding up, Mrs. Capone? How can I help?"

"Please call me Alice." Her hands were never still. "I still can't believe he's gone."

This wasn't a social call.

Jill came back with the coffee. Alice wrapped her hands around the cup like it was a lifeline.

"Craig said if anything happened to him, I should find you."

"You found me."

"My niece—Craig's brother's girl—has been missing a week. The cops don't have leads, and with staff shortages... they're not making it a priority. Every day that goes by, I feel them losing interest. I can't let this case go cold."

Her voice trembled under the weight of it. I put a hand on her shoulder. "I'm sorry, Alice. We'll get her back."

And I meant it. Time was already working against her. Another week and we'd be looking for a body instead of a girl. Craig had never turned me down when I needed help—I wasn't about to fail him now.

"Craig said you had... different tactics than the police," she said. "That you'd stop at nothing to get answers. Ty, I need your help. Find my niece."

I looked into her eyes. They weren't asking for mercy—they were asking for results.

"I will."

CHAPTER
THREE

Jill stared at me, her curiosity as sharp as a tack. "What was that all about?"

"We have a missing person case," I said, the words feeling heavier than they should this early in the day. "Frank!" I yelled toward his office.

"Present!" came his voice, cutting through the clutter.

I stepped into his office and immediately shook my head. Unpacked boxes everywhere. Paper, tools, and who-knows-what stacked in teetering piles. The man could rebuild a Chevelle with surgical precision but couldn't unpack an office to save his life.

"Craig Capone's niece, Ava Capone, is missing," I said. "Alice asked for our help."

That got his attention. His grin evaporated like a puddle in July. "What's the situation?"

"Ava's thirty, lives in Logan Square, works in the Loop. Alice gave me the names of her two close friends—Sophie Rodriguez and Brent Rogers."

"Any boyfriends?" Frank asked, already thinking two steps ahead.

If there was one thing Frank knew, it was that missing women and boyfriends often went hand-in-hand in the worst way.

"Alice didn't know about any," I said.

Frank's eyes narrowed. "Not good, Ty. How long's she been missing?"

"A week." Saying it out loud felt like dropping a brick on the table.

He took a slow breath—the kind you take when you already suspect the answer isn't going to be good. "I'll handle the police, see what they've gathered."

"I'll talk to her friends," I said. "Samantha can come with me. If they see someone their own age, they might be more willing to talk."

Frank nodded. "Good call. Sam's presence can make a difference."

Yeah. That, and she had a way of making people forget they were even in a conversation until she'd already gotten what she wanted.

Samantha and I pulled up to a brick apartment building in the heart of Logan Square, Chicago. The neighborhood hummed with a cocktail of cultures—Polish bakeries elbow to elbow with taco joints, neon bars blinking like they were winking at you, and street art splashed across brick walls like graffiti gods had run out of patience.

We hit the buzzer for Sophie Rodriguez.

Her voice came through the intercom, thin and crackly. "Hello, who is it, please?"

"Ms. Rodriguez, Tanner York, York Investigations. My partner, Samantha Rhodes. We're looking into Ava Capone's disappearance. Can we come up? You might have information that could help."

A pause. People always pause when they're deciding whether to tell you the truth or hang up. "I've told the police everything I know."

"We're in touch with them," I said. "But going over it again might jog something. Something you didn't even realize was important."

Another pause. I could almost hear the mental door closing. "I don't know what I could say that would help."

"She was your best friend," I said. "That's reason enough."

Samantha jabbed my arm, her own way of telling me to holster the cross-examination. "Ty, be nice," she muttered into the mic. Then, to Sophie: "Look, I promise we'll be quick, and it was a long-ass drive to get here, I could really use your bathroom. A girl's gotta pee, you know?"

A hiss of static. Then, "Okay. Hang on."

Seconds dragged. Long enough to wonder if she'd gone for the shotgun instead of the buzzer. Finally, the lock clicked.

The elevator groaned its way to the third floor. The hallway smelled like fresh paint and carpets that had never met a muddy shoe. Sophie's apartment carried apple-cinnamon warmth, with a trace of perfume underneath. Nice place. Too nice for someone in sales unless she had help.

"Can I get you anything?" Sophie asked.

"I'm good, thanks," I said, letting my eyes make a quick sweep of the room. Sleek furniture, all edges and angles. Money leaves fingerprints if you know where to look.

She pointed down the hall at Samantha. "It's just past the first bedroom on the right."

"What is?" Samantha asked.

"The bathroom. You wanted to use it, correct?"

"Oh, yes—silly me." Samantha rolled her eyes, stuck out her tongue, and twirled her finger at her temple. Then she vanished down the hall like she'd slipped into another scene entirely.

While she was gone, I got Sophie talking. She and Ava met through mutual friends, clicked fast, spent holidays together. Sophie worked sales at Lively Fashion; Ava was in marketing at Kensington, which handled Lively's ads. The lines between work and friendship blurred until they were one and the same.

"Ava shared inside info from Kensington?" I asked.

Sophie's eyes shifted. "And I'd share Lively's numbers. Costs, budgets. We'd work out figures ahead of time so both sides got what they wanted."

"That's not exactly by-the-book."

She smirked faintly. "We looked like stars in meetings. Bigger raises, promotions. We knew who had power and who'd fold. It was just smart business." She glanced down the hall. "Your associate's been in the bathroom a while."

Bathroom, or trouble. With Samantha, it could go either way.

"You tell the police about this arrangement?"

"Are you kidding? It might not have been legal." Her foot started tapping—quick, staccato. People tap like that when they want the conversation to end.

"Why tell me?"

She hesitated. "Before I let you up, I called Brent. He thought it'd be okay since Ava's aunt hired you. But... I think you should go now."

The hair on my neck prickled. "Samantha!" I called. No answer. Rookie mistake—I should've asked about other tenants the second we walked in. I scanned the apartment, ready to move. Two steps toward the hall—then Samantha appeared.

"Sorry. Long line for the ladies' room," she snickered.

"Thanks for your time, Sophie," I said, steering Samantha toward the door. "When you call Brent—and you will—tell him we're coming."

"Ava's a good person," Sophie said quickly. "We didn't do anything to deserve her getting kidnapped."

Samantha froze. "We were told Ava was missing. You said kidnapped. How do you know someone kidnapped her?"

Sophie's face tightened. "You need to go. I've said too much."

"Answer the question," I said.

"That's what Brent told me. Ask him."

As we stepped out into the street, the air had that late-afternoon heaviness, like the neighborhood was holding its breath.

I glanced at Samantha. "What were you doing in the bathroom so long?"

She grinned like a kid caught with her hand in the cookie jar. "Saw this detective show once—while one cop grilled the witness, the other excused herself to the bathroom and snooped around. Figured I'd try it. Checked the medicine cabinet. Nothing weird—cold meds, mouthwash, makeup. Then I peeked in her bedroom closet."

I gave her a side-eye. Samantha didn't just peek; she probably took inventory.

"She had two main wardrobes," Samantha went on. "One was work clothes and around-the-house stuff. The other? Pure sexy apparel."

"You've got some sexy stuff." I kept my tone casual.

"Sure," she said. "But not like this. For a sales rep, I'd expect modest clothes. This wasn't date-night lingerie—it was performance gear. Matching platform shoes, animal prints—leopard, cheetah—one- and two-piece outfits. You wear these, you're not going to the grocery store."

Maybe she had a steady guy with deep pockets. Guys like that buy clothes they want their girls to wear, not clothes the girl wants to wear. "Could be a boyfriend."

"Maybe," Samantha said. "But when I worked at the news station with Meghan, I saw her closet once. She had a few sexy pieces for dates, but eighty percent was work stuff."

I made a left turn, watching the traffic thin ahead of us. "Conclusion?"

"If I had to guess, she side-hustles as a stripper. And—" She reached into her purse, came up with a tiny baggie holding two pastel-green pills. They looked like they belonged in an Easter basket. "Found these in her nightstand."

"Party favors?" I asked.

"My guess—something to get her in the mood to dance in front of a crowd. Maybe fentanyl-laced. Everything's laced with that crap these days."

The street rolled past us, but my mind was still upstairs in Sophie's apartment. Stripping, drugs, corporate leaks—it was a cocktail that could make people disappear.

Samantha's eyes lit with a sharper edge. "If she's involved in stripping and drugs, it's possible someone at work found out about her sharing company secrets and her moonlighting job. We should check out her workplace—see if anyone had a motive to hurt her."

I nodded. "Good start. Talk to her coworkers, look for anyone nervous or suddenly flush with cash. And see if the company's security is a revolving door."

Samantha leaned back in the seat, already thinking ahead. "I'll dig into the company's background. Feels like we're just scratching the surface."

She was right. And the surface already looked dirty.

CHAPTER
FOUR

We stepped into Carter Frozen Packaging, and the AC hit like a wave off Lake Michigan in February—instant goosebumps. The foyer was all clean lines and muted tones, the kind of place where everything had its purpose. Somewhere in the background, machinery hummed—a steady, low grind that made me picture conveyor belts loaded with frozen dinners crawling toward cardboard boxes.

Behind the reception desk sat a woman who looked like she'd been here since they first plugged in the freezers. Warm eyes. The kind that made you think of Sunday dinners and unsolicited advice about your love life. A small silver cross resting against a modest blouse caught the light as she shifted. The name on her badge—Ruth—was printed in bold, as if anyone here would dare forget it.

"Good afternoon," she said, and her voice had the kind of kindness that could make bad news sound like a weather report. "How may I help you today?"

Samantha leaned in, all innocence and charm. "Hello, Ruth. I'm looking for my brother, Brent Rogers. Can you tell him Sammy and Ty are here?" She could sell ice to a guy in a parka.

Ruth's fingers danced across the keyboard. "He's working on the line now. What's this about?" There was concern there, soft but pointed.

Samantha didn't miss a beat. "I have some news about our Aunt Sophie. Her condition isn't improving, and he's not answering my texts. Mom's fit to be tied—she was ready to storm down here and pull him by the ear to the hospital."

I almost smiled. Not bad, Rhodes. Give the lie just enough detail to smell like the truth.

"Oh dear," Ruth murmured, sympathy pooling in her eyes. "I'll say a prayer for your family. Let me see if he can take a break."

While she was on the phone, Samantha adjusted her stance, as if preparing for a prolonged conversation. I leaned on the counter, watching Ruth's lips move. She didn't rush, but she didn't waste a syllable either—someone who got things done without needing to prove it.

"Good news," Ruth said finally. "His supervisor agreed to let him take a break. Here are your visitor passes. Follow me. First room on the left is an open conference room. I'll send him there. God bless you both."

She ushered us into a windowless box of a room. Neutral paint, no personality. The kind of place designed to be forgotten the second you left it.

A minute later, Brent arrived in a hurry, hair net half-cocked on his head like he'd wrestled it on during a fire drill. His apron had a constellation of stains, and I had the sense this wasn't the first shift he'd ended looking like that. He glanced at me, neutral. Then at Samantha—and his smile flickered. He tugged the apron straight, yanked off the hair net, stuffed it in his pocket. I've seen suspects with cleaner poker faces.

"I'm Tanner York, this is Samantha Rhodes," I said. "York Investigations. Did Sophie tell you we'd be coming about Ava's disappearance?"

Brent's eyes darted—wall, floor, ceiling, camera. His voice dropped. "I thought you'd come to my place. Not here. They listen to everything here. Everything is recorded."

Samantha's tone sharpened. "Who's listening, Brent?"

He looked at the camera again. "I'll tell you, but not here. Meet me tonight behind the Remington Hotel. I valet there. Nine o'clock."

Nine p.m., behind a hotel, with a guy already sweating bullets? My gut tightened. "If you're a no-show," I said, "I'll come looking for you."

"Me too," Samantha added.

We stepped back into the street, the humidity hitting like a wet towel to the face. Horns blared, machinery rumbled somewhere down the block, voices collided in the din. Samantha scanned the street like she expected trouble to come walking toward us.

"Think he's hiding something, or just paranoid?" she asked over the noise.

I shook my head. "Doesn't matter. We'll know tonight." My gut was already telling me the same thing my cases usually did—what we'd just stepped into was bigger, messier, and a hell of a lot stranger than we'd planned for.

CHAPTER
FIVE

The Remington Hotel's grand lobby radiated old-world elegance. Marble floors gleamed beneath soaring ceilings, the soft clink of glassware and low murmur of conversation drifting from the lounge. Polished mahogany mingled with fresh florals and a hint of aged whiskey. Crystal chandeliers cast deep pools of light across gilded columns and velvet chairs, wrapping the space in quiet luxury. I arrived an hour early, letting it all soak in. Pretended I belonged. Never really did.

I made a beeline for the in-house bar, the Incognito, and found an empty bar stool. Ordered a bourbon—my usual. The bartender shrugged, their supply of my brand had run out months ago. Figures. The bartenders probably hoarded the good stuff for their regulars. I scanned the shelves, landing on a familiar bottle.

"Neat, please. And may I know your name?" I asked, keeping my tone light.

He poured, sliding the glass to me. "Nick."

"Tanner York, but call me Ty," I said, shaking his hand. That amber warmth hit my chest, slow, rich, smoothing some edge off the day. I debated asking Nick about Brent, but that was a trap I wasn't ready to spring. Brent wanted to play it his way. Fine.

Nick swung by. "Like another?"

"Yes. And I was wondering if you knew someone." I gestured toward the details. "A woman. Erika. Platinum hair, sapphire eyes, early thirties. Nice figure. Friendly."

"Sounds like a knockout. Wish I did, Ty."

I pushed a fifty toward him. Subtle charm. He smiled, left it. "I was here a few months ago and spent some time with her. Mike set up the appointment. I'm just looking to say hi, catch up a bit. We're old friends." I took a sip of my drink. Erika was a bright flicker in the hazy corners of my life, but my heart—my heart was someone else's. Samantha. I kept that thought pressed against my chest, private and untouchable.

"You know, after thinking about it, the name Erika is ringing some bells." Nick stated, then looked at his watch, went over to his cell phone, and made a call. He came back a few seconds later. "You're in luck, Ty. I called Mike, and you checked out. He says you're on Erika's priority list. Mike said she was free. I'll see if I can track her down. He also said I should take care of you, and drinks are on his tab."

"Excellent Nick, thanks." I held up my glass. "Cheers to Mike." I took another sip.

She appeared like a warm sun breaking through clouds, brushing my shoulder. Pearl-white teeth, that smile, magnetic. I hugged her, a proper hello. Charisma, smarts, ambition—Erika had it all. But none of that dimmed the pull Samantha had on me.

"You still go to Uptown Coffee?" she asked.

"Now and then." I caught movement—a man, late sixties, early seventies, with a worn straw fedora and a just-as-worn sport coat, eye-fucking Erika out with eagerness. Noted him, slid my arm around Erika's waist. Safety in numbers.

"How's business?" I asked.

"On and off." Nick topped my drink, gave her something mixed. "Thank you, sweetheart." She smiled at him.

"Sorry to hear work's not going well. You look fantastic; not sure why your business would be down."

She took a swallow of her drink. "It's part economy and part the club."

"What club?" I asked. I looked to see if the guy in the hat was still there. He was but now playing with his phone.

"It's on the north side. High-end gentleman's club. Lots of themed rooms, members only, VIP stuff. I went once and checked it out. It's not for me. You know that girl you met with me the last time we were at Uptown Coffee, Jennifer? She left Mike and went there. Tried to get me to go, but I like it here with Mike."

I filed the information mentally. North-side high-end club, members only. Side hustles. Connections. A faint nagging in my gut told me all of this was going to intersect with Brent, Ava, and whoever had started this chain of events.

"Ever come across Brent Rogers? Works valet here," I said casually, scanning the room, noting shadows, exits, cameras.

She laughed, easy and genuine. "That guy from the packaging company? Yeah, made a few advances. I declined. Why what's up?"

"Investigating a missing person case, and he might have some details I need. Supposed to meet him here," I explained, taking a sip of my bourbon.

"I hope you get the answers you're looking for. Are you and Sammy still together?"

"Yes, we are. And I have to say, things are going well. We are in business together, York Investigations. Stop by and see us sometime. Check the place out." I gave her our business card.

We talked a few more minutes before Erika's phone buzzed. I caught the time—nine-fifteen. Time to move. I asked where the alley was, and she pointed. We said goodbye, and I slipped out of the bar.

Outside, rain stung my face, the air thick with wet pavement and garbage. Darkness folded over the alley, broken only by two overhead lamps. No Brent.

"Help, over here," the voice, ragged and raw.

I rounded the corner, and there he was—Brent, slumped against the brick wall between dumpsters like a ragdoll the city had tossed aside. His body was a grotesque still life, soaked in blood that pooled beneath him, black-red and glinting under the sickly glow of the alley lights. His clothes were shredded, clinging to him like a second, stained skin. Gunshot holes marred his flesh, frayed and darkened at the edges, oozing a slow, relentless river of crimson.

I dropped to my knees beside him, the stench of iron and wet asphalt punching me in the face. Nausea clawed at my gut, and panic skittered up my spine. His breaths came shallow, ragged—each one a negotiation with death. I could feel the thump of his heart under my hand, a faltering, stuttering drum that mocked the order of the world. His eyes, glassy and wide, searched nothing, and sweat slick on his pale forehead.

"I'm here, Brent," I rasped, my own voice foreign to me, thick with fear. "You're going to be okay. Just hang on." The lie tasted bitter, sharp as whiskey, but I swallowed it anyway. My hands trembled as I fumbled for my phone, one hand pressing rags to the worst wound, the blood seeping through in dark, unrelenting streaks.

"911, what's your emergency?"

"A man's been shot—behind the Remington Hotel on Superior Street. Brent Rogers. My name's Tanner York. Hang in there, Brent. Help is coming," I said, letting the words fall in sync with the rapid hammering of my heart.

Panic threatened to take over, hot and wild, crawling up my throat. Every second Brent hung on, the alley seemed to close in, concrete cold and unforgiving beneath us. I pressed harder on the wound, imagining sheer force of will could hold back the river of blood, could keep him tethered to this world.

"I called for help, Brent," I whispered, desperate. "Just hang on. Who... who did this?"

"I... don't... want... to die in an alley, please," he rasped, voice trembling, shaking like the last ember in a gutter fire.

"Help is coming."

"Talk... to... Ava's boyfriend. I'm cold," he coughed, blood flecking the pavement.

"Hang on, Brent. Don't... don't let go."

"Phil... Phil Hol... Holland. Where I work. Check the... Ka... Ka... lub."

"Phil? Did he—did he do this?"

Brent shook his head weakly, "doc...tor." Then he pointed upward, his eyes full like moons. "Th... th... the Asian."

A sharp pain lanced through my skull, white-hot and unforgiving. The alley dissolved into shadow, rain drumming a relentless tattoo on my shoulders. Darkness edged my vision. Alley fading. I collapsed against the dumpster, letting it all close in.

CHAPTER
SIX

Sammy Rhodes pushed open the heavy wood door, a burst of excitement coloring her voice as she stepped into Jillian Sinclair's Oak Brook residence. "I'm here, baby!" Her arrival was fashionably late, the clock ticking twenty-five past eight. Dropping her sleek overnight bag, Sammy ventured further into the spacious kitchen. Surprised not to find Jill in her typical welcoming stance, Sammy called out, her voice ringing through the house. "Where are you hiding, Jill?" Her eyes scanned the familiar surroundings. Nothing was out of place. Jill kept a clean house. Everything in the kitchen sparkled and had a fresh lemon scent. Her eyes landed on an unexpected sight—a neatly stacked pile of paper on the counter.

In a whirl of motion, Jill emerged. "You're late." Her presence carried a curious blend of maternal warmth and mild reprimand. She wore a plush robe that spoke more of indulgence than bedtime. Her hair was sleek and meticulously styled, her smoky silver eyeshadow framing high, apple-shaped cheeks with a natural flush. The matte crimson of her La Rouge Avant-Garde lipstick gave her lips a bold, modern edge.

Sammy hugged Jill, savoring the moment. The familiar scent of *Guerlain Mitsouko* wrapped around her, one of the two fragrances Jill reserved for life beyond work, the other being *Hermès 24 Faubourg*. In Jill's arms, Sammy found her haven—an embrace that felt less like contact and more like immersion in her very essence.

Jill led Sammy to the living room, where they sat down on the sofa together. Sammy poured Jill a glass of wine, and they clinked glasses in a silent toast.

Jill, a mosaic of endurance, resilience, and tenacity, stood as a symbol of survival. To Sammy, she was not just a mentor but a role model, someone she admired and respected deeply. In these shared moments, Sammy's admiration for Jill flourished in various shades, akin to a vibrant tapestry of affection and reverence.

As they sipped their wine, Sammy asked, "What's with the stack of papers in the kitchen?"

Jill glanced up nonchalantly from her glass. "Oh, that? Just some writing I've been tinkering with."

Sammy, now curious, asked, "You're writing a novel?"

"I've been dabbling in storytelling lately."

"You've never mentioned this before."

Jill stood, walked over to the bookshelf. She ran her fingers over the spines of the books. "Not everything is worth mentioning. Besides, it's a work in progress. Don't make a fuss. It's just a way to pass the time. Books are a great way to escape."

Sammy got up to find her purse. She dug around in her bag and pulled out her vape pen, then took a hit, held in the smoke for a moment, then exhaled. She offered it to Jill, "Need a hit?"

"Not tonight, baby."

As they moved through the room, Jill's gaze found Sammy's, her smile slow and deliberate. Sammy's heart skipped a beat. They continued to the window, where Jill drew back the curtains to reveal the night sky.

Sammy slipped the vape back into her purse and wrapped her arms around Jill, holding her close. Jill smiled again, and they shared a kiss—soft and lingering.

When they pulled apart, Jill's expression turned serious.

"I want to talk to you."

They returned to the sofa and sat down together, still holding hands.

"Our time together is special. You're such a free spirit—forward-thinking, unashamed. And when we play?" She gave a playful smile. "Wow, you make me tingle in places I didn't know I could tingle. And girl, your flexibility is Olympics good."

Her tone shifted again, more reflective.

"But Ty and you, need to figure out where your relationship is going. I know he has deep feelings for you. Right now, he's willing to... share. But eventually, that could change. He might resent us or get jealous. I can't go through that again.

"You and Ty are so good together. I don't want to come between you guys down the road. So maybe... we should slow things down—or stop altogether."

Sammy's face fell, and she looked at Jill in shock. "Wait, what? This isn't how I thought this night would go." She stood up, looking at Jill. "No way, no ma'am. First off, if Ty wants to be with me, he'll have to accept me for who I am. And I think he does. We're not cheating on him. He knows the deal. We've talked about our relationship, and he's cool with it. As long as he knows where I'm at and who I'm with, that's all that matters. Besides him, you're the only one I have sex with. And I want to be your friend, your bestie. I want to hang out, have wine, talk about work and our lives. My sister's in Florida, and even if she were here, I wouldn't want to hang out with her. You're it. I choose you. If the sex part's not working, well hell, fuck me, that would suck. But being friends is more important."

Tears welled up in Jill's eyes. Sammy grabbed the tissues from the sofa's end table and gave them to her. "Look, baby, you've been through a lot the last few months. Wait, strike that. The last few years. You deserve to be happy. If we make each other happy, what's the problem? Ty's not like Donny. I know you didn't get happiness from Donny, and I can't help that he didn't see how great a person you are. You're an awesome mom, I know. Caprice told me that herself, last time I saw her." Jill chuckled as Sammy continued. "You're fucking exceptional at work. You ran the WAR law firm and had to deal with Randolf Rockwell. God help us."

Jill laughed some more. "You got that right."

"And if I started in on what a great lover you are, we'd be up all night. Which is what I thought we'd be doing by now."

Sammy stroked Jill's hair, trying to soothe her. "Oh sweetheart, you're always thinking of everyone else." She kissed Jill's forehead. "Jill, look at me. You're one of a kind. I love you. I've learned so much from you. I want to keep learning. Teach me French, the language, the culture. We can go to Paris, see all the sights. I want to learn from you sexually. Your advice on life and love. And most important, someday, your advice on being a mom." With that, Jill fell into Sammy's lap and sobbed. It had been a long time coming. Jill was letting it all go. And her best friend was there to take it from her.

Jill giggled as she poured herself more wine, then offered the bottle. Sammy held out her glass, and Jill obliged—but as she poured, a splash missed the rim and hit the floor.

"Careful," Sammy warned, laughing.

Jill put the bottle down and grabbed a napkin, her hands moving with a quiet efficiency as she dabbed up the spill on the rug. "Fuck," she muttered through clenched teeth.

Sammy waved a dismissive hand at Jill. "Leave it, honey. The maid will get it in the morning."

Jill's anger cracked, giving way to laughter. "You know I don't have a maid," she said, her expression softening, eyes lit with amusement.

"I know, silly."

As their giddiness faded, Sammy's gaze fell to a droplet of wine clinging to Jill's fingertips. Smiling, she took Jill's wrist and drew her hand closer. Her lips brushed the tips, tongue tracing each curve, mouth closing gently as if tasting both the wine and Jill's skin.

Jill, mesmerized, as Sammy's lips and tongue worked their magic. "What are you doing, Sammy?"

Sammy continued to lick and suck Jill's fingers. "Helping you clean up."

The world slipped away, leaving just the two of them. In the quiet, the gentle sounds of Sammy's mouth on Jill's fingers drew them closer, the tension humming in the silence.

"We're both drunk," Jill said, her voice gentle. "It's been a long day, and I know you wanted to play tonight, but I just... can we cuddle in bed and watch a movie?" Jill's face softened, and she reached out to stroke Sammy's hair.

"But you got all dolled up," Sammy said, her voice teasing. "I just want to see what's under here. Just a little peek?" A mischievous gleam lit Sammy's face as she pulled at Jill's robe tie.

"*Allez-y*," Jill said.

Sammy pulled the tie, and the bathrobe slipped open, revealing Jill's naked body beneath. Her hand moved deliberately, tracing an invisible path through the air toward its target.

Her fingers roamed Jill's skin, pausing at the side of her abdomen. Delicately, her manicured French nails touched Jill's ticklish spot. Jill's eyes flashed a warning, and she bared her teeth. "*Pas de chaton*," she growled, low and menacing. "Don't you dare."

Sammy's serpentine smile curled as her fingers struck with surgical precision, dismantling Jill's anger. Within seconds, her defiance broke into laughter, helpless and bright.

Their wrestling rolled them off the sofa and onto the floor, laughter and breathless giggles filling the room. Tangled together, their bodies wrapped around each other.

Finally exhausted, Jill looked up at Sammy with a grin. Laughter spilled between them, unrestrained and breathless, until they clutched their sides and wiped tears from their eyes.

"Don't worry, honey," Sammy said, still chuckling. "The maid will pick us up in the morning."

The merriment faded, and they settled into comfortable silence, hands entwined as they gazed at the ceiling. Only their gentle breathing and the occasional creak of the house broke the stillness.

Just as they were about to get lost in more playfulness, Jill's phone pierced the quiet, its ringing shrill and insistent. Her expression shifted, eyes narrowing as she sat up and reached for it.

Her face fell as she read the screen, concern creeping into her voice. "Hey, Frank's calling me," she said, her pitch rising slightly.

Sammy scanned the room, spotted her purse, and rose swiftly, rummaging through it until she found her phone. The screen showed missed calls from Frank and the hospital.

CHAPTER
SEVEN

Ava Capone stirred awake, the dawn's gentle light filtering through the sheer curtains, coaxing her from slumber. The bed, a haven of opulent comfort, cocooned her in silky bamboo blended sheets that whispered against her skin, while the plush pillow-top mattress cradled her in a regal embrace. Stretching gracefully, she stepped out of bed and draped herself in a soft nightshirt before walking toward the bathroom for a swift morning ritual. The invigorating scent of freshly brewed coffee made her smile. In the room was a small fridge and a microwave, amenities that offered a slice of convenience within her sanctuary.

As the fragrant brew beckoned, someone rapped on the door with a sense of urgency to its rhythm.

"Come in," she said.

The door opened. It was the doctor. Her rigid tension melted away. Thankfully, it wasn't the Asian woman, Jayde, the no-nonsense head of security at the Farm, a mysterious facility situated on the outskirts of Kickapoo, Illinois, where the cornfields stretched as far as the eye could see. The single-story dormitory-style building was home to Ava and several other subjects, all of whom were monitored and studied by Dr. Donavan and his team.

Ava offered a smile as she greeted the doctor, "Morning, Doctor Donavan." She tried to hide any nervousness, but his imposing presence was hard to ignore.

Dr. Donavan looked her over with those sharp, assessing eyes that seemed to see right through her. "Good morning, dear. How are we today? Still sleeping well? Anyone here at the Farm given you any trouble?" He asked, his voice a mix of concern and authority.

Ava shook her head, trying to keep her voice steady. "No sir, I'm good." She didn't want him to think she was hiding anything.

The doctor reached into his bag, pulled out a compact flashlight and hooked his stethoscope around his neck. His hands, weathered and lined with experience, moved with a practiced ease as he began his examination. The flashlight cast eerie shadows across his serious face, his brow creasing with concentration.

Ava noticed how, despite his age, Dr. Donavan carried himself with an air of dignity and control. His salt-and-pepper hair was always neatly combed, and his clean-shaven face gave him a distinguished look. Tall and lean, he cut an impressive figure, and Ava felt the weight of his experience in every check-up.

His examination was thorough and methodical. He scrutinized her pupils, checking their response to the light, and listened intently to her breathing and heartbeat. Ava knew he was looking for any signs of irregularity, any hint that something might be amiss.

"Everything's looking good, Ava," he said finally, a small smile playing on his lips. "I can issue you two candy pills today. Would you like that?"

Ava nodded eagerly, holding out her hand. "Oh yes, I would, Doctor." She hoped that today would be a good day, that the pills would help her feel normal again.

"I have the pink and green pills today. You like the pink ones, don't you? I'll put them on the table, dear, but we need to look at one more thing." He placed a little baggie on Ava's table, which was in the middle of the room. "Now, just hop up on the bed and spread your legs open for me. Real wide now." He gave Ava a devious smirk.

Without hesitation, Ava obeyed.

The doctor pulled up a chair close to the bed and sat between Ava's legs. "I'm just going to have a look. I won't touch. You've come a long way from when I did your first examination. Do you remember?"

"Not really, Doctor Donavan. If you want to check my tightness, can I get another candy pill? It doesn't have to be pink, but I do like the pink ones."

"I didn't bring the instruments I need, dear. That wasn't on the schedule for today."

"I know, I just thought... Well maybe you could use the one in your pants like you did that other time you forgot your instruments..."

The door burst open with a thunderous bang, causing Ava to jump and retreat to the other side of the bed, clutching the sheets tightly around her. Startled, her heart raced, and her breath quickened. Her eyes widened in a mix of surprise and fear as she recognized the intruder. She trembled, and her voice quivered. "W-what are you doing here?"

The doctor's annoyance was unmistakable; his features tightened in irritation at the interruption. As his gaze shifted to the unwelcome guest, a sigh escaped his lips. It was evident he was familiar with this kind of disruption. He stood up abruptly, the chair scraping against the floor, and swiftly gathered his medical instruments. His actions conveyed his decision—the examination was suddenly over.

The tense silence filled the room, charged with Ava's surprise, the doctor's annoyance, and an underlying tension that hinted at an unspoken history between the doctor and the intruder.

"You're not supposed to be doing that, Doc," the intruder said, her voice firm but laced with a hint of frustration. "There's no reason to check her cunt. You're just getting your rocks off."

The doctor smiled. "Jayde Kato, I wouldn't say it's a pleasure. She wanted me to do the exam today."

"With what, your tiny cock? Please, she's been on the stuff for a few days now. She'll do anything to get more pills, even fuck you." Jayde laughed.

Ava's eyes widened at the imposing figure of Jayde. Tall and athletic, Jayde's toned legs were proof of her disciplined workouts—ones Ava knew she never skipped. Her form-fitting black leather pants and tight, low-cut white T-shirt emphasized every contour. Between her breasts hung a shuriken charm on a gold chain. Jayde's sleek black hair fell in straight strands, and her flawless skin was marked only by a long, jagged scar running from left elbow to wrist. Ava wondered how a wound so brutal had left such a fierce mark.

Ava's gaze fell to Jayde's boots, knowing they were more than just footwear. She had heard Jayde refer to them as her "ball crackers," and Ava could only imagine the force behind the kicks that had earned them that nickname. Jayde moved with a fluidity that was almost hypnotic, her strikes as sharp and precise as a katana blade. Ava could feel the command that radiated from her.

Jayde pulled out her notebook, flipping through the pages with a sense of purpose. "The little snatch is only supposed to have one pill today and two tomorrow," she said, her voice firm and commanding.

Ava was amazed that someone could talk so rough. Jayde's language was a barrage of curse words and abusive phrases. Ava wondered if this was a form of intimidation, a way to assert her dominance and strike fear into those around her. Whatever the purpose, Ava didn't like it. The harsh words grated on her nerves, and she found herself tensing up whenever Jayde spoke, bracing for the next verbal assault.

Jayde turned to the doctor. "Stick to the schedule."

The doctor shrugged. "I was just trying to help her out, Jayde. She's been doing well. A little reward."

"You're not following protocol."

Ava's eyes widened in anger, but Jayde just smiled a cold, calculating smile. "Don't get your panties in a twist, Ava. You'll get your pills. But you'll follow the schedule, or you'll deal with me."

CHAPTER
EIGHT

I stirred from a foggy haze, senses clouded by the incessant beep, beep, beep. My arm lay stiff, the IV needle making any movement unbearable. Struggling to bend it, I squinted at the ceiling, a punishing headache throbbed like a relentless hangover. Brent. That alley. Did he make it? My stomach churned at the memory.

Something warm nestled beside me. Strawberry-mint shampoo. My lips curved in a faint, guilty smile as I planted a gentle kiss on her head. Samantha stirred. "I suppose this proves I'd sleep anywhere with you."

The sharp pulse in my skull reminded me I wasn't out of the woods yet.

A nurse appeared, glancing at the machines hooked to me. "How are you feeling?"

"Never better. When can I leave?"

"The doctor will be in. Police want to talk, but not before you're cleared." She looked at Samantha. "She was insistent on being here. If it's uncomfortable..."

"She's fine." I grasped Samantha's hand. Her warmth anchored me. "Exactly where I want her."

"Anything else?" the nurse asked.

"Coffee. And what about the other man in the alley? What happened to him?"

"That's a question for the police." She left, leaving the quiet hum of the hospital to press against my ears.

Hours blurred. I dozed in and out, waking to Samantha pacing. I broke the silence. "How was your evening?"

"Jill and I fucked our brains out. How did your night go, honey? Let me guess—dark alley, creepy guy, clonked on the head, left for dead?" She paced with purpose, energy spilling into every word.

"Close. You skipped the conversation with Erika, the escort."

She froze, arms crossed. "Funny man here this morning. No more danger, Ty. I don't want more hospital visits. Did you even check if the shooter was still there?"

"I thought Erika would be the tricky part," I muttered.

"Really? Joke now? Jill's mad. Frank's chasing leads. You, in an alley." Her glare could cut steel.

"Come here." I extended my good arm. She hesitated, then bent down and hugged me. Her warmth seeped into my chest.

A tap at the door. "Hello, I'm Doctor Stafford. Can I come in?"

"Sure," I said. Samantha moved to the foot of the bed.

"Let's take a look. You've got a mild contusion on the scalp—nothing serious. The scan came back clear. No concussion or internal bleeding. The ER doc didn't find other injuries, so we kept you overnight for observation."

He flipped through his clipboard. "How's your vision? Any nausea or dizziness?"

"No, just a nasty headache," I replied, trying to sit up. Samantha rushed to support my back as I swung my legs over the bed.

"To be expected. I'm willing to release you, but the police have questions. They're outside. Can I send them in?"

"Yes," I said, trying to stand. Samantha grabbed my arm, steadying me as I swayed.

"It was nice meeting you. If the police aren't detaining you, you'll be free to go." The doctor nodded and left.

Moments later a man stepped in—college frat president turned seasoned cop. Polished, approachable, mid-forties. His gaze checked out Samantha.

"Maybe you should step out?" He pointed at the door.

"I'll stay. Who are you?" she said, unwavering.

"Are you family?"

"Girlfriend," she replied firmly.

He lingered on Samantha's answer, quiet assessment in his gaze—me, older, experienced; her, younger, confident. He studied her a beat too long, weighing something behind his eyes.

"I'm Detective Luke Hammett, Chicago Police Department. I have a few questions, Mr. York."

"Ask."

Hammett's questions came steady—probing but fair. I recounted the night: Remington, the alley, Brent—careful to protect what Brent told me. Missing person. Ava Capone.

"Craig Capone's niece? Someone asked me about her."

"Tall, athletic guy, Frank Brannon?"

Recognition. "That's him."

"Free to go?"

"One more." He glanced at Samantha, seeking permission. I nodded. "Video shows you with a blonde woman at the bar. Cozy. Explain."

I didn't want to get Erika or Mike in trouble. "Her name's Rachel Cavanaugh, a friend of Samantha's. She was in town visiting friends. Samantha told her I'd be at the Remington, where Rachel was staying. I got there early. She came down, and we talked."

"Close? Did you date?"

"I just know her through Samantha."

"Why didn't you visit your friend?" he asked Samantha.

"I was at another girlfriend's house."

He nodded. "We've connected Rachel—aka Erika—to a high-end escort service. Been chasing leads for months, no solid proof. Now here you are, tangled in her world, and she in yours." He looked at Samantha for a reaction; none came. "I don't think Ms. Cavanaugh connects to your case or the Rogers case."

"Did Brent make it?" I asked, bracing for the answer.

Hammett rubbed the back of his neck and exhaled slowly, a flicker of regret crossing his face. "Afraid not," he said, voice subdued but steady. He handed me a business card. "If anything comes up, here's my number. Don't hesitate to call."

I felt punched in the gut. Samantha stepped forward and took my hand. I gripped hers tightly as the reality of Hammett's words sank in.

"Take care, Mister York," Hammett said softly, almost apologetic.

"You too," I murmured.

I struggled to stand. Samantha helped, supporting my weight. Outside, sunlight hit hard, crisp wind cutting through the hospital's sterile calm. Relief? Not a chance. Something was coming, and I wasn't sure we were ready. Every breath tasted of uncertainty. Every shadow whispered warning.

CHAPTER
NINE

After leaving the hospital, we quickly arrived at our residence. Samantha handed the car keys to the valet, and I approached the front desk of Lake Point Tower, the glassy downtown sentinel on the banks of Lake Michigan. Sean, the assistant manager, greeted us.

"Sir," he nodded. "Ms. Rhodes, it's always a pleasure to see you."

"Have Jill or Frank gone up yet?" I asked, my eyes scanning the lobby. Too quiet. Too calm. Felt like the calm before a storm.

"No one yet, sir."

We reached the elevator bank, where Torrence, the attendant, met us with a wide grin.

"Sir, Ms. Rhodes, seeing you is the highlight of my day."

"Aren't you sweet, Torrence. Up to Wayne Manor, please."

"Right away, Ms. Rhodes."

The doors closed, and I leaned back slightly, feeling the familiar hum of the elevator. The condo had earned the nickname "Wayne Manor," an ode to its luxurious grandeur and my secret residence for years. When the girls discovered it, they compared me to Bruce Wayne. Now, with Samantha living here, it had become our shared space. The moniker stuck, even gaining favor with the staff. If Frank managed to engineer a secret entrance to the office building, I might start believing I really am Bruce Wayne.

The view from the sixty-ninth floor hit like a slap of clarity. Blue sky, Lake Michigan stretching endlessly, a few fishing boats dancing lazily. The city looked peaceful from up here. Too peaceful.

Shower first. Alley grime and hospital remnants washed down the drain, the warmth of water a rare comfort. Clean again. Human again.

In the living room, I poured a sip of bourbon—small luxury, but necessary. Samantha paced, on a call, words spilling like rapid gunfire: "working... I'm busy... broke up... I can't... Mom... Dad... No!" Tiff, probably. Her elder sister in Florida. Family always had a way of complicating things.

I grabbed a notebook and jotted down details—Brent's information, Ava's boyfriend, Phil Holland, the cryptic "k... lub... The Asian." Samantha's theory that Sophie was an erotic dancer. The green pills. Fentanyl. My brain refused to pause; notes were all I had to keep the chaos organized.

Phone buzzed. Sean: "Jill's on her way up."

I found Samantha lounging in the La-Z-Boy, legs over the armrest. "Jill's on her way."

"Tiff, I've got to go. Jill's here, and I have to work. Just take it easy. Relax. Tell Mom and Dad hey and love you." She ended the call.

"I need a glass of wine right now," she yelled.

"Make that two." Jill entered.

"Have you heard from Frank?" I asked.

"On his way. Feeling okay, sweetie?"

"Good enough." Jill leaned in, a soft, lingering kiss to my cheek. Nothing romantic, but enough to blur the lines between friendship and intimacy. I caught myself thinking—this is the kind of connection that makes life feel steady, even when the world's falling apart outside.

"Everything okay back in Florida?" I asked.

Looking at Jill, Samantha replied, "Tiff broke up with her boyfriend. She wants to erase him from her memory ASAP. Come up to Chicago and have a long girls' weekend with me—and you."

"Me? Why me?" Jill raised an eyebrow.

"Because I talk about you a lot. She met you briefly at Addy's funeral. Wants to meet Ty. Says we must be serious if we've lasted this long."

Timing's off, I thought. But family's family.

Doorbell rang. Frank. About time.

"Sorry I'm late. Been digging into stuff—think I found something big."

"What is it?" Samantha's curiosity sharpened.

Frank's expression tightened. Jill's narrowed. "Frank, what's going on? You're starting to scare me."

He pulled a small notebook from his pocket. "Ava's disappearance. I think it's tied to a larger organization. Human trafficking. Big time."

The words landed like a sledgehammer. Samantha froze, lips parted. Jill's color drained. I felt the air thicken, the gravity pressing against my chest.

"What makes you think that?" I asked, trying to keep my voice steady.

"Sources—Ava was seen with shady characters before she vanished. She was in over her head."

Samantha whispered, "What does this mean for us?"

Frank's face remained grim. "We need to be careful. If this is a human trafficking ring, we're in way over our heads. Maybe we should hand this off to the police. Or at least get them up to speed. Fast."

Jill's expression flashed with anger. "We can't sit back. We have to help Ava."

I leaned back, shoulders heavy with the weight of the night ahead. The room pulsed with pressure, and I knew one thing for certain: this was no longer just a missing person case. We were standing at the edge of something far darker.

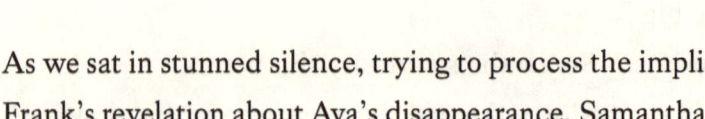

As we sat in stunned silence, trying to process the implications of Frank's revelation about Ava's disappearance, Samantha suddenly stood and turned on the stereo. Chopin's Nocturne in E-flat major, Op. 9, No. 2 floated through the condo, the delicate notes curling around the tension, easing it just enough for our brains to start turning again. I let it wash over me, though my mind refused to rest—there was always another angle, another shadow waiting.

Frank took a sip from his beer and set the bottle down. "I think Ty and I should question Phil Holland. Let's find out where he lives, and we'll do it there. I like Sammy's theory on Sophie's stripping job."

I nodded, thinking: Phil Holland—a punk creep with more social media influence than brains. This could get messy fast.

"I'll investigate—search the web, see what places she might work near where she lives. Maybe I could just ask her, say I'm interested in dancing there," Samantha said, already scheming.

"How are you going to bring that up without admitting you snooped in her bedroom?" I asked, eyebrow raised.

"I'll think of something," she answered, tossing her hair like she had this under control.

"Or you might just tell her the truth. Sometimes direct is the best way. Might build trust—between you and her," Jill advised. I could hear the logic, though honesty wasn't always a survival tactic in our world.

"Don't go question her alone. She seemed more nervous the longer we were there," I warned. Too many variables. Never go in blind.

"Invite her for coffee. Tell her you have a friend who's also interested—me," Jill said. "I'll go with you. Sometimes these girls get a cash bonus for bringing in new dancers."

"Good idea, Jill," Frank said. "That leaves us with the Asian and the other word. We need to get into Ava's apartment."

My stomach tightened. Apartment searches meant evidence, meant risk, meant getting tangled deeper than any of us had bargained for.

"What's your take on Detective Hammett?" I asked Frank.

"I think he's a good cop, someone we should get to know better. If we find something out, we should let him know to build some trust. He seems like a guy who would work with us. Samantha, you met him. What do you think?"

Sammy glanced up from her phone, a sly smile curling her lips. "He's cute. I liked him. Seemed... solid, but pushy." She shrugged, tossing her long blonde hair over her shoulder.

"Maybe I should meet this Detective Hammett," Jill said, teasing.

"Ty, the workday's wrapping up. Let's try questioning Phil Holland, then head to Ava's apartment. What do you say?" Frank asked.

"Let's do it."

"I'll call Sophie and see if Jill and I can meet her tomorrow," Samantha said.

Jill nodded. "Sounds good. I'll hang out here a bit longer with Sammy, pick up the kids from Mom's in a couple of hours, then head home. I'll keep my phone close—call if you need anything." Her voice was warm, though worry frayed the edges.

Frank headed for the door, hugging Samantha goodbye. Jill followed to see us out. As Frank reached for the handle, Jill caught his hand, her fingers holding his. She leaned in, pressing a soft kiss to his cheek.

"Be careful," she said.

Frank's mouth twitched into a grateful grin. "Will do."

Jill held his gaze a second longer than polite—something unspoken passing between them before he slipped into the hallway. Samantha caught it too, a knowing smile tugging at her lips. This wasn't casual. Not by a long shot.

I could feel the energy in the room shift—the subtle spark that could change everything. And me? I kept it in check. Observing. Not getting involved. Not yet.

CHAPTER
TEN

We pulled up to Phil Holland's place in Naperville, Illinois. The house was the kind of place that stopped you cold — big, bold, and polished like a trophy on a mantel. Nestled among manicured lawns and bright flower beds, it was a fortress of quiet wealth. The façade was a smooth mix of modern lines and classic shapes, perfectly balanced, like the architect had read every rule and then thrown them out.

A red brick path, laid out like a winding river edged by trimmed hedges, led us to the entrance. The oak door was a masterpiece—carved with more care than most folks put into their homes. Tall, arched windows flanked it like sentries guarding a secret, while a security camera above peered down like a hawk on prey.

Frank broke the silence, voice low but teasing, "How much you wanna bet they don't open the door when they see a black man standing here?"

I gave him a sideways look. "I'm taking that bet. Cameras don't watch; they just blink and pretend."

Before we could make more noise, the door clicked open.

"You owe me," I said, stepping forward.

The man at the door looked about my age, early fifties, fit like he ran from problems instead of facing them. Close-cropped beard, face sharp but polite. I knew the type — too smooth to trust, but maybe not dangerous. Not yet.

"Yes?" he said, voice steady but with a hint of 'what do you want?'

"Tanner York. This is Frank Brannon. York Investigations. We're looking for Phil Holland. You his father?"

He chuckled, a short, bitter sound. "No, son's Jackson. I'm Phil. Senior director at Carter Frozen Packaging."

We flashed our IDs. He stared at them like we were rattling his cage, then surprised me by stepping aside. "Want to come in? I take it Ava's still missing?"

Before I could say more, a woman came into view — jeans, Cubs sweatshirt, arms crossed like she owned the place. Susan Holland. Her smile was warm, but her eyes told another story. Sharp. Watchful. She sized us up quick.

Phil introduced her, and we moved inside to the study — leather chairs, polished wood, the kind of place that hides its skeletons behind framed degrees and expensive art. Frank suggested talking alone. I could tell Susan wasn't about to be shuffled out so easy.

Phil leaned back, voice clipped like he'd been rehearsing lines for a bad play. "Brent told you I'm Ava's boyfriend?"

I shot Frank a quick glance. Brent's name was like a ghost in the room, dead but still haunting every word. I decided to skip the pleasantries.

"Do you know where Ava is?"

Phil's face tightened, irritation simmering just beneath the surface. "No. Brent didn't fill you in much."

I didn't sugarcoat it. "Before he could, someone shot him. He's dead."

The room dropped a few degrees. Phil's hand twitched, a gold pen slipping from his fingers. Color drained fast. That crack in his polished armor was the first honest thing I'd seen all night.

"Brent's dead? Jesus... Who did it?"

"I was hoping you'd tell me."

Phil's mask slipped completely. "I swear, I had nothing to do with it. Or Ava's disappearance. I'd never hurt them."

I leaned forward, voice hard. "Then tell us what you know."

His breath hitched. "Ava was helping Susan with a project. Lately, she got these weird calls and texts. She shut us out. Then she vanished. I was frantic. Went to Brent, but he wasn't straight with me. He looked scared."

"What did Brent say?"

Phil's voice cracked like old paint. "Ava was in danger. People were after her."

Sue squeezed his arm and said, "We were out with friends that night. I can give you names, numbers, if you want to check."

Frank nodded, already filing it away.

Phil stood slow, walked to a cabinet, and opened it with a deliberate clink of glass. "Gentlemen, you might want a drink for what I'm about to say."

The room seemed to close in, every shadow hiding something unsaid. Whatever was coming next wasn't going to be clean or pretty. Just like this city, it was going to be messy.

CHAPTER ELEVEN

Jayde's computer screen flashed an alarm, indicating that the door to a room had been opened. The tenants' rooms were locked from the outside, requiring a key to access. Jayde could only think of one person who might have done this. She quickly looked up who was currently in Room 1123.

"Motherfucker, that bitch," Jayde said to no one. It was Ava Capone's room.

Grabbing her key card, Jayde hustled to Room 1123, fearing the worst. Upon arrival, she scanned the card on the door and burst into the room, her eyes scanning the space with a mixture of anger and disgust. She had always known the doctor was a pervert, but she had never suspected him capable of something like this. Ava's lifeless body lay on the bed, her skin pale and clammy. The doctor was on top of her, his pants around his knees, his hairy behind pumping up and down.

Jayde took in the scene, her mind a fury of thoughts. The doctor looked up briefly, then returned to his grim task. No one was supposed to die on this mission. She had controlled this assignment from the start. But this wacko doctor got in the way, and she was under orders not to touch him. They were getting close to the end, and then she'd be able to take her retribution on him for the lives he had taken.

"You're a monster," she spat, her voice low and venomous. "You're a disgusting, degenerate monster."

The doctor cowered, his head darting back and forth between Jayde and the door. He knew he was in trouble and was frantic to escape.

"Get the fuck off her, you psycho nut job!" she yelled. With one swift kick of her leg, she slammed a ball breaker boot into the doctor's side, flipping him off Ava. He screamed in agony, grabbing his side. Jayde bent down and checked Ava's condition. Ava didn't move, but that was one effect of the pills—a zombielike state. Jayde noticed Ava's skin had a blueish tint to it. Jayde pressed two fingers to the side of Ava's neck but did not find a pulse.

"She OD'ed," the doctor wheezed, his breath labored.

Jayde stood up, her body trembling with rage. "You gave the little cunt too many," she spat, her voice a low, dangerous growl. The room seemed to shrink around them. She paced back and forth, her boots clicking sharply on the linoleum floor, each step a countdown to the explosion she was barely containing.

"She died, and you wanted to get one more fuck into her," Jayde continued, her voice rising with each word. "I knew you were a pervert, wanting to see their snatches every time you did these examinations, but fucking a dead girl just makes you demented. Did you kill her on purpose? Like the others? This delays the testing now. We don't have any more subjects. Do you see how important she was? She showed the best results from the drugs. Now I have to go fishing for someone else and start all over. Fuck!"

She reached for her radio, her movements sharp and precise, a stark contrast to the chaos of her emotions. "I need a pickup and planting in Room 1123," she said, her voice cold and detached, all trace of emotion stripped away. The voice on the other end of the radio responded, and Jayde nodded, her gaze never leaving the doctor's face. "Copy that," she said, her voice firm and resolute, leaving no room for argument.

When the men finally arrived, they moved with efficient, almost clinical precision, their footsteps resonating in the sterile hallway. Jayde watched as they took Ava's body away, a sense of finality settling over her like a shroud. She had never liked Ava, but she didn't deserve to die like this. Nobody deserved to die like this! Fuck, why did this have to happen? Jayde felt a wave of nausea as she blinked hard to keep the feelings locked inside her.

She knew she had to keep it together, to maintain her composure in the face of this tragedy. But as she turned back to the doctor, she couldn't shake the feeling that something had shifted, that the world had tilted ever so slightly on its axis, and nothing would ever be the same.

The doctor, on the other hand, seemed to be feeling something entirely different. Jayde watched as he rose from his seat and moved with a slow, calculated deliberation. He approached the spot where Ava had lain; he bent down and picked up Ava's panties, the fabric clutched in his hand like a twisted trophy.

Jayde caught his expression, a mix of triumph and depravity that made her blood run cold. He brought the undergarment to his nose, inhaling deeply, his eyes closing in a moment of sickening ecstasy. The sight was so revolting that Jayde felt a surge of bile rise in her throat, the room spinning around her as she struggled to maintain her composure.

Before she could do something she would regret later, Jayde turned on her heel and stormed out of the room, slamming the door behind her with a force that shook the walls. The sound boomed down the hallway, a final, resounding declaration of her disgust. As she walked away, her steps heavy, she left the doctor to his victory and the haunting memory of Ava's final moments.

Jayde knew she had to act, to bring justice to Ava and the others and put an end to the doctor's twisted games. But for now, the mission came first.

CHAPTER
TWELVE

Sammy sat at her desk, Jill perched on the edge, listening intently as Sammy dialed Sophie's number. The office was quiet, the hum of the city outside their window was the only background noise. Sammy had filled Jill in on her encounter with Sophie the day before, and they were both eager to see where this lead would take them.

"Hey Sophie, it's Sammy from yesterday," she said, trying to keep her voice casual and friendly. "I hope I'm not catching you at a bad time." There was a pause before Sophie's tentative voice came through the line.

"Oh, hi. No, this is fine. I told you everything yesterday."

Sammy took a deep breath and launched into her fabricated story about disliking the investigator's job.

"I've got a bit of a credit card problem... and a serious weakness for Louboutin shoes. I was hoping you might have some advice. You strike me as someone who's got their finances together."

A beat of silence made her cringe—maybe she'd laid it on too thick.

Sophie's reply was hesitant. "Um, maybe you should try shopping at Target or something? Their shoes are cute and way more affordable."

"Yeah, maybe," Sammy said, trying to sound noncommittal. Then she decided to push a little further.

"Maybe there's a way we both could make some money."

"How?"

"Well, this might sound bold, but I saw some of your outfits in your bedroom when I passed by on the way to the bathroom. They were really nice. I couldn't help but notice they looked a bit... sexy for a regular job."

There was a longer pause this time, and Sammy could almost hear Sophie's mind racing on the other end.

"You snooped? I'm hanging up. Goodbye," Sophie snapped, her voice barely concealing her nervousness.

"Come on, Sophie. No judgment here. The way you were acting yesterday... it felt like there was more going on. If something's up, you can talk to me."

Sophie let out a shaky breath. "I do some dancing on the side. It's just a way to make extra money. But I don't want it to get out, you know?"

They were getting somewhere.

"I get it, Sophie. I just want to know more about the place where you dance. Don't girls get a finder's fee—so to speak—for bringing in new girls? Can you tell me about it? Actually, my girlfriend wants in too. That's even more money for you."

Sophie hesitated. Sammy could sense the internal tug-of-war. Then, finally:

"Okay. I'll meet with you. But just for coffee. And just to talk about dancing."

Sammy grinned, trying to hide her excitement. "Great. How about Uptown Coffee, tomorrow at one o'clock?"

"Sure. That works," Sophie said, her voice a little stronger now.

As Sammy hung up, a ripple of satisfaction washed over her. They were one step closer to solving the case—and she had a feeling Sophie might be the key.

Jill leaned over and kissed her on the cheek. "You're a genius, Sammy."

"Thanks, Jill. I think we make a pretty good team."

"I never punished you for the antics the other night."

"Was I bad?" She batted her lashes.

"Do you and Ty still have those handcuffs?"

CHAPTER
THIRTEEN

Phil Holland's liquor collection could've stocked a speakeasy. Bottles lined the shelves in a parade of bourbons, ryes, and vodkas—labels gleaming like polished trophies. Every choice looked carefully picked, the kind of shelf that told you the man had money and wanted you to notice. Frank went with a beer, Susan curled her fingers around a white wine, and Phil and I poured ourselves into a sixteen-year bourbon that burned just right on the way down.

"Gentlemen, I think my wife is a better person to explain how we know Ava. Dear, would you?"

"Of course, love," Susan said. Her voice had polish, like a professor in front of a class. "When I was in college, I specialized in sexuality studies throughout the twenty-first century, focusing on partnerships that deviate from established norms."

I hadn't expected that angle, but it got my attention.

"I've always been drawn to human connections—intimacy, orientation, preferences, desires. But studying them isn't enough. I need to experience them firsthand. That's ethnographic immersion—stepping into other people's worlds and living them."

Her words ran smooth, too smooth, like a stream with no rocks. Easy to get carried away if you didn't keep your feet planted.

"By fully engaging, you adopt their ways, their habits, and you learn who they are and why they do what they do," she went on, her eyes lit with passion. "For me, that means exploring my own needs, finding fulfillment in ways that aren't always conventional."

Her speech painted a picture all right—one dripping with velvet shadows and locked doors. I couldn't help but wonder how far she was willing to go in the name of her "research."

"Wonderfully done, my dear." Phil's smile was a salesman's. He turned to Frank and me. "I can see by your expressions Susan's explanation was a bit overdone."

I tried to play it cool. "Not at all." The words came out flat. I wasn't fooling anyone.

Frank wasn't playing at all. He cut through the perfume of Susan's monologue like a bayonet. "What's this got to do with Ava?"

Phil didn't flinch. "Because of my wife's education, and her openness to explore, we went to the new club that opened recently. That's where she met Ava." His voice was steady, controlled.

"I was curious why women work at such establishments," Susan said. "So, I asked Ava."

"And?" Frank's jaw tightened.

"Long story short, we started seeing her outside the club," Susan said. "I'm writing a book on empowering women to embrace their sexuality without shame. Ava fit a certain age group, experimenting with sex outside traditional roles."

"In other words, bicurious," Phil chimed in. "But let's be clear—we didn't have relations with Ava. My wife only interviewed her."

Susan moved to stand beside him, a picture of solidarity. Phil carried on. "Brent and Sophie were two of the names Ava mentioned. She had no feelings for Brent, though Brent made his interest known. Sophie, on the other hand, intrigued her. She wanted to explore that curiosity but didn't know how to approach Sophie. I advised her to be honest with Sophie, to let Brent down easy, and to pretend I was her boyfriend if it kept Brent off her back. Looks like she took my advice."

Frank drained his beer and rose. "It's been interesting, Phil. Thanks for the conversation—and the drink." He shook Phil's hand, grip firm, eyes harder.

We made for the door. One last thought hooked me. "Phil, that club you mentioned. Where you met Ava. What's the name?"

"Of course—the Kinky Kitten Club. North side."

"Was Ava one of the dancers?" I asked.

"Just a server,"

"Thanks for the information."

We left, but my head was buzzing. Too many doors had opened at once, each one darker than the last. Kinks, lifestyles, experiments—it was a jungle of appetites out there. Was Samantha my kink? Was her being with Jill another? Or was I just the older guy in her story, the one she'd grow out of?

The bourbon in my gut turned to fire, but it didn't burn off the doubt riding shotgun in my head. Sammy was young, sharp, and full of light, and I was fifty-one with more miles than I cared to count. Some nights I wondered if she deserved better than an old dog like me. And Jill—steady, dependable Jill—she had two kids waiting at home, yet here she was, knee-deep in our mess. Maybe I was dragging her down a road she didn't need to walk.

We had Ava's place next, and the closer we got, the more the city seemed to hum—low and dangerous, like it knew the answers before I did. Something ugly was waiting out there, something important. And I couldn't shake the feeling that, one way or another, the people I cared about would pay the price.

As we drove to Ava's apartment, the rhythmic hum of the tires on the pavement filled the car, a steady backdrop to our conversation. I was looking up the club Phil mentioned on my phone.

"The club looks impressive," I told Frank.

"We might have to check it out. You have the key code Alice gave you to Ava's apartment?"

"Yeah. Don't have to break in this time. What do you make of what Susan said?"

"People study all kinds of things, and if her book helps others, great."

"I just wonder about Samantha. She's young. Am I being selfish by having her as my girlfriend? Will she resent it after a while, dating an older guy? I don't think I can give her what she may want later on."

"What's that supposed to mean?"

"I don't know. Maybe she would be better off without me."

"Hey, I'm not sure where this is coming from, but let me tell you what I see. You and Sam? You're like two peas in a pod. The way she looks at you? It's like watching Michigan Avenue light up at Christmas. And you care for her, Ty. It's plain to see. Sam's not one to stick around if she doesn't want to. She's put her time and money into York Investigations. That's a sign, don't you think? She's in it for the long haul. Look, we're brothers. We can talk straight, right?"

"I hope so."

"I think you respect each other enough to trust each other. We're all on this big ride we call life. It's the greatest thing in the world, and we only get one. So don't worry about what others think or say. You have each other, you have Jill, and, of course, yours truly. Do you love Sam?"

"She's my dream come alive. Yes."

"Then what the hell are you worried about? I know Sam and Jill have a special bond. And if Sam wants to spend some time with Jill, what's the big deal?" Frank's laugh was deep, almost comical.

"Thanks, man," I said, feeling gratitude toward my friend.

Frank reached over and gripped my shoulder, a gesture of solidarity in our friendship. "No problem, Ty. We're in this together."

I gazed out the window, replaying my conversation with Frank in my mind. As we passed under a streetlight, its glow briefly illuminated the road behind us, catching my eye in the side mirror. Among the scattered headlights, an old, beat-up white panel Chevy minivan trailed at a steady distance.

As we approached Ava's apartment, tension built inside me. What would we find? Would there be any clues that could help us solve the case?

Frank pulled into a parking spot, and we both got out of the car. My breath misted in front of me. I took in the distinct vibe of Bucktown, a spirited neighborhood crackling with creativity. Ava's building, just north of Armitage Avenue, radiated urban charm, mirroring the area's artistic spirit. Bold street art covered nearby walls—bursts of color and character that spoke to the neighborhood's flair. The lively bar scene added its own layer of energy to the atmosphere.

We reached the apartment building, and Frank punched in the key code Alice had given us. The door clicked open, and we stepped inside. The place was dark and quiet; the only sound was the low hum of the refrigerator in the kitchen.

"Okay, let's get to work," Frank said, his voice low. "We need to find out what happened to Ava."

CHAPTER
FOURTEEN

"What are we looking for?" I asked.

"I'm sure the police and family have been through here already, so look for something out of the norm. We could get lucky and find something written, but with phones these days..." Frank let the thought trail off.

Ava's living room had a modest charm, with wide crown molding standing guard over a high popcorn ceiling, a touch of old elegance clinging to the place. Paintings of fruit baskets hung along one wall, the kind of thing you'd find in a church basement, while the others were covered with photos—family, friends, the soft snapshots of a life lived quietly. An area rug sprawled across the creaking hardwood, soaking the place in warmth. One photo snagged my attention: Sophie and Ava against the city skyline at North Avenue Beach, both smiling like they had the world at their feet.

The small apartment made for a quick sweep, and we were down the hall in no time. The bedroom wasn't much—just a queen bed jammed between walls, leaving little space to breathe. Like the rest of the place, it showed no sign of panic, no sign of a rush. Just a quiet life, suddenly snatched away.

"This is one small bedroom," Frank said.

"Check the closet, and I'll take the dresser," I said.

I sifted through the drawers with care, pulling out the scraps of an ordinary woman's life—blouses, jeans, sweaters folded neat. Nothing to whisper of trouble.

But one drawer sat a shade shallower than the rest. That got my attention. I pulled out the sweaters and pressed the base. Something was off. A false bottom.

How the hell did the cops miss this? Maybe they were short on manpower. Maybe they just didn't care enough to dig.

I worked the bottom open. Passport. Birth certificate. Social security card. A manila envelope, edges browned with age and coffee stains. The tape clung weakly to the flap. Handwriting scrawled across the front—looping and twisted, like it came from another world.

I slipped a finger under the flap and tore it open. Two photographs slid out—one showed Ava in overalls and boots, standing in a cornfield like she'd stepped out of a harvest postcard. The other put her in a ball gown, on the arm of an older man in a tux, under the glitter of banquet hall chandeliers.

One more thing in the envelope—a small plastic bag of pills. Vivid pink. Same size, same markings as Sophie's.

I pocketed the photos and the pills, then slid the clothes back in place.

Frank opened the bedroom door, and hell came with it.

A body slammed into him, knocking him onto the bed. His skull cracked the headboard with a thud that made the walls shake.

"Ugh!" Frank barked, pain and rage all tangled together.

Before I could move, a boot plowed into my ribs, and the air rushed out of me in a gasp. My vision swam. Another kick cracked across my face, and I hit the bed beside Frank, the taste of iron filling my mouth. Blood. Spit. A cocktail for the damned.

The attacker moved like smoke, fast and silent. Frank fought back, swung a fist like a piledriver. It missed. The wall didn't. The crack of knuckles on plaster made my teeth ache.

I lunged with the only thing I could grab—a pillow—shoving it like a shield against the figure and pinning them to the dresser. Dark eyes glared through the mask, sharp and female. She swung an arm down hard, a hammer blow to my neck that set fire to my nerves and dropped me back a step.

Frank had his Glock out, but she was faster. A kick sent it spinning across the floor, metal clanging like church bells.

Then she was on him. The cord from the blinds whipped tight around his neck. His choking gasps filled the room, ugly and desperate. Eyes bulged, veins stood out.

My gut turned cold. Frank's life was bleeding out by the second, and I was the only one left who could pull him back from the edge.

CHAPTER
FIFTEEN

When the Southwest 737 airliner from Orlando landed at Midway Airport in Chicago, Tiffany Rhodes felt a spark of excitement. Eager to make the most of her solo adventure, she navigated the bustling baggage claim, a sense of liberation washing over her. In her early thirties, she had always been the responsible one, the safe bet. But after her long-term boyfriend's infidelity, she was ready to reclaim her independence and embrace the unknown.

Tiffany had always been curious about the world, but life had a way of keeping her grounded. Now, with a few days to herself in Chicago, she was determined to experience everything the city offered. She dreamed of sipping a cocktail at a chic rooftop bar, indulging in a gourmet meal at a Michelin-starred restaurant, and perhaps even meeting someone intriguing who could help her forget about her past and embrace the present.

The driver skillfully navigated the bustling streets, dodging cars, bikers, and pedestrians as they approached her destination. Tiffany had chosen this hotel as her home away from home for the next few days. Its prime location in the city center offered easy access to Chicago's attractions, and she had booked a room with a breathtaking view. The hotel boasted a renowned five-star restaurant and an elegant cocktail bar. She thanked the driver, tipping him generously, and he returned the favor with a friendly wink.

As Tiffany stepped into the lobby of the Remington Hotel, she was struck by the opulent decor and the sound of jazz music. Fresh flowers and polished leather filled her with a sense of excitement and possibility. A friendly receptionist greeted her with a smile as she approached the registration desk.

"Good evening, ma'am. How may I assist you?"

Tiffany's eyes widened, taking in the lobby's elegance. "I'm checking in. This hotel is stunning."

The clerk nodded and turned to her computer, her fingers moving swiftly across the keyboard. "May I have your name, please?"

"Tiffany Rhodes." As the clerk worked, Tiffany noticed the other guests in the lobby, likely investors or businesspeople, engaged in lively discussions.

"Ah, yes, Ms. Rhodes. You have a city view room with a king-sized bed."

"That's correct."

The clerk provided details about the restaurant and bar hours, and Tiffany made a reservation for the day after tomorrow. As she turned to head to the elevator, her eyes wandered, and she noticed a blonde woman sipping a drink at the bar. The woman's confident demeanor and enigmatic smile drew Tiffany's gaze, and she found herself slowing her pace, curious about the woman's allure and the secrets she might hold.

Tiffany's room offered a spectacular view of the city and a glimpse of Lake Michigan. She sat on the bed, flipping through her notebook, a sense of liberation washing over her. This trip was about her, a departure from her usual role of caring for her family. Flipping to the "Things to Do" page, she checked off her reservation for the hotel restaurant. Other culinary adventures included a French restaurant Sammy had talked about, trying Chicago pizza, and sampling the famous Italian beef sandwiches. For sights, she had Millennium Park, The Bean, Willis Tower, and The Art Institute on her list. A Chicago Bulls game against the Denver Nuggets was also on her radar, given her appreciation for the athletes' physiques and skills.

Tiffany's delicate beauty was striking, with high cheekbones, full lips, and warm, inviting brown eyes framed by natural lashes. Her hair, a rich chestnut hue, was thick and lush, a trait shared by all the Rhodes women, each with their unique shade. Slightly taller than Samantha, Tiffany had a similar build but carried herself with a quiet, sophisticated power. While Samantha radiated confidence, Tiffany preferred the background, observing more than engaging.

As she looked out at the moonlit city, Tiffany felt a mix of determination and worry. She was looking forward to seeing Jill but felt uneasy about meeting Ty, her sister's older boyfriend. Tiffany wondered if Samantha was truly happy or just seeking validation and stability. She sighed, knowing she couldn't control her sister's life but feeling a sense of responsibility as the older sibling.

With a steadfast determination, Tiffany decided to make the most of her trip and ensure her sister was okay, whatever the outcome.

CHAPTER
SIXTEEN

The Donavan Pharmaceuticals Research Center was on the outskirts of Kickapoo, Illinois. There were two buildings on the 343 acres of farmland, which was one of the bigger properties in Kickapoo. The larger of the two buildings housed the labs used for the research and development of the products and the quality control lab. The second building housed the offices of the engineers, the sales and marketing teams, and CEO Warren Donavan.

As Warren sat in his office, staring out the window at the sprawling complex, he felt a sense of pride and accomplishment. The window was slightly open, allowing a gentle breeze to carry the scent of fresh-cut grass into the room, reminding him of the company's carefully manicured lawns. The rustling of leaves from the nearby trees provided a soothing backdrop to his thoughts, creating a moment of quiet reflection amidst the bustle of the research center.

But as he turned his attention to the phone call with his brother, Herbert, his mood shifted. The sound of Herbert's voice was like a grating noise, and Warren's eyes narrowed as he listened to his brother's complaints.

"Do you know where Jayde is? I haven't seen her tonight, and there was an issue. Did she tell you about Ava?"

"Jayde is out on a project," Warren said, not giving much thought to the Ava situation. "Besides, she tells a different story."

"Well, she's wrong, as usual."

Warren Donavan had always been burdened by family. His mother's long, agonizing battle with cancer had instilled in him a sense of duty—one that became an obsession after she made him promise to take care of his younger brother, Herbert. He was a constant source of frustration. A man who insisted on being called "the doctor," Herbert was a habitual liar and a self-aggrandizing parasite who seemed to harbor an unexplained animosity toward Jayde. But a promise was a promise, and Warren kept his word, even if it meant dragging Herbert along with him into the pharmaceutical empire he had built from the ground up.

Warren's initial foray into the pharmaceutical world was fueled by a noble cause: to find better ways to manage cancer. Driven by grief, he poured his energy into advancing treatments, hoping to spare others from the pain he had witnessed his mother endure. But as the years passed, his ambition outgrew his moral compass. Curing cancer wasn't enough anymore—he wanted to eradicate it completely, no matter the cost.

Funding his lofty vision required resources far beyond what his legitimate ventures could provide. To secure the capital he needed, Warren began cutting corners. He skirted FDA regulations, fast-tracked experimental drugs, and brokered questionable government contracts. Most were insignificant, such as agreements to reduce prescription medication costs, but one particular military contract had changed everything. The project required him to develop a drug capable of manipulating decision-making on a massive scale. The concept was simple yet horrifying: an airborne substance that, when inhaled, would render entire armies compliant, obedient, and incapable of independent thought. Officially, the government claimed the drug was a defensive measure—a safeguard against other nations pursuing similar weapons. Unofficially, the project had the potential to reshape the battlefield and redefine warfare.

The contract offered more than just financial backing. It gave Warren the freedom to push boundaries. By blending his cancer research with this new endeavor, he discovered that certain opioids, such as fentanyl, had properties that could enhance the drug's effectiveness. But progress was slow, and human testing became an unavoidable necessity.

Desperate to continue his work, Warren created a dormitory-style facility where subjects could be housed and monitored. To manage the day-to-day operations, he put Herbert in charge. While Warren despised his brother's personal habits—especially his inappropriate behavior with the female test subjects—he turned a blind eye. Herbert's transgressions, he reasoned, were irrelevant as long as the data proved useful.

Initially, Warren sought volunteers for the trials, but as the drug's nature became more controversial, secrecy became paramount. Volunteers were no longer an option. Warren distanced himself from the grittier aspects of subject procurement, delegating the task entirely to Herbert. He never asked questions about where the subjects came from or how they were acquired, and Herbert never offered answers. Warren didn't need to know the details.

In his mind, the potential cure for cancer outweighed the ethical compromises. Breaking a few eggs was a small price to pay for cracking the ultimate code of life and death.

Due to stringent government regulations on opioid procurement, Donavan Pharmaceuticals encountered significant obstacles in acquiring the volume needed for its experimental drug development. While legally permissible sources provided a limited supply, it was far from sufficient for large-scale testing. To circumvent these restrictions, Donavan turned to alternative methods, including exploiting vulnerabilities along the northern border. The southern border, with its heightened scrutiny and cartel activity, was deemed too risky. In contrast, the Canadian black market offered a quieter, less patrolled route for obtaining the raw materials they needed.

This covert operation served multiple purposes. Beyond securing additional opioids, it became an unorthodox means of testing their experimental subjects. Individuals undergoing early-stage trials were sent on dangerous "retrieval missions," tasked with crossing the U.S.–Canada border to acquire small quantities of illicit substances. The objectives were twofold: to observe how the drug affected decision-making and emotional responses in high-stress, high-stakes situations, and to ensure plausible deniability for the company if the subjects were caught. After all, who would believe that a respected pharmaceutical company orchestrated such operations?

While the approach yielded mixed results—some subjects failed the missions outright, either apprehended by authorities or succumbing to the drug's side effects—Warren considered these failures collateral damage. For him, every setback was a step closer to success. Each test provided critical data for refining the drug's formula, especially its ability to induce compliance and suppress cognitive resistance under duress. The casualties were justified—a small price to pay on the path to revolutionary progress. The potential rewards, both financial and military, far outweighed the human cost.

"Herbert, Jayde's an asset we can't lose," Warren said, his voice firm and commanding. "I'll tell her to keep her distance from you. Does that work for you?"

The line went quiet, and he could sense his brother's anger and frustration in the deliberate silence that followed. But he didn't care. He was too busy thinking about the next step in his plan—the next move he needed to make to achieve his goals.

CHAPTER
SEVENTEEN

I couldn't believe what I was seeing. Frank, my best friend, choking. The cord tight around his neck, his face red and clawing, gasping for air.

Panic surged, sharp and hot, but I shoved it down. My eyes darted around the room. Lamp. Dresser. I grabbed it by the base.

I lunged. The cord ripped from the wall with a snap, recoiling like a whip. I swung.

The assailant turned just in time. As I jabbed the lamp forward, shade first, they lashed out with a brutal kick. The lampshade flew off, and the bulb shattered with a sharp pop. Shards of glass sprayed like shrapnel. What remained in the socket glinted in the dim light—jagged and deadly, like the teeth of a saw.

I faked another thrust. They kicked at my hand. I jerked back. Their momentum carried them slightly off balance.

No fakes now. Lamp, broken bulb, jabbed into their side, just below the ribs. A grunt, and their grip on Frank loosened. Frank rolled off the bed, coughing, gasping for air.

My adrenaline roared. I kicked right where the lamp had struck. The assailant doubled over, shrieking, then straightened quickly, sharp and purposeful—but done. They darted for the door.

I leaped, but it slammed shut before I could reach it. Footsteps faded into the apartment. Silence.

Frank crumpled against the wall, pale, clawing weakly at his neck.

"T... T... Ty. No," he rasped.

I froze. Halfway to the door. My heart thumped.

"He... hel... elp."

I went to him, kneeled, pulled his hand away from the rope. Red welt darkening already.

"Come on, buddy. Deep breaths," I said. His voice was weak, but steadier now.

"Thanks... don't chase. Could be more outside. I can't... back you up."

"Let's get you up first." His legs shook as he leaned on me. I guided him to the kitchen, eased him into one of the creaky chairs, filled a glass with water.

"You tagged it pretty good," he said, ghost of a grin.

"Yeah, and they tagged you better," I muttered, scanning the apartment. Shadows stretched long. Streetlamp flickered outside. No one.

I picked up Frank's Glock from the floor, checked it, tucked it into my waistband. Slowly, I moved through the dim apartment. Every corner, every shadow on high alert.

Returning to the kitchen, Frank clutched the glass, his other hand gingerly touching his neck.

"Our intruder?" I said, sliding into a chair across from him. "Female. Eyes said Asian."

"Agree," Frank uttered, strained, but firmer now. Glass clinked as he set it down.

"Hospital?"

"No. No hospitals," he waved me off.

I studied him. Hellish, stubborn as ever. Good sign.

"Five minutes, then we go. You still got the envelope?"

"Right here," I said, patting my coat pocket.

"Must have been after those pictures, the pills." He winced, shifting in the chair.

I crouched, inspecting his neck. Nasty rope burn. Red, deep, bruising already.

"You're gonna have a hell of a rope burn for a few days," I moved to the bathroom. The medicine cabinet was stocked with the basics—aspirin, mouthwash, and a nearly empty tube of aloe lotion. It wasn't much, but it was better than nothing.

"Okay, Doc. I take back what I said about bedside manner," he joked.

"Yeah, yeah," I said, tossing the tube onto the table.

"Could use a drink."

"Ditto," I said, standing. "But not here. Not now."

The parking lot outside was dead quiet, the only sound a car's distant hum. Streetlamps cast long shadows across the pavement, the night pressing in close.

I scanned the lot, eyes hunting for movement. Nothing. Just the wind rattling branches.

We walked side by side. At the car, we slid in, the leather creaking under us. I started the engine. Relief bled through me as we pulled away from the complex.

But it didn't last. Driving through the empty streets, I couldn't shake the feeling we were still being watched. I checked the rearview mirror. Nothing there. Just the dark city stretching out behind us, waiting.

As I arrived at Lake Point Tower, the night staff greeted me with polite smiles and ushered me up to our condo. Samantha's perfume—something French—hung in the air, sweet and familiar, a brief reprieve from the shadows I carried with me. She was waiting, and my heart skipped a beat.

Samantha lay in bed, arms handcuffed to the headboard, asleep but vulnerable. Naked. My mind flicked over the day's violence—the fight, the bruises, the fear—and then back to her. How long had she been waiting like this, trusting me to return? Her arms must be sore. I took the keys off the nightstand and unlocked the cuffs, letting my fingers brush her skin as I freed her, careful not to disturb the fragile quiet.

"Tiger," she murmured as her eyes blinked open. "Jill left me like this for you."

"Not tonight, baby." I pressed a kiss to her forehead, feeling the softness of her skin, the slow rise and fall of her chest, the small sounds of her breath in the dim light. Her hair was a mess, a golden halo across the pillow, and I stroked it gently, letting strands slip through my fingers. "Did you have fun with Jill?"

"Always do." She said, her voice weak with sleep.

The hooks and chains rigged in the bed were there, silent witnesses to their play, but tonight they were irrelevant. I wasn't thinking about games or fantasies. I wanted nothing more than to hold her close, to feel her warmth press against mine and forget the world for a few stolen hours.

Even with aches from the day's fight gnawing at me, her presence wrapped around me like armor, a fragile cocoon shielding me from the darkness lurking just beyond our door. But even in this sanctuary, I could feel it—the pull of the streets, the weight of the city, the knowledge that danger never really slept.

Her soft snores tugged me toward sleep, the glass windows holding back a restless city below. I had her warmth, her trust—but even in each others arms, I couldn't shake the feeling that danger still had a key to the door.

CHAPTER
EIGHTEEN

Samantha entered the kitchen with a quiet purpose, her movements deliberate but softened by the remnants of sleep. She reached for a glass, filled it with water, and slid it across the counter toward me.

"You can't live on coffee, bourbon, and sex," she said, her voice low and raspy.

I smiled at the familiar jab. "It's working so far," I replied, taking a sip of my coffee.

She'd been nudging me to eat better and work out, and I had to admit—it worked. I was down ten pounds, muscle starting to show where soft edges used to be.

"Let's have it," she said.

"I think Frank and I figured out who the Asian is. A female. We got jumped in Ava's apartment. She knew judo or something. Did you call Sophie?"

"We did. Did you put ice on your ribs? I looked at them last night while you were sleeping. How's Frank?"

"Fine. He's Frank." I shifted, pain stinging my side. I tried not to let her see it.

"We're meeting Sophie today in Uptown."

"This Kinky Kitten Club ties into the three of them and the Hollands. We may have to poke around there," I said.

"You know me—always up for poking around." She wrapped her arms around me, rose on her toes, and kissed me slow and deliberate. It seemed to last forever. When she finally lowered herself, she kept her arms tight around me. "I loved cuddling with you last night."

"Me too."

There was a pause. Her gaze slipped somewhere else. "What's on your mind?"

"Oh, nothing. Just something I noticed last night."

"What's that?"

"Did you see the weird way Jill and Frank said goodbye?" she asked, brow furrowed.

"I did."

"Do you know what's going on with them? Something you're not telling me?"

"Nope. Didn't give it a second thought. Obviously, you have."

"She hasn't said a word." The puzzled look on her face said plenty.

"As far as I'm concerned, it was just a goodbye. And please—leave it alone. We've got a case, and I don't want people's minds tangled up. Promise me."

"If Jill and Frank have the hots for each other, why wouldn't she mention it?" Her eyes narrowed, gears turning.

"Look, don't do anything. Just wait till after the case."

The shrill ring of my phone cut through the kitchen, shattering the weight of the moment. I answered, expecting Frank's voice.

"York, this is Detective Luke Hammett, CPD," a voice said. The name landed like a punch. "Kickapoo PD just called. They found a girl matching Ava's description, buried in a soybean field. I'm headed out there. Thought I'd throw you a bone—see if you want to tag along, maybe ID the body."

My heart dropped. Dread seeped in fast. I looked at Samantha. Worry had carved lines into her face.

"Yeah, sure," I said, steadying my voice. "We'll meet you at KPD and head out."

As I hung up, Samantha's voice broke the silence, barely above a whisper. "What is it?"

I drew in a slow breath, steadying myself against the news. "Kickapoo PD might have found Ava," I said. "Frank and I are heading there. I want you and Jill to still meet with Sophie, but don't tell her about Ava. Just get the info about the club."

The sun dragged itself over the horizon, bleeding pink into orange like a knife wound that wouldn't close. I thumbed the phone button on the steering wheel.

"Call Frank."

He picked up after a few rings, voice rough as sandpaper. "What the hell's with the early call?"

"Hammett called. They think they found Ava's body. In a Soybean field out in Kickapoo."

"Fuck." A pause, heavy. "I'm not home. Meet at the office."

I pulled in, brewed coffee—one for me, one for him. He showed right on time, same as always, even with a hangover in his eyes.

"Why'd Hammett call us?" he asked as we headed for his pickup. "And aren't you supposed to lay off the coffee?"

I handed him his cup. "Because the department's drowning. And Hammett knows we get results. He needs friends. I brought what we found in Ava's place—maybe we trade notes. And don't worry about my coffee intake. I'm a big boy."

"Yeah, until Sam tells you otherwise." He gave me a look, then softened. "I never really thanked you for saving my ass."

"Don't start. You know better. You'd do the same for me. Always have."

"Still. I owe you a beer."

"That, I'll take."

We laughed, but it faded fast. "Neck holding up?" I asked. "And where the hell were you last night?"

Traffic was already clogging the streets, brake lights bleeding red against the windshield.

"Didn't feel like sitting at home. Went out. Drank too much. Crashed with... a buddy."

I raised an eyebrow, kept it even. "A buddy, huh? Hey, no judgment. After what you went through, a night with company's a hell of a lot better than drinking alone. You could always crash with us."

He barked a laugh, clapping me on the shoulder. "And listen to you and Sam go at it all night? Hard pass."

I smirked, staring at the traffic ahead. Out there, in a field of beans, a dead girl was waiting. And here we were—cracking jokes, hiding from ghosts we didn't want to name.

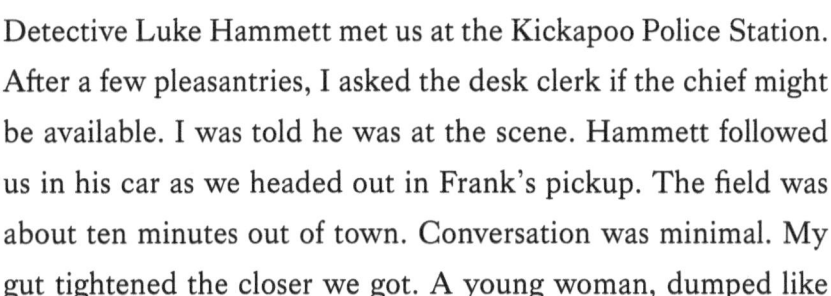

Detective Luke Hammett met us at the Kickapoo Police Station. After a few pleasantries, I asked the desk clerk if the chief might be available. I was told he was at the scene. Hammett followed us in his car as we headed out in Frank's pickup. The field was about ten minutes out of town. Conversation was minimal. My gut tightened the closer we got. A young woman, dumped like trash in a field—maybe she'd trusted the wrong man, maybe she never had a chance. Either way, I couldn't shake the feeling we were about to stare at something ugly.

As we neared the crime scene, Hammett caught up to us, his gaze sweeping the landscape. He tried to cut the tension.

"Pleasant country out here," he said, his voice low.

I nodded, my eyes fixed on the coroner's van up ahead.

"Yeah. Good place to clear your head," I replied.

"I came into town on a curvy stretch. The scenery was beautiful, but you really had to keep your eyes on the asphalt. Wouldn't want to drive that on snow and ice. It seems you know the area, York. And the cops here."

"I have a cabin out here on five acres of land. We come out on weekends and when we need time away from the city," I said.

"By we, are you referring to the young lady I met when you were in the hospital?"

"Yes, Samantha."

"She's young for you, don't you think?"

Hammett was a detective all right. His questioning about my relationship was forward, but with the job he had, it was probably impossible to turn it off. I kept my answers short. He didn't need to know our history. Not yet anyway.

"She's young, but mature at the same time." The words sounded thin even as I said them, but I wasn't about to let Hammett dissect my personal life on the side of a country road.

The regional CSI van was parked beside the medical examiner's. I spotted the chief and walked over, extending a hand.

"What brings you out here, Ty? Hey Frank. How are things? Sorry you sold the shop. Now I've got to drive to the next town over to service the cars."

That was small-town Illinois for you—news traveled faster than the mail, and everyone carried a mental Rolodex of who fixed what, who sold what, and who married whom.

"I'm good. All things must change," Frank said. "Chief, this is Detective Luke Hammett of the CPD."

They shook hands.

"Ah, you're Hammett. We called because the girl we found matched your BOLO. Thought you'd want to check the scene out. You know Ty?"

"We met on a case Frank and I are working—the disappearance of Ava Capone. Detective Hammett called, said you might have found Ava," I said.

The chief's mouth tightened. "We got a call from a farmer. Last night he saw two men digging in this field. It isn't his land, but he's got permission to work it. When he came back this morning, he noticed fresh dirt and found her arm sticking out. That's when he called us."

We moved toward the field. The soil was raw, damp, unsettled. A shallow grave—sloppy, careless. If the farmer hadn't stumbled on her, coyotes would have done the work by nightfall.

"Any footprints? Who owns this land?" Hammett asked.

"It belongs to Donavan Pharmaceuticals," replied the chief. "We'll notify them once we're done here. Our team will make plaster casts of those tire tracks over there." He pointed to a set of ruts by the edge of the field.

"The forensics team can use a laser to create a 3D profile. I've seen it done before, and it's quite impressive," Hammett said.

"Maybe in the city, but not in our small town. Well, let's not waste time. Let's see if we found your missing person," said the chief, leading us toward the coroner's van.

The medical examiner stood waiting with a stretcher and a black body bag. The chief's eyes shifted to me as the zipper rasped open. My chest tightened. I braced myself for Ava's face—but the woman inside wasn't her. Relief and dread twisted together in my gut.

I shook my head. "That's not Ava Capone."

CHAPTER NINETEEN

The lifeless body of Sophie Rodriguez lay before us, her eyes frozen in a permanent stare, as if death had claimed her with unsettling swiftness. My stomach tightened, a cold knot of guilt twisting inside me. We'd been trying to help her, trying to uncover the truth about Ava's disappearance, and now she was dead. Did we somehow push her closer to this? Could we have prevented it? I didn't dare answer.

Frank's voice cut through my thoughts, low and serious. "Ty, we need to talk about this."

I nodded, my mind a whirlwind of questions and doubts. Who could have done this? And why?

The medical examiner's voice was calm, precise, almost clinical, yet tinged with morbid curiosity as he pointed to the telltale signs on her arm. "The marks suggest she may have been injected with a lethal dose of fentanyl or heroin. The lack of rigor mortis and livor mortis indicates she's been dead less than eight hours."

Frank and I exchanged a look, the silence between us thick with unspoken questions. Who could do this to someone like Sophie? And why?

The examiner continued, his words detached but sharp. "Given the absence of visible trauma or defensive wounds, she was likely killed elsewhere and dumped here. Toxicology tests will confirm the cause of death, but it's clear this was no accident." He zipped up the body bag with clinical finality.

The chief's voice cut through the stillness, firm but tinged with concern. "Ty, I'll need a statement from you. This case just got a lot more complicated."

Restlessness pricked at me, a familiar itch I couldn't scratch. I wanted to do something—anything—to move this investigation forward. "Let's get out of here," I said, turning to Frank and Hammett. "We can talk more at my cabin."

Hammett nodded, a subtle acknowledgment passing between us. He followed in his car as we wound through the desolate landscape, the world around us quiet and unforgiving.

I checked my watch. 1:00 p.m. I needed to call Samantha, break the news that Sophie wasn't going to show.

In the distance, the faint wail of sirens cut through the valley—a grim reminder that Sophie's death was just one turn in a twisted, ongoing game, one that would push us all to the edge and beyond.

Jill walked out of Uptown Coffee with Sammy to meet Sophie, and they sat at one of the small cast-iron tables. Uncertain whether Sophie would show, Jill glanced at Sammy, who was checking her makeup in a compact mirror. Her thoughts drifted back to the conversation they'd had earlier, and she wondered again if she should take a step back to give Sammy and Ty the space to grow their relationship. But the idea of losing Sammy—of being pushed aside—made her heart ache.

Sammy, oblivious to Jill's inner turmoil, closed her mirror and turned to Jill with a bright smile. "I hope this works, we need info fast, she better show."

Jill's expression softened. "We will get the info." she said, trying to sound casual despite the flutter in her chest.

Sammy reached out and gently brushed a strand of hair behind Jill's ear.

"Why do you look so serious? I know what you're thinking, Jill," she said. "You're thinking about that conversation we had the other night. We're good. You have nothing to worry about. So, can we get past this?"

As she spoke, Sammy's gaze drifted toward the entrance of Uptown Coffee. She thumbed toward the door. "I saw you checking out that cute barista. She's a hottie—maybe I'm the one who should be concerned," she teased, trying to lighten the mood. "And we need to talk about that long goodbye with Frank. Don't think I didn't notice."

Jill's face flushed. She held up her hand, palm out. "Stop."

Just as she was about to defend herself, Sammy's phone rang, cutting through the moment. She answered, her gaze still locked on Jill's. The call was brief.

When she hung up, her expression shifted. "That was Ty. Sophie's dead. That's who they found in the field—not Ava."

A pang of grief struck Jill. "Poor girl. First Brent, now Sophie…"

Sammy moved closer and wrapped her arms around Jill, pulling her into a gentle hug. Their fingers found each other, lacing together naturally. The weight of the news settled between them, heavy and raw.

Jill looked up, overwhelmed by a rush of emotion—and love. They kissed, soft and sincere, a quiet balm against the pain. It was their first public kiss, unguarded and real.

For a moment, Jill forgot the fear of being seen, the secrets still tucked away from family and friends. All that mattered was the woman in her arms, and the fragile comfort they gave each other in a terrible moment.

They got up to leave when she felt a growing sense of unease, like a shadow creeping up behind her. She scanned the café, her gaze drifting over the crowded tables, until she landed on a man in a beat-up straw fedora, sitting off to their left. His face was weathered and worn, and his eyes narrowed into slits as he watched them with an unnerving intensity. His eyes seemed to be judging them, like a juror weighing a verdict of guilty until proven innocent.

The oak and pine trees that guarded my cabin stood tall, their autumn glory a vibrant backdrop to the tension waiting inside. My key turned the lock, and the door creaked open, revealing the warm, inviting interior. Hammett's eyes widened, brows rising as he took in the space. He wandered over to the floor-to-ceiling bookshelf, letting his fingers trail along the spines as he whispered the titles under his breath.

"Quite a collection you have here," he said, voice a mix of awe and curiosity. "First editions, if I'm not mistaken."

I nodded, a faint smile tugging at the corners of my mouth. "Most of them are. I have a fondness for rare books. Bridget's Book Nook in the city is my go-to spot."

Hammett's eyes lit up. "I know the place. It has that old bookstore feel..."

Frank, ever the host, cut in. "Beer, anyone?" He headed to the kitchen, and I nodded, grateful for the distraction.

"Not for me—on duty," Hammett said, glancing around the room, taking in the cozy furnishings and warm atmosphere. "This is quite a place you have here, York. I was expecting a rustic fishing shack, not a cabin on five acres."

"It's home," I said, pride seeping into my tone, though my chest tightened a little.

"And it comes with an owl," Frank added.

"A what?"

"A great horned owl—likes to visit around dusk. We call him Dash," I said.

Hammett's interest piqued. "We?"

I glanced around and spotted Samantha's bra and panties on the couch. Quick reflexes scooped them up, tucking them into an end table drawer. "Samantha considers this her cabin, too," I explained, trying to keep my tone light.

Frank handed me a cold beer, passed one to himself, and gave Hammett a bottle of water. We settled in, the tension in the room refusing to dissipate entirely.

"Ava's still missing," Frank said, voice low. "We've found some things we'd like to share—see if we can work together to get her back."

Hammett's expression hardened, guarded. "I appreciate the water, but you know I'm not supposed to discuss an open case. I hope you didn't take anything from a crime scene."

My jaw clenched. Frustration simmered beneath the surface. "Cut the bullshit, Hammett. We're trying to help. You could have identified the body without us. What do you want from us?"

Hammett met my gaze, a subtle challenge in his eyes. "I need to know I can trust you. I've worked with other investigators before, and it didn't end well. You two seem different. I'm willing to overlook minor infractions if it helps the case."

Frank pulled a small cellophane baggie from his pocket and handed it to Hammett. "We found these pills in Ava's and Sophie's apartments. I sent some to my CIA contact to see what they are. When I get that report, I'll share it with you."

Hammett's eyes narrowed as he examined the pills, thoughtful. "I've seen these before around the city," he said. "The feds came through asking questions. They're all over this."

I passed him the photos we'd found. "One of her dresser drawers had a false bottom. We're not sure who the old guy is, though."

Hammett's gaze lingered on the photos before he looked up, a hint of a smirk playing on his lips. "Maybe she likes sugar daddies, like your girl does, York."

I felt a surge of anger, but Frank stepped in before it escalated. "Let's focus on finding Ava. We're trying to help, Hammett. Can we work together?"

The tension eased slightly as I sipped my beer. Hammett's voice softened. "Sorry, York. Didn't mean to ruffle your feathers. Maybe I'm just jealous. I'm not dating anyone at the moment."

I nodded. "We're cool. Let's just focus on finding Ava."

As we discussed the case, Hammett's demeanor grew more serious. "I don't recognize the man in the photo, but I can run it through our database. Before Brent Rogers died, you said he told you something. What was it?"

I hesitated, weighing how much to reveal. "He mentioned an Asian. We didn't know what it meant, but I think we found out in Ava's apartment. The assailant seemed to have Asian features and knew judo or karate."

Hammett's gaze intensified. "Did you see the face?"

I shook my head. "No, they wore a neck gaiter. We only saw the eyes."

Hammett nodded, taking notes. "Anything else?"

Frank spoke up, voice low. "The Kinky Kitten Club. Brent tried to tell Ty the name, but didn't get it out. We figured it out. Ava worked there part-time as a server; she met Phil Holland and his wife, Susan, there. Susan's working on a book Ava was helping with. Sophie also worked at the club, but as a dancer..."

Hammett's eyes gleamed. "Is this the new place on the north side?"

I nodded. "Yes. Everyone we've dealt with seems connected to this club."

Hammett's expression grew thoughtful. "Maybe I'll bring these people in and see what I can get. The interrogation room can be... persuasive. You'd be surprised what people say in a tight spot."

Unease slithered through me. I didn't want Hammett running the show. "Maybe hold off on interrogations. Let us dig into the club first. We don't want to tip anyone off. Can you help by looking into their backgrounds instead?"

Hammett rubbed his jaw, eyes narrowing in thought. "Okay, I'll give you some time. But keep me in the loop, or I'll slap obstruction charges on you in a heartbeat. Just poking around won't get much. You need someone on the inside."

I leaned forward, heart tightening. "Who?"

CHAPTER

TWENTY

Jayde stood in front of the bathroom mirror, topless. The fluorescent lights overhead cast a harsh glow on her skin. She winced as she applied a new dressing to her wound, the pain still throbbing from the fight with the two men in Ava's apartment. The door eased open, and Donavan stepped inside, his attention drifting from corner to corner, with a blend of curiosity and want.

"Don't you fucking knock, you perv?" Jayde snapped, her voice menacing.

Donavan chuckled, his interest fixed on Jayde's breasts, a leering grin spreading across his face. "I've seen you naked before, Jayde, remember how we met?"

Jayde spun around, hands on hips, her glare sharp enough to cut glass. "That doesn't give you the right to just barge in here, asshole. This better be good."

"They found Sophie in the field," he said flatly, his voice devoid of emotion. "Unlike Ava, she wasn't responding to the pills. I had the doctor take care of it."

Jayde did her best to conceal her surprise—and her anger. Another one lost. More innocent blood spilled on this mission.

She finished changing her bandage and spoke through clenched teeth. "I'm security. I should have handled this. I don't appreciate you going behind my back."

She couldn't help but think: if she'd been the one to intervene, she could've brought Sophie into her system—kept her alive and safe.

"You could have let the doctor take a look at that." Donavan pointed to her wound.

"Fuck him. He's a quack."

"Okay. Moving on. We'll need a new subject. Losing Ava puts us behind. We'll need to speed up the process. We have enough pills to last us until we have a full development of the product and complete the government contract. I was thinking of looking for another subject at a different club. Maybe something in the suburbs."

Donavan's words caught Jayde's attention. Changing locations now wouldn't be good. Everything she needed was in place at the Kinky Kitten. She had to think fast. "That's not gonna work for me."

"It's worked out in the past. Besides, it looks like we're making a pattern. We took two girls out of the joints on the south and west sides. Now we'll be going back to the same club and getting another about the same age as the last five. You see where this is going?"

"We have the Kinky Kitten scouted. If we switch clubs now, that will delay us further."

Donavan mulled it over. "You're right. And I thought I was the brains of this partnership."

"You are. It doesn't mean you're fucking smart." Jayde reached and grabbed her shirt.

Donavan reached out a hand and grabbed her arm, pulling her toward him. "You want to play with Jayde, baby?" she whispered, her voice low. She smiled a cold, calculating smile.

Donavan lit up with desire, and he leaned in, his lips brushing against Jayde's ear. But before he could continue, Jayde's knee shot up, connecting with his groin with a sickening crunch. The sound of his groan was like music to Jayde's ears, and she smiled a triumphant smile as he fell to the ground, writhing in agony.

Jayde used her boot to roll Donovan onto his back. "This is what we're fucking going to do. It's too late now to change clubs. So, I'm going to the Kinky Kitten Club, and I'll get who I want as a subject. I doubt those two fucking fools at her apartment found anything to link you to Ava. I searched that whole place before they showed up. Once we get this contract done, we'll have no need for subjects. The doctor is getting careless. With Ava, he left some DNA for the cops to find. That dick of his will be the end of him yet. We can pin this whole thing on him. Make sure he gets locked up. Have one of your morons dig Ava up and stick her up in a tree somewhere. That will throw the hick cops off for days."

All Donavan could do was grunt and nod.

CHAPTER
TWENTY-ONE

"That's insane. You're fucking crazy," I said. "I can't go along with putting Samantha at risk, let alone parading her around half-naked in a strip club with all those men pawing at her. Can't an undercover detective do that?"

"We'll be with her the whole time, York. We don't have the resources for this type of operation. Besides, I'd have to bring my superiors in on it, and that place would crawl with cops," Hammett noted.

"No," I declared.

"We've used civilians before. By doing so, we'll have better access to insider information. Sam can blend into the environment better than we could. She'll have the advantage of building trust, which could be crucial for gathering evidence and witnessing criminal activity firsthand. She can gain access to sensitive locations. I think she can handle herself," Hammett continued.

"Ty, I think it's worth a try," Frank said.

"Come on, Frank. You're not on my side? Don't you see how dangerous this is? Also, we lost her before, remember?"

"Ty, we didn't lose her. We tracked her the whole time. But this way, we control the situation. We say when shit goes down. Look, we can microchip Sam, use that to track her in case something happens. We'll have eyes on her the whole time. We'll use the chips the CIA uses, so if anything goes south, I can call them and they can intervene," Frank said.

"You guys have access to that stuff?" Hammett asked.

"If this is the place they took Ava and Sophie from, we could find a lot of answers there. And if Sam can get a job working the floor inside, we'd have a mole in the club and might uncover even more corruption. But we need her inside. We'll keep Hammett in the loop daily."

Hammett's expression grew serious. His voice was urgent. "We can't do this without her."

I felt a surge of resistance, my mind racing with every reason this was a terrible idea. But Frank's calm, steady voice cut through the doubt. "We'll be with her the whole time, Ty. We'll keep her safe."

I looked at Frank, searching for reassurance, but all I saw was quiet defiance—a strength I couldn't argue with. "This is crazy," I muttered.

Frank put a hand on my shoulder. "Young girls are being taken. For what, we don't know. It all leads to this Kinky Kitten Club. Just ask Sam if she'll do it. If she says no, we'll come up with something else. It's her call. I'd think you'd want it that way. Come on, let's start back."

I sat there like stone, knowing she'd say yes and think it was a blast. What bothered me—what shook me more than I'd admit—was that it turned me on. I pictured her up there, taunting those men, multicolored lights dancing over her half-naked body.

Spinning, grinding on the chrome pole. Strange men staring up, fantasizing. And I knew she'd get off on it, knowing I was out in the crowd. I imagined what coming home afterward would feel like.

But I loved her, and this was dangerous. I could ask her not to do it. Demand she not do it. But that wasn't us. Each of us made our own decisions. Samantha deserved that right. I could tell her how I felt, but in the end, it would be her choice. All I could do was be supportive—and make damn sure nothing happened to her. Or I'd unleash hell on everyone in that place.

"Ty, you ready?" Frank asked.

"Yeah, buddy." I rose from the chair, then glanced back, picturing Samantha draped across the armrest in nothing but my dress shirt, lost in her own world. I loved that image of her.

I set the alarm and locked the front door. Just as we were about to leave, I caught sight of Dash, perched high in the oak outside. He stared down at me, unblinking, sharp-eyed—a silent reminder to watch over our girl.

CHAPTER
TWENTY-TWO

Tiffany entered the Remington Hotel, her arms laden with shopping bags from the various high-end stores along Michigan Avenue, feeling a sense of carefree joy that only a vacation could bring. She was delightfully behind schedule, but it didn't matter; every decision was hers to make, from what to buy to where to dine, without anyone telling her otherwise. She had woken up late that morning, the aftermath of an unexpectedly late night and one too many fancy drinks, but the memories of the intriguing people she had met, particularly that one guy, made it all worthwhile.

The previous evening had been spent at the Incognito Bar, a peculiar establishment unlike any she had experienced before. The decor lived up to its name, transporting her to a different era. The main room was spacious, featuring a long wooden bar on one side, tables and chairs in the middle, and booths lining the opposite wall. It was as if she had stepped into the French resistance of the 1940s, an impression reinforced by the sign above the bar reading "La Résistance." The staff added to the authenticity: the bartenders, dressed in slacks, suspenders, and rolled-up dress shirts, and the servers in short navy-blue skirts and stripe shirts, complete with red scarves and black berets.

As the night matured, she'd discovered the Incognito had an enigmatic downstairs called The Catacombs. The darkness seemed denser there, a subterranean realm veiled in deeper shadows. Descending the stairs, she'd found herself with a choice to venture left or right. She followed the path on her right, which led her into a long, coiling corridor. The path wound around like a clandestine maze, each step taken shrouded in mystery.

Amid this obscurity, she encountered hidden alcoves seamlessly carved into the walls, resembling secret caves. These tucked-away retreats held snug sofas nestled against the walls, accompanied by petite black tables just spacious enough to accommodate a flickering candle and a pair of drinks. Passersby easily overlooked these cozy, hidden niches. Old-world French romance filled Incognito Bar's ambiance; soft background music resonated with this distinctive vibe. She began to understand her sister's fascination with all things French; the bar itself seemed to whisper tales of French elegance and mystique.

When she wandered back upstairs to the main bar, she met a group of three couples. Tiffany found out they were also there on vacation. After some conversation, they asked her if she'd like to join them at their table. The couples found Tiffany fascinating, having a father as a Florida state senator. One couple knew a guy who had come into the bar by himself, and they introduced her to him. He was older than her. Not the type of man she dated. Tiffany attracted college-educated men who worked in IT. But this guy had well-developed muscles, was rough around the edges, and looked like he had seen and thrown a few punches. To her surprise, she found herself attracted to him. He spoke well and was down to earth. As she sipped her wine and chatted with the stranger, she couldn't help but feel a sense of excitement and anticipation. The dim lighting and soft music of the bar created a sensual atmosphere, and Tiffany found herself leaning in closer to him, their bodies touching as they talked.

Tiffany felt a thrill as he touched her arm, his fingers tracing a gentle path along her skin. After the "getting to know you" conversation, the drinks kicked in. He suggested they go to The Catacombs. Tiffany let her guard down a bit. She had come here for an adventure, so why not have drinks with a handsome stranger?

As they made their way downstairs, Tiffany felt the weight of the stranger's gaze on her, his eyes burning with desire.

The Catacombs' dark atmosphere and hidden alcoves gave the place a scandalous air. Was this where spouses brought their secret lovers? They settled into one of the cozy niches, the soft cushions swallowing them into a cocoon. The candle on the table cast flickering shadows on the dark walls, and Tiffany felt like she was in a different world, one where anything was possible. She allowed herself some light kissing and touching. The stranger's lips were warm and gentle as he kissed her, his tongue tracing a path along her neck that left her breathless and wanting more. She was overcome with a rush of unrestrained liberation, a sensation of freedom and escape that was entirely new to her. As his hands explored her body, she got so aroused that she almost climaxed. He was a strong, confident man. She spent the rest of the night drinking fine wine, flirting, and kissing her stranger. Their bodies melted together on the small sofa. She was comfortable with him. This was a perfect evening after her breakup. If only she could get a photo of them together to post on social media. That would teach her ex that Tiffany Rhodes had moved on without him.

The spa this morning had put her back on track. She only got in a half mile of shopping along the Magnificent Mile. Impressed by the excellent selection of stores to pick from, her first stop was the shops at 900 North Michigan. She purchased a few things at Bloomingdale's, Kate Spade New York, and Gucci. She even bought a bra and panty set at Enchanté Lingerie, which fit and felt so good that she was going to wear it tonight. Tiffany wanted to feel sexy.

After that, she strolled along the Avenue and found Max Mara, Marcus, and Carlisle, who was featuring a black-and-white fashion collection. Her last stop was at Coach, where she found the perfect bag. She would switch purses when she got back to her room. Tonight, she'd go out in style.

She passed the concierge's desk and nodded, and he smiled back. She made it to the elevator, and a thought popped into her head. She turned around and headed back to the concierge's desk.

"May I help you, Ms. Rhodes?" He smiled.

"Oh, how did you know my name?"

"It's my job to know all our guests who stay with us. I'm Orlando." He picked up his phone. Tiffany thought it was funny that a big fancy hotel still used a landline, but she guessed it was in keeping with the whole ambiance of the place. "Please send up someone to help Ms. Rhodes with her packages." He put the phone down.

"You don't have to do that."

"My pleasure. I bet your shopping excursion exhausted you. I hope you had a successful day." Orlando waved at someone who came right over. "Take Ms. Rhodes's packages up to 1018." The person took the bags and left.

"Don't worry, Ms. Rhodes. They will be in your room safe and sound."

"Thanks. I stopped by to ask a question."

"Of course, anything. What is your wish?"

"Do you know where I can get a Bulls ticket for tonight's game for a lower price than the prices online?"

Orlando's eyes lit up, and he nodded enthusiastically. "Ah, a basketball fan. Let me see." He unlocked a drawer, pulled out a tablet, and tapped through a few screens. "Here we are—two tickets for Bulls vs. Nuggets, section 101, center court, row 8." He turned the screen toward Tiffany, then tapped to send them. "Just sent them to your phone. Enjoy."

"Wow, I only need one. How much do I owe you?"

"Please, take both. Maybe you'll bring a friend—or meet someone new. And they're complimentary, of course."

"How kind. Can I tip you?" Tiffany dug through her purse. But Orlando waved her off.

"If at the end of your stay, you feel I've helped in making your stay more enjoyable than expected, I would appreciate any gratuity you deem appropriate for my service," Orlando said.

"Hola, Orlando."

Tiffany looked up and saw the beautiful blonde woman walk by arm in arm with a tall, dashing man. She waved at Orlando, and he nodded in response, his cheeks flushing with a hint of embarrassment.

"Afternoon, Ms. Erika," Orlando said.

While walking by, Erika put a hand to her mouth and blew Orlando a kiss, then waved goodbye. He looked down, unable to meet her eyes, a flush of red creeping across his cheeks.

Tiffany felt a pang of curiosity, wondering who this woman was. "You know, I could swear I know her. But I can't think of where it was," Tiffany said. Her thoughts were broken by Orlando asking if there was anything else.

"No, thank you so much. I better get going if I want to make the game. Thanks again."

"My pleasure, Ms. Rhodes," Orlando said.

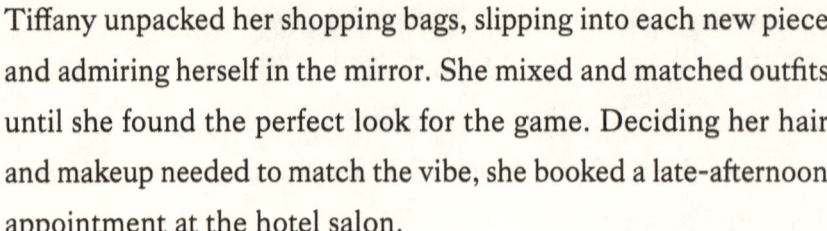

Tiffany unpacked her shopping bags, slipping into each new piece and admiring herself in the mirror. She mixed and matched outfits until she found the perfect look for the game. Deciding her hair and makeup needed to match the vibe, she booked a late-afternoon appointment at the hotel salon.

While she waited, she ordered tea and macarons from room service. Curled in a chair by the wide window overlooking the city, she sipped, flipped through a fashion magazine, and let the hours drift by.

When it was time, she threw on sweats and headed downstairs. The hairdresser and makeup artist each had their opinions, and Tiffany had hers. A little back and forth, a little compromise—and the result was everything she wanted. Sexy. Confident. Beautiful.

On her way back to her room, a bold idea struck: that extra basketball ticket. Should she text him? It was short notice; he was probably busy. But the thought of going alone nagged at her—late nights, dark streets, all the things she'd been warned about. Then again, wasn't this the independence she'd always wanted?

She hesitated, thumb hovering over her phone. Then she smiled. She'd do it. She'd text him.

Hi, it's Tiffany from last night. I enjoyed hanging out with you. I know it's last minute, but I have an extra ticket to the Bulls game tonight. Are you interested?

There, she'd done it. The text was sent. She set the phone down, waited a few seconds, then a few minutes. Still nothing.

Tiffany slipped into her black ankle-length jeans, sleek and snug, then pulled on the new white charmeuse blouse—fitted at the chest, flowing at the waist, a hint of skin showing between fabric and denim. She checked her phone again. Still blank.

Heels next. Pointed stilettos with ankle-strap bows she'd been dying to wear. Then the black faux leather jacket—oversized, sharp, and just the right amount of attitude.

One last mirror check, a tousle of her hair. She looked ready to kill. Maybe she should send him a selfie—show him what he'd be missing.

As if on cue, her phone buzzed.

Tiffany picked it up. A slow smile creased her face as she read the message.

She texted back. *Meet u out front in 10, babe.*

Tiffany put down the phone and did one last check of her outfit, hair, and makeup. She was pleased with the results. She picked up her new Coach handbag and examined its contents, put the phone in, threw in two condoms, and snapped it closed.

Tiffany took the elevator down and walked past the Incognito Bar. She glimpsed the blonde woman sitting in the bar with a new man. A tiny, insistent voice in her head whispered questions as she wondered what the woman's story was and how she attracted so many men. She pushed the thought aside and focused on the evening ahead, as she stepped out of the hotel and into the cool night, the sound of the city came alive. She pulled out her phone and checked the time, and then, just as she was getting anxious, she saw him standing outside the hotel with a smile on his face. "Hey, babe," he said as he walked toward her. "You look amazing."

CHAPTER
TWENTY-THREE

"I'll do it." Samantha's voice was firm, unwavering, and it hit me like a cold splash of water.

A surge of resistance attacked me, my gut twisting and my chest tightening. Every instinct screamed at me that this was a terrible idea.

"Like hell!" Jill shouted back, sharp as a whip.

The room fell silent. The only sound was the steady hum of the air vent, a low mechanical heartbeat in the quiet. Frank's calm voice cut through, steady and sure. "I think Sam can handle this."

"I'm with Jill on this. Too risky, and I'm not crazy about her being a stripper," I said flatly, my voice tight, like I'd swallowed a fist.

"Hey, there's nothing wrong with being an exotic dancer," Jill shot back. "Just not her."

"That's not fair," Samantha said, her tone cutting, but not angry. Sharp enough to pierce my self-restraint.

Late afternoon shadows stretched across the office, long and lean, sneaking across the walls like predators. Hammett had gone back to the station to check phone records and scan for any surveillance cameras that might have caught something. He'd also monitor the reports filed by the Kickapoo Police Department. The construction crew had packed up for the day, leaving the office hushed, almost conspiratorial. We sat in one of the conference rooms, breaking down the plan. As expected, reactions split the room like a blade.

"You all trust me, right? We will protect Sam. Keep her under constant surveillance the whole time. Only stage performances, no lap dances. She can go backstage to give us eyes on the workings, who's who in there," Frank said, his voice calm, steady, a rock against the storm in my head.

"She'll be taking her clothes off in front of you, Frank. You're fine with that?" I asked, jaw tight, the words tasting like ash.

"Ty, this is business. We have a missing person here. We're desperate for clues, and we all agree everything leads to the Kinky Kitten Club." Frank's gaze flicked to Samantha. "I promise I won't look... long." He chuckled, but I felt none of his levity.

"Oh, fuck it. Here." Samantha pulled her top over her head and handed it to me. My pulse jumped. She arched her back, reaching behind with unhurried grace as she unclasped her bra. It fell into her palm, her breasts exposed, rising gently as she inhaled. Her nipples hardened—I couldn't tell if it was from excitement or the cold air.

The breath stalled in my chest. For a heartbeat, all I saw was her—bare, defiant, unflinching. Fear and want twisted tight inside me, but beneath it was something fiercer: respect. Samantha wasn't being reckless—she was fearless. She knew exactly what she was doing, and it took more guts than I'd ever seen.

"There. Now we all know what they look like. Satisfied?" Her teasing voice hit me like a spark to dry kindling.

Frank cleared his throat. "Very."

"It's my decision, right?" Samantha walked toward me, her serpentine smile sliding across her face, dangerous and intoxicating. "Tiger, look at me. I won't do anything to hurt you or our relationship. I'll do what Frank wants and not put myself in danger. You'll have eyes on me the whole time. And won't that be fun? Seeing your girl strut her stuff." She leaned close, her breath warm against my ear. "Just think of the great sex afterward."

My hands shook slightly as I returned her shirt, fingers brushing the fabric like it was a lifeline. My chest thudded, my thoughts a knotted tangle of fear, desire, and helpless anticipation. I could feel the pull in me, the raw, impossible want to see her shine and survive the danger all at once. I knew this was going to happen. I knew I couldn't stop it. And, God help me, part of me didn't want to. A part of me was already living through that strut, that sway, imagining the multicolored lights splashing over her skin, imagining the heat that would follow once the mission ended, once she was back in my arms.

I swallowed hard and exhaled, a slow, deliberate breath, trying to anchor myself. This was her choice. Always her choice. I could only stand guard, keep the shadows at bay, and promise that if anyone so much as touched a hair on her head, they'd wish they hadn't.

We went over everything two more times, and as we reviewed the plan, Jill's and my doubts were slowly fading. Frank had a solid plan, and Samantha agreed that if Frank and I felt it was unsafe at any point, we'd pull the plug. That thought loosened the tight band around my chest, though not entirely. My mind kept flicking between worry and reluctant acceptance—she could handle herself, but the stakes were high, and I couldn't shake the sense that danger was licking at our heels.

Frank's phone buzzed, and he read the message. "It's from Quinn, my CIA contact. She'll send over the breakdown on the pills soon."

"Let's get a copy of that report to Hammett," I said, thinking ahead. We needed eyes on this from every angle, and the more intel Hammett had, the better.

"I'm heading out," Jill said, gathering up her things. She gave Samantha a quick kiss. "Bye, baby. Love ya. Bye, Frank, bye, Ty."

Frank and I lingered a moment, talking quietly about the renovations of the building. He was showing me plans he'd drawn up for a secret entrance when his phone buzzed again. He glanced at the screen, then smiled, fingers flying across the keyboard like a pianist mid-concert.

"Guess my plans have changed for tonight. I'll see you in the morning."

As he slung his bag over his shoulder and moved toward the door, I couldn't help but ask, "Where are you off to in such a hurry?"

He grinned, that easy, devil-may-care grin of his. "Just got invited to the Bulls game."

I watched him go. The office was quiet again, but the hum of the city and the hum of my own racing thoughts filled the space. This wasn't just a mission anymore—it was a game of survival, a delicate balance between risk and trust, and I knew the next few days would stretch me in ways I wasn't sure I was ready for. But we had a plan, we had each other. All I could do was make sure we'd make it back in one piece.

CHAPTER
TWENTY-FOUR

We arrived at the office and headed straight for the conference room, where sleek fluorescent lights threw a cool, sterile glow over the oval table. The wall screen blinked to life, revealing Detective Luke Hammett. His face was cut from granite—tight-lipped, focused, unreadable—even pixelated through the glass.

"Hello, can you hear and see us?" Jill asked, her voice carrying a brightness that didn't belong in a room like this.

Hammett's face softened into a smile. "Yes. Hi. Who are you?"

Jill's warmth could've thawed ice. "I'm Jill, Jillian Sinclair. My part of this operation is in the office more than in the field."

Hammett's eyes crinkled at the corners. "Nice to meet you."

"Likewise. We can get started. I'll be taking notes in case we need to go back."

Frank leaned forward. "Ty and I will scout out the club tonight. Before tomorrow's—"

"You know, I was thinking we should speed this up," Hammett cut in, his voice steady but urgent. "Time isn't on our side, and waiting another day could prove detrimental. I found out who Ava was with in the photo. It's Warren Donavan—he owns Donavan

Pharma in Kickapoo and the land where we found Sophie. If you take the picture and ask around the club, maybe someone saw him. That gives me cause to push for a warrant for his home and office. Right now, a judge won't touch it."

Frank's voice was cautious, but it carried weight. "We could, but it needs to be discreet. We don't want to raise any red flags that we're searching for someone—"

Hammett cut him off again, sharp as a blade. "I have a better idea. Take Sam with you tonight. The three of you can get a feel for the place, scope the layout, and see if she can get started right away. We're running out of time, so we move quickly and quietly."

It was a dangerous play, putting Samantha in the crosshairs. And yet, no one else fit the bill. The thought of her walking into that club, bathed in that cruel neon glow, made my blood run hot with both fear and something I didn't care to name.

"All right," Frank said, steady again, "we'll need full cover IDs that can pass a deep scan. Not the cheap kind you buy online—these have to hold up if someone runs them through federal databases. Real credentials, synthetic backgrounds, clean credit, full digital footprint. Everything has to line up."

"And what if they ask for a second form of ID when I apply for work?" Samantha asked, her tone calm, like she was ordering coffee instead of volunteering to walk into the lion's den.

Frank nodded, already ahead of her. "We'll backstop everything—utility bills, pay stubs from shell companies, even a fake lease if needed. The whole picture, airtight."

"Right," I said, my throat dry. "What about tracking? We'll need to monitor her once she's inside." The words scraped coming out. I hated saying them—but the thought of losing her was worse.

"I was thinking subdermal RFID, maybe micro-GPS," Frank said. "Small enough to hide under the skin. Live feed, encrypted. We'll be able to follow her in real time."

My eyes narrowed. "How secure is it? We can't risk discovery."

"Encrypted, closed loop—our server only," Frank replied. "Still, there's always a risk. If the implant fails, or if they scan her with the wrong tech..."

Samantha nodded, eyes sharp and unflinching. "I understand. I'll take the risk."

Jill's voice cracked with concern. "Are you sure this is necessary? There's got to be another way to track her without... cutting her open."

Frank shook his head. "Anything external—AirTags, jewelry, wearables—they'll sweep for them. This is the only method that stays invisible."

I nodded, the agreement cutting deeper than I let show. "Fine. But she has to consent to it fully."

Samantha looked straight at me, her jaw set, fire in her eyes. "I'm in. No hesitation."

Hammett leaned closer to the camera, his cop's skepticism edging through. "Implanted chips, forged credentials... that's a long way from a standard PI gig."

Frank didn't blink. His voice came out calm, gravel steady. "Then it's best you don't ask too many questions, Detective. Call it plausible deniability."

Hammett held his gaze for a long beat, then gave a slow nod—the kind a man makes when he knows he's better off not knowing more. "Understood. Keep me in the loop, no matter the hour. And Jill—good to meet you."

"You too, Detective." Jill smiled before ending the Zoom meeting. Silence settled like smoke before the screen went black.

"Now you've met Hammett, Jill, what do you think?" Samantha asked.

"He doesn't look like a real cop. He looks like a Hallmark movie cop," Jill quipped.

I chuckled. She was dead-on with that description. Hammett had the clean-shaven jawline and squared-off smile of someone better suited for a Christmas card commercial than a homicide detail. Still, I trusted him more than most men who carried a badge.

"Do you still want to do this?" I asked Frank.

"Yes. I agree with Hammett. We'll take Sam tonight. The sooner we check this out, the better."

"Did Randolph get that report?" Frank pressed, his voice low and serious as he sipped his coffee.

"Samantha sent it out yesterday," I replied, the clack of my keyboard filling the room as I double-checked my inbox.

"Ty, I'll make sure nothing happens," Frank promised, his gaze steady and reassuring.

"I know," I admitted, though part of me couldn't stop running the odds in my head. Trusting Frank wasn't the issue—he'd always had my back. What kept me awake at night was whether fate felt like playing dice with our lives. "Did you find anything going on where Ava and Sophie worked?" I asked, leaning back and steepling my fingers like I had all the answers, when really, I was grasping for one.

"It's looking like a dead end," Frank muttered, frustration thick in his tone. "I think this club is where we need to focus." He leaned forward, elbows planted on the table, a man ready to dig in.

I nodded, then remembered Frank had gone to the game last night. "How was the game?" I asked, more curious than I wanted to admit.

"Fantastic," he said, a grin spreading across his face like the sunrise on Lake Michigan.

"Didn't they lose?"

"They did. I didn't."

"Whoa. Is that what I think it means? Dish, man," I teased, giving Frank a dap. The echo of our palms snapping together filled the office, sounding bigger than it was.

"What did you tell me? Oh yeah, a gentleman never tells." His laughter boomed like a bass drum.

"You dawg, you." I shook my head, though I couldn't help but laugh with him. Some things never changed.

"Come on." Frank stood and clapped a hand on my shoulder, his grip firm and reassuring. A man could build a bridge on that kind of steadiness. "Let's get Sam a job at a strip club."

"Awesome." I followed him out of the office, though deep down I wondered how long this ride would stay on the tracks before everything came apart.

CHAPTER
TWENTY-FIVE

Tiffany awoke, but her body resisted. Every muscle screamed in protest as she moved, particularly her vagina, which she affectionately dubbed *the duchess*. Sliding off the bed, her feet sank into the plush carpet, the soft fibers tickling her toes. With unsteady legs, she made her way to the bathroom, caught a glimpse of herself in the mirror, and groaned.

After taking three Tylenol tablets, she called room service for a pot of coffee. Draped in a robe, she fluffed her hair and reached for the remote, intending to catch the morning news. Sunlight streamed through the window, dust motes drifting lazily in the beams, and Tiffany squinted against the brightness. To her surprise, the television displayed the afternoon news instead. She settled in, waiting for the coffee while her discontent duchess made its complaints known.

"I know, I'm sorry," she murmured, acknowledging her body's protests. How could she have had such a fantastic time last night, only to feel so miserable this afternoon? Still, she smiled as the memories rushed back, filling her with joy.

Frank had been a delight—sharing her passion for basketball and talking animatedly about the Chicago Bulls. He had pointed out the championship banners from the 90s, Michael Jordan's retired number, and the statue outside the United Center. Tiffany marveled at the six championship trophies displayed on one concourse, savoring Frank's stories about the Bulls' glory years. Watching the team play live had been electrifying, and she had appreciated his companionship.

Frank's well-mannered, polite nature—not just toward her, but toward others as well—had made a lasting impression. When he asked for a nightcap, she accepted, and they shared a drink at Incognito. Then, with a touch of nervousness, she invited him to her room. They had used the two condoms she brought along, as well as one of his own.

"No wonder you're angry at me," she muttered softly, sympathizing with her irritated duchess.

Despite the discomfort, she couldn't deny the pleasure she had experienced. Frank's lovemaking had been gentle yet powerful, devoid of roughness or force. Every touch, thrust, and kiss held meaning, and he knew precisely how to arouse her. Multiple climaxes swept over Tiffany throughout their intimate moments, surpassing any previous experiences. He had awakened a world of ecstasy with only his hands and mouth, and thinking back made her giggle at the sheer bliss.

Older men like Frank had shattered her notions about their prowess. Her sister Sammy dated an older man named Tanner, but nobody ever took her seriously; she was the wild one, rebellious and self-absorbed, always chasing trouble.

Room service arrived, and she tipped the server generously. The aroma of freshly brewed coffee filled the room, stirring her senses. Opening her notebook, Tiffany began a new list of the day's activities. Frank had said he was busy tonight, but maybe they could see each other the day after. That was fine with her. She needed time to recoup—time for the duchess to rest.

One change she made was to cancel her dinner reservation. Instead, she would stay in, watch television, and call home to check in. She would call Sammy tomorrow. It was time to let her know she was in town. For the afternoon, she planned more shopping, with another stop at Enchanté Lingerie for something new.

A knock at the door interrupted her thoughts. Tiffany set down her coffee cup, wondering who it could be. Had Frank decided he couldn't stay away, showing up at her door to embrace her and recreate last night's magic?

Rushing to the mirror, she fussed with her hair and checked her breath for any hint of coffee.

"Shit, ah, be there in a sec," she muttered, squeezing toothpaste onto her brush. She scrubbed her teeth and tongue for fifteen seconds, rinsed quickly, and darted to the door.

Opening it, she found a bouquet of perfect purple blooms—roses, miniature carnations, and other delicate flowers arranged with care.

"Delivery for Tiffany?" the courier asked.

"Yes, that's me," Tiffany said, signing and placing the bouquet on the side table. "Wait, I'll get my purse."

"No need," the courier replied. "Gratuity's already taken care of."

Closing the door, Tiffany felt a rush of elation. She pressed a hand to her mouth, then opened the card.

Dear Tiffany, beautiful flowers for a beautiful lady. I remembered you mentioned your fondness for purple. I had an amazing time with you and look forward to seeing you before you leave. Best, Frank.

A warm flutter spread through her chest as she gazed at the flowers, her mind replaying the gentle way Frank had touched her, the way he had listened. This was a man who knew how to make a woman feel seen, and she couldn't help but be drawn to him.

She had to give Sammy some credit—maybe older men really did know how to get things right. But Tiffany reminded herself this could never be more than it was. Her father's re-election campaign was about to start, and they expected her to play an active role. An interracial relationship might sway votes, one way or another, and she would have to weigh the risks.

Besides, long-distance relationships rarely worked. She would return to Florida, and Frank would remain in Chicago.

Shaking her head, Tiffany reminded herself they had agreed to keep things casual—no last names, no attachments. Just two consenting adults enjoying a moment in time. It would stay their secret, a cherished memento of her trip to Chicago.

No one needed to know. And no one ever would.

CHAPTER
TWENTY-SIX

The three of us arrived around ten o'clock that evening. The bass from inside the club thumped through the walls, rattling my bones as we approached the entrance. Frank walked beside me, shoulders squared but jaw tight. Samantha was a step ahead, all confidence and sway, as if she'd been born to charm her way past bouncers and red ropes. I wished I felt half as calm as she looked.

A bouncer waited at the door, wand in hand. He checked Frank first—quick sweep, no fuss. Then me—one pass down the sides, another across my chest. Nothing.

When it was Samantha's turn, she lifted her arms, smile effortless. The wand beeped once—sharp, fast. My heart stopped.

The bouncer frowned, waved it again. Silence. He tapped the handle, gave her a long, lazy grin. "Enjoy."

She smiled back, easy as breathing, but I caught the flicker in her eyes—the one that said she'd felt it too.

Samantha turned heads the second she stepped into the Kinky Kitten Club, radiating confidence and style. Her black mid-thigh dress dipped low in front, the neckline hinting at her elegant cleavage, while sheer lace side panels gave it an edge. The fabric hugged her frame like it had been custom-stitched to her curves, leaving little to the imagination.

Her accessories hit the mark too. Oversized hoop earrings caught the shifting lights, a sleek clutch matched the dress, and black strappy heels made her look like sin served on stilts. Jill had worked her magic on Sam's hair—loose, tousled waves that framed her face perfectly. Subtle makeup sealed the deal, topped with a muted lipstick that whispered mystery.

A plush carpet ran under our feet as we passed through the door, the lighting dim and deliberate. Behind a reception desk stood a woman in a leopard-print bodysuit, something that look straight out of Sophie's closet, that plunged low enough to get the imagination humming. Cat ears perched on her head, a collar with a heart-shaped pendant reading Penny at her throat. I couldn't see below the desk, but I wouldn't have bet against her sporting a tail to finish the look.

"Good evening, I'm Penny the leopardess. Can I help you?" she purred. The ID scanner sat on the podium like a black trap waiting to snap shut.

"Hello, Penny. We'd like to explore the club. First time here. We've heard great things and wanted to see for ourselves," I said, keeping my tone polite, professional. Frank and I in suits, Sam dressed to kill—on paper, it worked. But I knew one bad scan, one flicker of doubt, and the whole thing went up in smoke. Don't screw this up, Ty. Not here, not now.

"I see." Penny's smile didn't shift. "Welcome. It's always great to hear positive reviews. I can arrange for one of our kittens to give you a tour, and I can book a VIP table with an excellent view. If you like what you see, you can consider membership. Your kitten will explain the benefits."

"That sounds lovely, Penny. Are there other rooms besides the VIP area?" Samantha asked, smooth as glass.

"Yes, we have the Cat Nip Lounge, the Purr Palace, and our most exclusive room, the Lion's Den—for members only."

"For now, we'll take the VIP table," I said, sealing it.

"Wonderful. I think you'll be quite pleased. Normally, there's a fifty-dollar cover for men, but with a VIP booking, your admission is free. And would the beautiful lady like her own pair of cat ears? You can choose black cat, leopard, lion, tiger, cheetah, or jaguar."

"How fun. I'll go with the tiger, of course." Samantha nudged me playfully.

Penny handed her a pair of tiger ears. "Great choice. You look super sexy. Welcome to the Kinky Kitten Club. Now, may I have your IDs and a method of payment?"

Samantha went first. She smiled like she owned the joint and slid her ID across without blinking. Penny raised a brow, unimpressed, and swiped it. The scanner beeped, the light froze, and my heart did the same. Penny studied the screen a beat too long, and my stomach flipped. Then she handed the card back.

"You're good. Next."

Sam turned, winked at me like walking a tightrope over a canyon was all in a night's work.

Frank followed. No smiles, no charm. He shoved his ID across like it was a toll booth and Penny was blocking traffic. It wasn't flashy, but I respected it. She scanned, the light blinked, paused, then settled. Penny's lips pursed, but she returned the ID.

"Go on."

My turn. I swallowed hard and slid my ID across like it was made of glass. Blank face, bored eyes, but inside, I was unraveling. The guy who made our IDs came recommended, but recommendations didn't guarantee a damn thing.

Penny took the card, compared my face to the photo, then swiped it.

The scanner blinked. And blinked. And kept blinking.

My pulse pounded in my ears. One bad read and we were finished.

I didn't breathe. The screen hadn't beeped, hadn't given me anything. Penny tapped the scanner again, her frown cutting deeper. My stomach dropped. Great. The damn thing's glitching, and now we're about to get dragged out like amateurs.

"Security," Penny called over her shoulder, waving to a guy built like a brick wall. He started lumbering toward us, and I fought the urge to grab my ID and bolt. That'd only get me tackled faster.

I glanced at Frank. He wasn't looking at me—he was locked on Penny's hand like a sniper. Samantha, cool as ever, kept that polite smile pasted on her face, though I caught the faint twitch of tension in her jaw.

"Just a sec," Penny muttered, giving the scanner a hard smack like it had just insulted her mother.

Suddenly, the light flicked green. The machine let out a cheerful beep, like it hadn't just tried to shave ten years off my life. Penny's frown deepened, as if the thing had betrayed her at the worst possible moment.

"You're good. Sorry for the delay. Sometimes you just gotta give it a good whack," she said.

"Tell me about it, girl," Samantha chimed in, smooth as silk.

I took my ID back slowly, forcing myself not to snatch it out of her hand like a drowning man clutching a rope. "Thanks."

We stepped past the entrance, and the door closed behind us, sealing us inside the pounding beat of the club.

"Thought we were toast," Frank muttered under his breath.

"Me too," I said, finally letting the air out of my lungs. First hurdle cleared, but I knew better than to think we were home free. "Let's keep our heads down. We're not out of the woods yet."

Samantha just smiled, feline and fearless. "That's the fun part."

I hoped she was right. To me, the fun part felt a hell of a lot like walking on black ice with a blindfold on.

A young woman appeared, moving with a dancer's grace. She wore a lion bodysuit and ears, with a tail that swayed behind her like it had a mind of its own.

"Welcome. How exciting—your first time at the club. My name is Sapphire, the lioness. You're in for a treat tonight. DJ Mick is spinning in the main room, and he's one of the best in Chicago, if not the country. I'll show you to your VIP table." Her voice carried enthusiasm like she bottled and sold it.

A fresh surge of music hit me square in the chest. The bass pounded like a war drum, lights flashing and spinning in a frantic hunt for something only they understood. A burst of blue light swallowed the room before shifting to green, the rhythm chewing up the air itself.

The stage was shaped like a T. The vertical walkway split a curtain, a chute for the dancers to come and go. The horizontal bar held a chrome pole at each end, and two topless dancers clung to them like living neon, bending and twisting for an audience drunk on the spectacle.

As we wove toward the VIP section, a man in the corner caught my eye. Black suit, black tie, posture too stiff for this place. His eyes were locked on Samantha like she was the only person in the room. I nudged Frank and tilted my chin toward him. Frank gave the briefest of nods. But when I turned back—the man was gone.

The Kinky Kitten Club opened wider the deeper we walked. It was by far the most expansive joint I'd ever seen. A balcony on the upper floor ran along an L-shaped path, tables and chairs stacked along the rail, giving VIPs a predator's-eye view of the stage. At the far end of the balcony, another smaller stage glowed in half-light, invisible from the main floor. Something special, just for the chosen few.

"This is a fantastic place. How does one go about working here?" Samantha asked, her voice equal parts curiosity and bait.

Sapphire gave her a quick once-over and smiled. "I can check on that. You're very attractive. Have you danced before?"

"Thank you. A little, back home," Samantha said, playing the line just right.

"Great." I slipped Sapphire a couple of hundreds, folding them into her palm. It wasn't just generosity—it was a signal that we weren't here on a whim.

We settled into our VIP table, upholstered seats giving us the kind of view that made you forget the price tag. But in the corner of the room, another kind of show was happening. A group of people sat huddled together, laughing too hard, smiling too wide. To anyone else, it looked like friends enjoying a private game. To me, it looked like something else. Something calculated.

I leaned back, scanning them from the corner of my eye. Whatever they were playing at, it wasn't poker.

CHAPTER

TWENTY-SEVEN

Across the street from the Kinky Kitten Club, in a drab concrete building, the stale scent of coffee and burnt popcorn clung to the air beneath the harsh buzz of fluorescent lights. Marty Shay leaned back in his chair, gray eyes fixed on a bank of monitors streaming high-definition footage from the club's IP cameras. He sipped from a chipped mug that read *I See You Naked*.

Three unfamiliar figures had just entered the club—faces half-obscured by the dim, pulsating lights and drifting shadows. Marty's credentials came from INSCOM—the Army's Intelligence and Security Command. Not the spookiest outfit in the intel world, but they trained their analysts to read shadows like stories. And tonight, the story was getting interesting.

"What do you make of these three?" Marty asked, voice low and skeptical as he pointed to the screen.

Jayde's boots thudded against the tile as she approached. She stopped short, tilted her head, and let out a mock gasp.

"Well, look at her," she said, cupping her hands under her chin like a teenage girl fawning over a boyband. "Isn't she just a little motherfucking hottie? With her tiger ears on, no less." She batted her lashes, then stiffened, eyes narrowing. "Hold the phone, Batman. I ran into those two clowns she's with yesterday. The white guy's the one who jammed a busted light bulb into my ribs."

Marty winced. "Oof. Romantic."

"Yeah, I was touched," Jayde muttered. "Now they show up here? They're sniffing around. I'd bet a bottle of Yamazaki they're looking for Ava."

"Cops?" Marty asked, recalling how badly things went last time law enforcement got nosy. "Wouldn't be the first time. Remember that club on the South Side?"

Jayde shook her head. "More like PIs. If they were cops, we'd hear them rattling around with warrants. And the scanner's been quiet."

Marty checked the duty roster on his tablet. "We've got Sapphire and Tiny working tonight. DEA detail."

Jayde gave a slow nod. "Good. Call Tiny. Tell him to get close—but keep it chill. We don't want them bolting like squirrels."

Marty picked up the secure line and dialed. "Tiny, we've got a situation. See if you can get a read on the three newcomers—low profile, no spook vibes. Got it?"

While Tiny responded, Jayde's attention stayed on the woman in tiger ears. Several dancers approached the trio, but they weren't biting. No money flying. No smiles. Just scanning.

"They're not here for the bump and grind, titties-in-your-face night," Marty muttered. "They're fishing. Tiny says the woman's asking about employment. What's the play?"

Jayde's lips curled into a calculating smile. "Hire her. Roll out the red carpet. Give her the main stage—solo. Make her feel like a damn queen. People loosen up when they think they're the ones holding the leash."

Marty nodded, fingers dancing over the keyboard.

"Tell Tiny to ask the guys if they want to work security. Make it easy. If they're here for her, they'll stay close. Let's keep them right where we can see them. Oh—and have Tiny collect their drink glasses. I want prints."

"Copy that," Marty said. "You want someone to tail them?"

Jayde's smile went razor-thin. "Nah. They'll come back. We're gonna have some fun tomorrow."

Marty glanced at her, watching her move through the room like she owned it. He remembered Jayde was born and raised in Japan, trained in the disciplined arts that made her fast, and deadly. Charming, until she wasn't. She moved like water over stone, she thrived on precision, wit, and a psychological edge that turned enemies inside-out before they knew the blade had slipped in. He remembered the first time she came over for dinner years ago—helped his wife mash potatoes, had the kids ninja-flipping across the living room, swore like a sailor while doing it. Which he had to point out, not in front of the kids. Marty wasn't sure anyone knew her real name. Hell, he wasn't sure she even remembered it herself. His wife once said, only half-joking, *If you ever screw up, I'm calling Jayde. You'll vanish.* Marty laughed at the time. Now? He wasn't so sure she'd been joking.

CHAPTER

TWENTY-EIGHT

As the seconds ticked by, Frank's patience thinned. His back straightened, shoulders squaring—a signal flare that something was off. Sapphire was nowhere, and her silence pressed heavier with each beat.

The music thumped like a heartbeat, syncing with mine in a rhythm I didn't trust. Strobe lights slashed the room in jagged bursts, painting everything in fractured glimpses. The other kittens had melted away, prey vanishing into the shadows at the scent of a predator.

Then he appeared—a large Black man moving toward us with the kind of calm that promised trouble. My brain started running numbers, odds stacking against me if things went south. Frank's glance locked with mine: stay cool, stay sharp, don't make it worse.

From the left flank, a server swooped in with drinks, her timing too clean to be chance. Two beers for Frank and me. But it was the tray of four fruit-colored concoctions she set in front of Samantha that made me sit up. Before Sam could speak, the server leaned in, her voice cutting through the bass.

"This one is the one you ordered, and the other three are from the kittens over there." She pointed, and we looked. Three ladies by the bar held up their drinks in a toast. Samantha lifted hers, nodded slightly, and sipped. Damn, she made it look effortless.

The server left, and the big man approached our table.

"Hello folks, my name is Tiny. Just checking to see if everything is to your liking." His grin was wide, disarming the tension like a well-placed shield.

"Tiny? That's an unusual name," Samantha said.

"More a nickname, pretty lady."

Frank pointed to Samantha. "She wants to be a kitten."

"The house mom, Angie, will handle that. I'll let her know." Tiny pressed a button on his radio and spoke. With the music pounding, I couldn't catch the words.

Frank and I noticed the tattoo on Tiny's forearm: a knife pointing up through two crossed arrows, encircled with a U-shaped scroll. At the arch of the scroll were the words *De Oppresso Liber*.

"Hey brother, what group you with?" Frank asked, nodding at the tattoo.

Tiny met Frank's gaze. "Fifth Special Forces Group, Second Battalion, Bravo Company."

"That's Fort Campbell, Kentucky, right?" Frank asked.

"Yeah. Were you there?"

"I was at Fort Campbell for a few months," Frank said. "I was part of a special ops unit. We did some training with the Fifth Special Forces Group."

Tiny nodded, understanding clear in his eyes. "Sometimes I miss it, you know?"

"I hear you, brother."

Tiny cupped his ear, listening, then nodded toward us. "Angie will see you now."

"Great," Samantha said, standing. I got up to go with her.

"You should wait here. Not a good idea to have a boyfriend hanging around for the interview," Tiny said.

"Right," I muttered, sliding back into my chair.

"I'm Puma," the kitten said, walking up to us.

"Puma will take you to see Angie," Tiny said to Samantha before turning to Frank. "I have a break coming up. Do you want to hang out until they're done? I'm looking to hire some security—could always use an ex-military grunt."

Frank shot me a glance. "You good?"

I nodded. Tiny and Frank went one way, Samantha and Puma the other.

The strobe caught the hallow spaces where my people had been, leaving me adrift in a sea of painted kitten eyes. My beer became a small lifeline, a liquid shield against the swarm. Take it slow, I told myself. Don't make eye contact. Don't breathe too loud.

A tall, toffee-haired cheetah kitten was the first to pounce.

Sammy slid into the chair in front of Angie's desk, crossing her legs with just enough poise to suggest confidence. Her fingers drummed lightly on the armrest, betraying a flicker of nerves beneath the cool exterior. The office was small, windowless, thick with cigarette smoke and cheap perfume, walls plastered with faded photos of dancers and old X-rated posters.

Angie's eyes roamed, calculating. "So, what's your story?" Her voice rasped, skepticism seeping through. "Pretty girl like you—surely you could find a rich guy to take care of you?" She exhaled a cloud of smoke, watching Sammy's reaction.

Sammy leaned back slightly, a flash of defiance sparking in her eyes. "I like being independent," she said smoothly. "Especially when it comes to my finances."

Angie's lips quirked, just the barest edge of a smile. She stubbed out the cigarette, the butt hissing against the ashtray. "Been in this business a long time, sweetie. Seen it all. Not always glamour, not always excitement. Some days, it's just showing up and doing the work. You get that?"

Sammy inhaled, letting the smoke sting her lungs, and nodded. Her palms rested lightly on her thighs, thumbs tracing invisible patterns as if she could will her confidence into the room.

Angie leaned back, rocking her chair with slow precision. "Ever dance before? AEL?"

Sammy handed over the adult entertainment license Frank had given her, keeping her hand steady. "Yes. Back home in Florida." She didn't mention it had been a one-off, amateur night, in a swimsuit.

Angie's gaze softened just enough to let her feel competent. "We're a topless-only club. You'll work as an independent contractor. I won't feed you to the wolves just yet. So stage work first, no VIP dances—builds anticipation, word-of-mouth advertising. We follow a set rotation, so when you clock in, check in with me for your spot. Arrive backstage at least two dancers before your turn to touch up your makeup. That way, you'll be ready to wow the crowd. Are we good so far?"

Sammy nodded, storing every detail.

"You'll share a makeup table. The girls get catty, keep your distance. Boyfriends—don't, this is work. Got it?" Angie's eyes flicked to the tiger ears on Sammy's head. "Tiger squad's colors: black, white, orange. We'll get you fitted for a two-piece—costs deducted from your first night."

Sammy absorbed it, posture unchanging, mind racing.

"Harold! Come 'ere!" A middle-aged man appeared, looking like he'd been interrupted mid-bite.

"This is Harold. He manages everything but the girls. Stage name?"

"I thought, Kylie," Sammy said, voice steady.

"Good. Tigress Kylie." Angie slid a stack of papers across the desk. Sammy caught them—contract, W-9, other forms—and brushed her gaze over the fine print.

Sammy reached down, collected her purse, and stood to say goodbye. Angie leaned forward, her stare sharp and unapologetic. "One last thing. We need to see those little titties, sweetheart." Her voice carried, robust and commanding.

Sammy froze, chest tightening. She swallowed hard, jaw clenching. But she lifted her chin, moving with deliberate calm. A deep breath. Her fingers hooked onto the zipper slider. Metal teeth parted with a slow, metallic purr, intimate and deliberate, like a secret being dragged into the open. She slipped a strap off one shoulder and then the other. Harold stiffened, his gaze locked intently on her. Sammy's dress fell to the floor, pooling at her feet. The cool air brushed her skin. Goosebumps surfaced. She held her gaze forward, pulse hammering in her ears. Her dignity felt on trial. But if Angie was hoping for shame, she'd be waiting forever.

Harold's stare devoured her, a low whistle escaping his lips.

"Very nice," he murmured.

Sammy forced a smile, smooth and controlled. "Thank you."

CHAPTER
TWENTY-NINE

Jill breathed a sigh of relief as she tucked her two children, Preston and Caprice, into bed. For the first time all day, she had a moment of solitude. She padded to the kitchen, the hum of the fridge the only sound. She poured herself a glass of rich Bordeaux—a 2015 Château Margaux, one of her favorites. The velvety aroma, the smooth taste, brought sophistication to what had otherwise been a messy, ordinary day.

She took her first sip, savoring the calm. The house bore evidence of the storm her kids had created—action figures, colored pencils, and storybooks scattered across the living room. Jill knelt and picked up Preston's toys, setting them neatly on the shelf where he would find them in the morning. Caprice's art supplies waited for her careful hands, each marker returned to its case, each sheet stacked into a tidy pile. The simple act of restoring order grounded her, reminding her that their home was a sanctuary.

Her glass followed her upstairs, each step a familiar creak. In the primary bathroom, the cool marble kissed her feet. She undressed slowly, the shower steaming as she turned the dial. The water cascaded over her, washing away more than physical exhaustion. In those minutes, she let go—of stress, of unease, of the gnawing edges of old pain. She whispered affirmations under her breath, soft but steady. She deserved this. She deserved love. She deserved happiness.

Wrapped in a towel, Jill's thoughts turned to her children. Preston had been struggling with a bully at school. She weighed whether to speak to his teacher or try to resolve things directly with the other parents. More than anything, she wanted to show him that strength could exist without cruelty—that he could stand tall while still being kind.

Caprice, on the other hand, was thriving. Bright, curious, endlessly creative. Jill often marveled at her daughter's focus, her ability to throw herself into projects with complete abandon. Perhaps an enrichment program could stretch her further. Jill made a mental note to explore the possibilities, determined to nurture her daughter's gifts.

By the time she slipped into fresh pajamas, her thoughts had drifted to what she missed most—connection. Frank, with his ex-military discipline and easy grin, offered steadiness. Sammy, fiery and magnetic, tugged at her imagination. Her body ached, her heart wavered. Two very different possibilities, yet both reminders she still longed for more.

She had built her life around stability for her kids, and anything new—man or woman—meant change. But wasn't that what she deserved too? More than just surviving, she wanted to live fully. She wanted love, connection, and desire.

Her children would learn from her choices. They would see that love could be expansive, that it could cross boundaries of expectation. Jill wanted them to grow up knowing compassion, openness, and the courage to follow their own hearts.

Now, tucked beneath the covers, she reached for her dog-eared copy of *Le Petit Prince*, its French words carrying an echo of streets and cafés from her youth. The pages whispered a lullaby of comfort, each line rocking her toward rest. Her eyelids grew heavy, and the book slipped gently from her hands as dreams claimed her—threads of love, resilience, and the fragile promise of tomorrow.

The neon lights of the city flickered through the steamy shower, casting eerie shadows on the tiled walls. I could feel the weight of the investigation, heavy as a stone, pressing down on my shoulders. As the warm water cascaded over us, I stole glances at Samantha, her curves silhouetted against the dim light. Her body was a map of strength and beauty, every line telling a story.

Samantha reached for the soap, her movements deliberate and sensual. The sight of her lathering herself sent a jolt of desire through me. I couldn't help but react, my hunger responding to hers with an urgency that was almost primal.

"Excited to see me dance tomorrow?" she asked, her voice a sultry purr cutting through the hiss of the water.

I grunted, "Yeah," trying to focus. My thoughts were tangled in danger, strategy, and worry. The idea of her walking into that chaos made me sick.

Samantha looked down my body, her eyes lingering, then back up with a devilish smile. "Something on your mind, Tiger?"

She pressed into me, her slick skin driving me wild. I pinned her against the wall and lifted her up. Hot water rained down, steam swirling around like a misty veil. I lowered her onto my length.

"Oh, Tiger. It's so good." She wrapped her arms around my neck, her kisses hard and demanding. Her moans were a symphony of want, her body trembling and convulsing against mine as my hips drove harder and faster.

Her voice grew heavy, threaded with something I couldn't quite place—an urgency, a playful edge, a trust I hadn't earned yet—and it cut through the fog of pleasure. "Oh god, yes. It's so good, Daddy. Just like that, yes."

I froze and looked at her with a mix of astonishment and intrigue. "What? Wait, what did you call me?"

She tried to brush it off, a pout playing on her lips. "What? I don't know. What did I say?" But there was a spark in her eyes, a challenge that dared me to question her.

"You called me Daddy, Samantha. Are you..." I let the question hang in the air, unsure if I wanted to know the answer.

She let out a gasp, her voice taking on a serious tone. "What? No, god no. Eww, I'm too young to be... I'm not even gonna say it. No. It's just a saying. Sexy talk. Is it okay with you?"

"It's just sexy talk?" I repeated, my voice a blend of skepticism and relief.

"Yes. Now fuck me, Daddy." Her eyes bored into mine, and she bit her lower lip, a wicked grin playing on her face.

I leaned in, my voice low and gruff. "Were you a good girl today?" I slammed into her and watched her eyes roll back and close.

"Yes, Daddy." Her grin was wicked, a promise of more to come.

I raised my eyebrows, slowing my pace. "Are you sure?"

Her words dripped slowly, each one a teasing drawl—thick, warm, rolling off her lips. "No... Daddy."

Curled up together, I held her close, letting her warmth steady me as sleep claimed her. My mind refused the same peace. Tomorrow at the club promised shadows and danger, pressing against my chest like a weight I couldn't shake. I squeezed her tighter, aware of her resourcefulness, her capability, the sharp mind that had carried her through situations that would swallow most people. Still, the grip of dread didn't loosen. Here, in the quiet, I felt the raw need to protect her with everything I had—and I would, no matter the cost.

Frank's bachelor condo blended ruggedness with urban sophistication. Dim lights threw shadows over vintage sports memorabilia, military photos, and scattered mementos of a life filled with action and late nights. He grabbed a beer, the hiss of the cap cutting through the quiet, and his phone buzzed, Tiffany.

Still working? Or are you tired of me?

Frank smirked. *No way I'm tired of you, baby. Long day. You?*

Lonely. Can you be my booty call?

Timing was the worst. *I would love to, but not tonight. Tomorrow's chaos... or that's today.* He sent it, drained half his beer, and shook his head.

Tiffany didn't relent. Another buzz—*Can I tempt you?* This time she sent a selfie in delicate blue topaz lingerie, lace and bows perfectly framing her skin. Desire flared in his gut, but he forced himself to focus on Sam and the mission ahead.

You're killing me, baby. Can't wait... I'll get to you soon.

Then a single, daring line popped up: *I'll be dreaming about you tonight...*

Frank's lips twitched. He set the phone aside, savoring the burn of attraction, and let the tension of the city wash over him.

He moved to the floor-to-ceiling windows. Below, Chicago sprawled in a tangle of lights and shadows. Honking horns and distant sirens created a rhythm that pulsed under his skin. The city always had a pulse, and tonight it throbbed with danger.

Back on the sofa, beer in hand, Frank let the condo's familiar clutter settle around him—TV chatter, empty bottles, sports gear. His sanctuary offered a pause before the storm. But even here, the weight of the upcoming operation pressed down. Sam needed protection, and he knew the streets held shadows that could turn lethal in a heartbeat.

Then there was the neighbor—a casual fling that had soured into a lesson in boundaries. Notes on the doorstep, dinner invites, constant persistence. He shoved the memory aside, focusing on what mattered: the job, the danger, the people he actually cared about.

His phone buzzed again. Quinn: *Report on the pills soon.*

Frank drained the rest of his beer and set the empty bottle down. Tomorrow wasn't about indulgence—it was about vigilance. He had to be ready, alert, prepared to protect Sam at all costs, no matter what lurked in the dark streets of Chicago. Ty was counting on him, trusting him.

CHAPTER
THIRTY

As the autumn morning unfolded, the vibrant city embraced the shimmering shores of Lake Michigan. The sun emerged from the horizon, casting its radiant rays across the water and creating a dazzling path of glistening diamonds on the gentle waves. As it steadily ascended, its warm light embraced the city's iconic skyline. It illuminated the towering skyscrapers in a dazzling display of pinks and purples.

The skyline served as a majestic backdrop to nature's masterpiece. Vibrant fall foliage filled the parks and pathways along the lakefront. The trees, dressed in a rich tapestry of fiery reds, burnt oranges, and golden yellows, provided a vivid contrast against the deep blue of the water.

The city came to life. Joggers, cyclists, and early risers ventured along the lakefront paths. Their silhouettes dance against the backdrop of the rising sun. Seagulls glided gracefully overhead, basking in the serene beauty of the crisp morning air.

I stood in front of my high-rise window, coffee in hand, letting the city's symphony of colors wash over me. The sky was a painter's palette, streaks of orange, pink, and gold cutting through the haze, but the tranquility didn't last long.

The phone buzzed on the table, harsh and insistent, yanking me back into reality. Hammett.

"Morning, Detective," I said, keeping my voice pleasant, though my gut already knew it wouldn't stay pleasant for long.

"York, how did things go last night?" Hammett asked. He had that edge—competent, but always trying to stay one step ahead, direct and pushy. The kind of guy who made you feel like a rookie, even when you weren't. I gave him a quick rundown of the previous night's events and outlined our plan for today.

"Things went well. She has an audition at noon. Frank made friends with security, and he asked if Frank and I wanted to join the security team," I said.

"Wow. You guys work fast. Do you think this guy's legit?"

"Him and Frank have some military connections. So yes, I believe so."

"Maybe this will change your mind about going any further. I have some news about Ava. Unfortunately, it's not good. Authorities found her body in that same field Sophie was found. Someone driving by discovered it," Hammett said.

The air seemed to thicken. I gripped the coffee cup tighter. "How did they spot her from the road?"

"They placed her body in a tree."

I shook my head, sorrow sinking deep. Ava. Beautiful, ambitious Ava, gone. Her dreams—career goals, new experiences, a life with loved ones—snuffed out by some deranged individual. My chest tightened, and the taste of bitter coffee suddenly matched the weight in my stomach.

"York, are you still there?" Hammett's voice cut through the fog.

"Yeah. Maybe it's not her. How do you know?"

"Fingerprints confirmed her ID."

"So, it's officially a murder investigation now, not a missing person's case?"

"Yes. Once we receive the coroner's report, I'll update you. Look, York, you and your team need to be careful tonight. If things go south, pull out fast," he warned.

"I believe we have a good handle on things."

"Any concerns about Sam dancing? You sure you want her doing this? This might be our only shot at catching this guy. I don't want you hesitating and causing a scene," Hammett said.

"Samantha and I discussed this extensively. We're both on board," I assured him, though a knot of anxiety tightened in my chest.

"Maybe I should be there, just in case," he suggested.

I couldn't help but smirk. Sure, Hammett, tag along so you can see Samantha topless on stage. Not a chance. "It's best if no cops are present. They'd find your badge, raise suspicions."

"I suppose you're right."

I called Frank, gave him the update, and made plans to meet at the office. Then, I gently woke Samantha and told her about Ava before heading into the shower. Breakfast was out—vanilla yogurt and blueberries, part of her plan to keep me on my weight-loss campaign. Effective, but I missed my three-egg omelets, hash browns, and toast at The Fast Track Diner. Still, the sight of her in my unbuttoned dress shirt beat any scenery the diner could offer, hands down.

I came up behind her, wrapped my arms around her slim waist, and inhaled the strawberry-and-mint scent of her shampoo. I nibbled along her neck, the way I knew drove her wild. She shivered.

"Oh, Tiger," she moaned. I spun her around, kissed her deep and long, hands roaming her back and settling on her rear. Her shirt slipped off one shoulder. My fingers traced the line from her lips down her cheek to her neck, and I gave her shoulder a soft bite.

"God, I'm still horny from last night..."

"I bet you are," a third voice said. We spun around. Jill stood in the doorway, smiling. She, Samantha, and Frank were on the list of people allowed up without notification, and they had a key.

"I texted you and said I'd be up. Guess you two were busy," Jill said. "Good morning. Did you see the sunrise? Gorgeous. Last night a success?"

Samantha and I lingered in one more kiss, then she ran over to Jill, shirt flying open, giving her a full-frontal look. Samantha wrapped Jill in a tight hug. Jill returned it. After a moment, Samantha looped her arm around Jill's and led her out of the kitchen. "Audition at noon. Want to see my tiger outfit?" Jill agreed.

I returned to the window, the city humming with its usual indifference, as heavy thoughts weighed on me. Each sip of coffee was bitter, mingling with grief. The sunrise now felt distant, stolen by death's intrusion.

Ava was gone, leaving questions and a void no answer could fill. Life had a cruel edge—snuffing out beauty and potential without warning.

I clenched my jaw. Justice for Ava became my singular focus. Every lead, every shadow, every whispered hint—I'd pursue it all until the killer faced the consequences. The flame of resolve burned hot, unrelenting. Justice awaited, and I'd seize it, one deliberate step at a time.

CHAPTER
THIRTY-ONE

Frank stepped into the office and dropped into the chair across from my desk. We shared a look that said everything and nothing.

"Hammett wanted to come with us tonight," I said, leaning against the desk. "But I told him no. They'd spot him a mile off."

Frank nodded. "True. But I don't think much will happen anyway. We don't even know who we're looking for. I've been digging into missing persons the last few months—there's a pattern. Girls vanishing out of strip clubs around the city. If Ava ties into that, would they risk hitting the same place twice? And why didn't Hammett mention the others? It's not adding up."

He got up and started pacing. Frank's frustration had a way of filling a room, sharp enough to cut glass.

"Sit down," I said, pointing at the chair. "You'll wear a hole in the floor. Look, Hammett works homicide, not missing persons. CPD's stretched thin, and he's a loaner. Hell, normal businesses can't hire, let alone the cops. Who wants to carry a badge these days? Not me. He may know more, but he won't show his hand. Doesn't owe us the truth—and he sure as hell won't give it."

Hammett was a cop, and cops guarded their cards like they were made of gold. I had the sinking feeling we were walking blind into something too big to handle.

Frank sat again, slow and heavy, as if the chair had dragged him down. The silence between us was thick enough to choke on.

Finally, I broke it. "What do you want to do? We check it out, see what shakes loose? Or we walk away and let Hammett figure out who killed Ava, Sophie, Brett—and maybe a dozen others?"

Frank sighed, shoulders slumping under the weight. "Ty, we don't have much to go on."

"What about Donavan Pharmaceuticals in Kickapoo? Or the Asian who nearly killed you?" My voice stayed steady, but my gut was replaying that night—Frank, half-dead, and lucky.

Frank's jaw set like concrete. "Now that's someone I want to find and stop. Okay. We go as planned. But we keep a sharp eye on Sam."

"Absolutely."

My phone buzzed before I could say more. Hammett's name lit the screen. My gut tightened—news from him was never good.

I answered. "Yeah?"

"We pulled a print. Not Ava's," Hammett said, voice clipped. "Coroner found semen. DNA's in the works. My money says it matches."

My throat went dry. A girl dumped was one thing. A girl used, then dumped—that was a different kind of rotten.

"What's next?" I asked.

"Kickapoo. Two bodies turned up on Donavan property. I've got warrants for the research center." His tone carried the grim thrill cops get when the case cracks open.

I glanced at Frank. One nod—that was all I needed.

"Fine. We'll meet you at KPD. Samantha's got an audition at noon. She and Jill are going. If Sam works tonight, we'll have to cut out early."

"Works. See you there."

The call ended, leaving a silence louder than words. Ava was dead. Two bodies in Kickapoo. Donavan Pharmaceuticals sat at the center of it all.

No turning back.

Kickapoo waited—and whatever prowled in the dark, we'd meet it head-on.

CHAPTER
THIRTY-TWO

Tiffany slipped into one of Chicago's iconic Italian joints and claimed a window table. She wasn't here for atmosphere—though the vintage photos and clatter of plates painted a lively picture of the city's past. She was here for deep-dish.

When the pizza landed, its aroma rose up in waves—tomato, cheese, buttered crust. She cut in, the molten cheese stretching, and took her first bite. The crust was crisp, the sauce tangy, the richness unapologetic. One bite and she understood why people swore by it.

She pulled a sleek black notebook from her purse, flipped to her to-do list, and crossed out deep-dish pizza. One more box ticked.

The server hovered. "Finished? Or should I box it up?"

Tiffany smiled, savoring the moment. "Leave it. I might go in for another bite. It's that good."

A momentary pause accompanied the server's response. "Thank you. Perhaps another glass of wine?" The waiter produced a crumb sweeper, its sleek metal scraping against the tablecloth to collect any fallen crumbs, a gentle chorus of precision.

"I would love one more glass."

As the line rang, Tiffany's stomach did a nervous little flip. *Should I have called Sammy the second I hit town?* Guilt nipped at her, but she brushed it off. *She's going to be surprised—hopefully the good kind.* She tapped her fingers lightly against the table, the rhythm betraying her jitters, then shook her head. *No use second-guessing now.* The phone buzzed in her ear, and she whispered under her breath, *"Here goes nothing,"* a crooked smile tugging at her lips.

"Hi Tiff, what's up?" Sammy's voice broke through the line, filling Tiffany's ears with familiarity and warmth.

Tiffany exhaled, her words flowing effortlessly, buoyed by the atmosphere of the restaurant. "Are you busy? Have time for a chat?"

"We just got done with something, and we're driving back home."

"Are you with Tanner?"

"No. Jill's with me, though."

"Hi Tiffany!" Jill's voice interjected.

"You're on speaker in the car. Tiger and Frank went to Kickapoo, working on a case. What's up?"

Tiffany's lips curved into a smart, teasing smile. "Hello Jill. You'll never believe what I'm eating right now. A deep-dish pizza."

A moment of silence stretched, heavy with the anticipation of Sammy's response. When she spoke, her voice held a mix of concern and curiosity. "Where are you?"

Tiffany's giggle, vibrant and infectious, danced through the room. The server returned, presenting her with a fresh glass of wine. She nodded her thanks.

"Chicago. Surprise! I'm here. Been here a few days." Tiffany's words brimmed with joy, carried by the sounds of serenity.

"Why didn't you tell me you were here? Why did you wait?" Sammy's voice held a blend of curiosity and concern, mingling with the rich tapestry of the surroundings.

With enthusiasm, Tiffany launched into an explanation. She weaved her tale, which formed a backdrop of her independence and adventure. She recounted her shopping excursions, the vibrant atmosphere of the Incognito Bar at the Remington Hotel, and the pulse of the city that had captivated her.

"Do you guys know that place I'm staying at? That bar is so cool."

In response to Tiffany's query about Incognito, the soundscape shifted as Sammy's voice held a mix of familiarity and caution. "Yes, we do. It's upscale, Tiff. Can you afford it?"

"I have been saving money, probably more so than you. And Dad kicked in a bit, you know, emergency money. Just in case." Tiffany's confident reply reverberated with a hint of amusement.

"Let me guess, that emergency was the Coach bag. Correct?" Sammy couldn't resist a teasing jab.

"Come on Sammy. You'd do the same thing."

Jealousy tinged Sammy's words as she playfully accused Tiffany of indulgence. "So, you ate like a pig, drank expensive cocktails, and shopped, blowing up Dad's credit card on Mag Mile. Anything else?"

"I went to a Bulls game."

"Is that the game they lost because the team couldn't keep focused on the game? Your aura of beauty was so distracting to them, they could only shoot 30% from the floor?" Sammy laughed.

"Be nice, Sammy. That sounds like fun, Tiff. Looks like you had a busy few days in our city," Jill said.

"I did, thanks Jill. And as a matter of fact, I'll have you know, a sexy, handsome gentleman bought most of those expensive cocktails for me," Tiffany said.

"Did you fuck him?" Sammy shot back.

"Oh Samantha, really?" Jill's gentle reprimand stressed the moment, as if the atmosphere itself had been momentarily hushed.

"Yes, I did." Amid their playful repartee, Tiffany dropped a blow, and a stunned silence settled over the conversation. The world seemed to hold its breath before Sammy's voice broke through, laced with a tinge of disbelief.

"Dish, Tiff."

Tiffany's emotions fluttered between delight and unease. She lifted her wine glass, her hand trembling just enough that the rim clipped her tooth. A splash of red dribbled onto her chin. Heat flushed her cheeks, but she dabbed it away with her napkin, recovering quickly. The lingering scent of wine marked the misstep, a small reminder of nerves she couldn't quite hide.

She cleared her throat, straightened in her chair, and caught the server's eye to signal for the check.

"I'll tell you when I see you. I want to meet Tanner and see Jill, of course. And the kids, Jill. I'd like to see the building you live in and the cabin..." Tiffany's words carried a rush of excitement.

Sammy's voice, mixed with practicality, cut through the soundscape. "Okay, slow down, Tiff. So, you'll be here a while, is that what you're saying? Look, we're on a case now, and tonight we are on surveillance. Look, we're about to head into the underground garage, so we might lose you. I'll call you tomorrow afternoon, and we'll work it out. You can stay with us, but..."

"Or me," Jill interjected, her voice warm and welcoming, added another layer to the conversation's melody. "I know how your sister can try your patience. You're more than welcome."

Tiffany's gratitude overflowed as she responded, her voice echoing with appreciation. "Thanks Jill, you're sweet. I can always just stay at the Remington. Call me tomorrow. Love ya."

"Okay, love ya back," Sammy said.

Tiffany ended the call, her heart lifted by Jill's invitation—a refuge of familiarity in an unfamiliar city. She gathered her things and walked to the exit, her heels clicking against the tile, drawing a few lingering glances as she passed.

Outside, the restaurant's warmth gave way to the rush of traffic, sirens, and the distant rumble of the El train. Her thoughts drifted to Frank, and a slow smile curved her lips. She was already drafting the message she'd send him—subtle, suggestive, full of promise. The city pulsed around her, its rhythm syncing with the anticipation rising inside. Whatever came next, she was ready.

CHAPTER
THIRTY-THREE

Hammett pushed through the glass doors of Donovan Pharmaceuticals like he owned the place, his team fanning out behind him. Frank and I followed in the slipstream, "consultants" in name, shadows in practice. The KPD was out in full force, badges flashing, latex gloves snapping, the air tight with tension.

Hammett's shoes clicked on the marble floor—too polished for a murder trail, but here we were. The office gleamed, sun slicing through tall windows. The usual hum of keyboards and half-whispered gossip cut dead as every head turned our way. Nothing makes a room freeze faster than cops with paper in hand.

The receptionist stiffened as we closed in. Élodi d'Aubert, her tag said, posture perfect until her eyes hit Hammett. Anxiety crept through her smile like a hairline crack in glass.

Hammett slid the warrant across the desk, voice steady, official. "Detective Hammett, CPD. We're executing a lawful search of these premises in connection with a homicide. We'll need security and management notified immediately. Cooperation's not optional."

She swallowed and nodded, French lilt leaking into her careful English. "Oui, of course. I—I will call zem now."

I leaned in just enough to soften it. "Relax, Élodi. We're not here to rattle cages. Just need eyes open. Anything unusual lately? Anyone out of place?"

Her hands fluttered, then stilled on the desk. "Non, monsieur... I 'ave not seen anyzing."

I gave her a small nod—whether she was hiding something or just scared stiff, keeping her calm was better than spooking her. Witnesses talked more when they weren't cornered.

Hammett motioned, and the machine started moving. Officers broke off in pairs, gloves on, shoe covers crunching soft against the tile. Evidence techs rolled in carts—paper bags, evidence tape, cameras. Every desk drawer opened got a photo before fingers went near it. Computers were logged, drives tagged for later imaging. The hum of the office turned into a chorus of zipper bags, camera shutters, and low muttering.

One officer read the search warrant aloud for the record, voice flat, while another noted the time in his log. Chain of custody wasn't a suggestion—it was the only thing that kept defense lawyers from shredding you on the stand.

Frank caught my eye as he leaned against the wall. He didn't need to say it—the scene had the smell of something off. Corporate gloss hiding rot underneath.

Hammett circled back to Élodi. His tone was colder this time. "We'll need access to the labs. Now."

She hesitated, eyes flicking toward the restricted hallway. Then she pressed the phone again, voice quick in French before she handed us off to a company guard—a broad man with a belly under his belt but the kind of authority that came from holding keys others didn't.

He swiped us through door after door, badge reader beeping with each green light. The hallways narrowed, clinical and sterile, silence broken only by radios crackling updates from KPD teams cataloging files and boxed samples upstairs.

The guard stopped at a set of steel doors plastered with red warnings and yellow biohazard triangles. He keyed in a code, swiped again, and the lock clunked heavy.

Inside, the labs glared with stainless steel. Counters lined with microscopes, centrifuges humming low, racks of vials under glass. Liquids in shades of blue and green shimmered under the fluorescents like bottled secrets.

We spread out. Evidence techs worked with tweezers and swabs, sealing samples in sterile bags, every item logged by time, initials, and badge number. Photos flashed, clipboards scribbled. Even dust bunnies were fair game.

I trailed the perimeter, eyes tracing the order of things—the lab benches too neat, the equipment calibrated, nothing sloppy. But underneath the shine, I felt it: this wasn't just science. This was a fortress with something ugly buried in the mortar.

Frank stood by the security guard, watching him more than the room. I knew that look. The guard wasn't just a guide—he was a wall. And walls meant something worth hiding.

The case had teeth now. Ava wasn't the only ghost rattling around Donovan's halls.

And Hammett? His face said it plain. He wasn't leaving until those ghosts started talking.

"York, Brannon. Over here," Hammett said.

I caught Frank's glance. We both hoped this was the crack in the case, the thread that might finally unravel the knot.

"What did you find?" I asked.

Hammett waved us into another lab. The sterile scent of disinfectants hit first, sharp enough to sting the back of the throat, mixed with the faint, sour whisper of chemicals.

The place was a temple of steel and glass—countertops polished to a mirror shine, equipment arranged like soldiers on parade. Fluorescent lights buzzed above, washing everything in white. The hum of refrigerators and ventilation fans never stopped, the kind of sound you only notice when you want silence and can't have it.

"This is Jenkins. He's in forensics," Hammett said.

Detective Jenkins bent over a workbench, loupe strapped to his glasses, a high-intensity beam pinned to his forehead like a miner hunting gold. The light swung toward us, blinding. I raised a hand to block it.

"Oh—sorry." He clicked it off.

"Anything?" Hammett asked.

Jenkins straightened, tugging at his gloves. "I'm afraid not, gentlemen. They keep clean labs here. Too clean. I'm impressed. But we've got a few more to check." He didn't wait for comment—just turned back to his work, the picture of quiet persistence.

The detectives moved with that same steady tempo, every step measured, every search methodical. But my patience was thinning. Ava, Sophie, Brent—still nothing. Clean labs, locked doors, polite lies. Too damn clean. A place this polished always had dirt, you just had to know where they swept it.

"Let's pay Mr. Donavan a visit," Frank said.

The double doors of the president's office loomed ahead. Plush carpet muffled our steps. Hammett didn't bother with ceremony—one sharp knock, then he pushed through like he owned the place.

Inside, it was mahogany and money. A desk that looked big enough to land a plane on, crystal decanters glinting in the light, and awards lined up like trophies from a long, indulgent war. Behind it sat Warren Donavan, gleaming like a silver set out for company, eyes tight despite the smile pasted on.

"Mr. Donavan," Hammett said, voice firm, steady. "I'm Detective Luke Hammett, CPD. I'm leading the investigation into the homicide of a young woman. I need to inquire about your whereabouts on the night of the incident."

Donavan leaned back in his leather chair, trying to look relaxed, trying to own the room. "Detective Hammett, I was at a charity gala that evening. Plenty of witnesses can confirm."

Hammett's expression didn't twitch. "I'll need the names of those witnesses, their contact information, and any documentation that verifies your attendance."

A flicker, just a flash, crossed Donavan's face before he masked it with another smile. "Of course. My assistant, Ms. Hayes, will compile the details and get them to you."

His poker face had a crack. Just a hairline fracture, but enough for me to see daylight through it. The man knew more than he was willing to say.

Hammett slid his phone out, thumbed the screen, and held it up. "Do you make these pills?"

Donavan slipped on reading glasses, studied the photo. He lingered longer than a man who had nothing to hide. "Can't say we do. I'd need the actual pill to run tests. I could tell you what it is, and whether it's manufactured here."

"We'll need a list of everything produced on-site," Hammett said.

"Anything you need," Donavan replied, his mouth curling into a sly smile that didn't reach his eyes.

I'd seen smiles like that before. They usually came with a knife tucked behind them.

Frank and I needed to start our way back to Chicago. We bid farewell to Hammett, who wished us luck and assured us of his availability should we encounter any difficulties during Samantha's shift at the Kinky Kitten. He emphasized that he would inform us promptly if he uncovered any pertinent information.

As we approached the front doors, we passed the reception desk where Élodi was seated, her troubled gaze finding mine. It was clear she had something left unsaid. The kind of look people give when their conscience wrestles with fear. Sensing it, I told Frank to wait and stepped toward her desk.

"Thank you for your assistance, Élodi," I said, offering a polite smile. "That is a lovely name. I assume you're of French origin?"

"Oui—oh, I mean yes," she replied, her accent slipping in with the words. "I was born zere, but moved 'ere for school and ended up staying."

Élodi, early thirties, had a quiet sort of charm—delicate features, bright blue eyes, a smile that softened the room's edges. With her sleek ponytail, librarian glasses, and unassuming grace, she radiated intelligence and kindness. She was the girl-next-door, if the next door opened onto Paris.

"My girlfriend and a colleague of ours have a deep fascination with French culture," I said, trying to build a bridge. "Our colleague, Jill, even spent a summer in France. I'm certain they'd love to trade stories with you."

Her lips curved up, tension loosening from her face. That was the trick: give people a safe lane to talk without the flashing red lights of the law crowding their rearview mirror. She didn't need cops sniffing around her visa file—she needed a way to be heard.

I slid her my business card. "Here's my contact information, Élodi. Feel free to reach out if you ever want to talk. I'm not a police officer, and I don't work for them. I can introduce you to my girlfriend, Samantha—she's about your age."

Her brows ticked upward, a flicker of judgment in her eyes. Maybe surprise, maybe curiosity. I let it hang. "She can show you around the city. It's much more vibrant and exciting than you might expect. It's not Kickapoo, that's for sure."

Élodi's grin grew wider as she studied the card. "Perhaps, Monsieur York. Bonne journée." There was a trace of hope in her voice—or maybe it was curiosity—but either way, it fractured her reserve.

When I rejoined Frank, I carried a quiet satisfaction with me. It wasn't much, just a card and a conversation, but sometimes that's the fuse that lights a bigger charge. In this line of work, the smallest steps often led to the loudest breakthroughs.

CHAPTER
THIRTY-FOUR

Samantha stepped into the spacious master bathroom, her adrenaline kicking up a few notches. Jill sensed it, as she followed her into the bedroom, her curiosity piqued, wondering what news Samantha had received.

"What is it?" Jill asked.

"Ty and Frank are on their way back, and the initial search was unsuccessful," Samantha replied. "It's a go for tonight. I'll need to get ready."

Jill nodded, understanding the importance of the mission they were undertaking. She looked Samantha straight in the eyes, her expression resolute. "I'm going with you tonight," she said, her tone leaving no room for argument. "You shouldn't have to face this alone. I've got your back, no matter what."

"Ty and Frank will be there, and I'm sure they can monitor me. Besides, I have this thing in my wrist." Samantha raised her arm, shaking her wrist, showing Jill where Frank had put the tracking chip.

"I know they can, silly," Jill said, her voice gentle. She knew Ty and Frank were capable, but her concern for Samantha's well-being couldn't be assuaged easily. She wanted to be there to provide moral support in case the performance went awry. "Besides, I'm not going to miss seeing you half-naked and bounce those cute tits I like so much."

They both laughed as the conversation took a playful turn. "You know you can see me naked anytime. Are you jealous I'll be around a bunch of half-naked girls?"

"No," Jill snapped. "Won't you be jealous that I'm checking out all those half-naked girls?"

"Of course. I'll just have to perform so amazingly that you can't take your beautiful green eyes off me." She kissed Jill on the cheek. "I guess if you're coming, we could go early. That way they won't scan your ID. I can also get a feel for the stage before they open. Ty and Frank could meet us there."

"Are you sure they would let me in?" Jill's voice was a little apprehensive.

"I asked at the audition, and Angie said it was okay. You'd still have to pay for drinks. They wanted to see a picture of you, and Angie was very interested in hiring you, just putting it out there."

"Forget it. Nobody wants to see this flabby body." Jill looked at herself, her ego waiting, and hoped Sammy would argue that point. And she did. Samantha responded with affectionate reassurance, countering Jill's insecurities with genuine compliments.

"I'd kiss, lick, and fuck that flabby body any day."

"Bitch!" Jill howled.

As daylight gave way to the encroaching night, Samantha sent a text message to Ty, arranging to meet at the club. They left their wine glasses in the kitchen, their arms intertwined as they stepped out, ready to face anything that awaited them.

CHAPTER
THIRTY-FIVE

Tires crunched over cold stones, the engine exhaling its last breath into silence. Nightfall stretched its fingers across the empty lot. He stepped out, leather shoes sinking into gravel, every movement deliberate, every breath a warning.

A subtle nod to the doorman, and he slipped inside. He moved with purpose—until he collided with someone. The man tipped a worn straw fedora, muttered an apology, and passed, eyes fixed ahead.

The hunt had begun. He descended into the club's depths. Darkness enveloped him, but the room's energy thrummed around him. Bodies flowed like currents, neon slicing through haze. His shoes whispered against the floor, silent, predatory. He didn't belong to the chaos—but he was here to navigate it, to watch, to measure, letting the night carry him forward.

"What the fuck are you doing here? Warren should have told you to back off. The cops raided the pharm today," Jayde bellowed, now in the Kinky Kitten Club, her voice reverberating through the room as she stomped her boot down, punctuating her words.

"We need a replacement. The shipment is only a few days away. We need to prep whoever we get and get them out of the country," the doctor retorted, undeterred by Jayde's display of power.

Jayde's voice was a low, venomous whisper, her eyes blazing with a fury that seemed to simmer just below the surface. "Quiet, you idiot! People can hear you. Fuck me. You realize you're going to be wanted by the cops once they get the ID on that jizz you left in Ava. You being here puts this entire operation at risk." She spat the words out. Behind the anger, Jayde's mind ran several steps ahead, calculating how to use this situation to her advantage. She wanted the cops to catch this guy and put him away for good, but she couldn't tip her hand just yet. The doctor's challenge cut through her thoughts, his voice a blend of desperation and rebellion. "No, you still need me. What about the examinations? Who's going to hand out the pills?"

Jayde's response was swift and cutting. "Not you anymore. If it wasn't for you, we wouldn't be in this mess. You should just leave." Her tone was sharp, seeping with disdain and contempt.

The doctor's jaw tightened, his nostrils flaring as his gaze sharpened, darkening with barely contained fury. Jayde could see the whirlwind of indignation in his expression, as if he was struggling to comprehend how she dared to speak to him that way. The doctor's fists curled, knuckles straining, a sharp tension coiling through his jaw and cheek.

Jayde braced for his response and just as he was about to snap back at her, his gaze shifted suddenly, drawn to a figure on the dance stage.

A young African American girl strutted onto the stage, her mere presence demanding attention. Her curly, voluminous hair framed her face. Clad only in a leopard print bikini bottom, her dance pole moves emitted a fierce energy onto the stage. The doctor spoke, breaking the trance she had on all of them. "She could be the one we need."

"You have to leave now, dirtbag. Go back to the fucking pharm." Jayde's patience had worn thin, and her tone annoyed. She noticed a few patrons looking their way. She didn't need this public exposure.

Warren had promised to handle the doctor, but Jayde knew she had to take matters into her own hands. Jayde moved with practiced ease, masking intent beneath casual motion. She brushed her knuckles across her chin, voice barely a breath. "Marty, we've got a problem."

Jayde seized the doctor by the collar, yanking him up from his chair to his feet. She signaled for Tiny, who swiftly approached. "Escort him out of here, and he's banned."

"Let's go," Tiny instructed the doctor, leading him away.

As Jayde made her way to the club's exit, her keen eyes scanned the crowd, always on the lookout for potential targets. Suddenly, her gaze landed on a woman who stood out from the usual crowd at the Kinky Kitten. This one wasn't the typical dancer or partygoer; there was something different about her.

She sat at a corner table, her posture relaxed yet alert. She wasn't flaunting herself or trying to attract attention. Jayde's interest piqued, and she took a moment to observe her more closely. Her attire was modest compared to the scantily clad women around her, but there was an undeniable allure to her presence. Her eyes, a striking shade of green, held a depth of intelligence and curiosity that Jayde hadn't seen in a long time.

This woman was a departure from their usual targets. The doctor typically went for the young, naive girls who were easy to manipulate and control. But this one... she seemed like she would be a challenge. And challenges, Jayde knew, often yielded the most interesting results.

Jayde continued to the exit, her steps measured and deliberate. As she passed by the woman's table, she allowed herself a brief, appraising glance.

Jill looked up, her eyes meeting Jayde's for a moment before Jayde moved on. There was a flicker of recognition, a spark of something unspoken passing between them.

With that, she exited the Kinky Kitten. The stage was set for a collision of fates, secrets, and ambitions that would soon entangle their lives in ways they couldn't yet imagine.

CHAPTER
THIRTY-SIX

Frank and I stood inside the Kinky Kitten Club, our senses sharp as switchblades, playing our undercover roles as security. Every muscle was keyed in, and our eyes scanned for trouble. The other bouncers threw wary glances our way—clearly unsettled by how fast we had inserted ourselves into the team. I counted heads, noted exits, and mentally mapped the cameras overhead, the blind spots, and the likely egress points. Nothing was safe tonight, and I wanted the first move to be mine.

One bouncer approached, extending a hand. "Don't worry about those guys," he said. "We've got plenty of coffee if you're interested. It comes in handy during the late-night shifts. Our number one job is to protect the girls. Most of the guys are decent, but yeah, we get some real wackos." My mental note: decent guys are manageable; wackos, that's where things go sideways fast.

Tiny posted me at the bottom of the stairs backstage where the dancers entered and exited the main dance area. It was the best vantage point in the house—eyes on the floor, on the performers, on every guy who looked like he might touch what wasn't his. And I won't lie, the ego boost was a nice side effect. Helping the dancers navigate the steps, catching their grateful smiles—it added a little shine to an otherwise dirty night. But I kept my mind running through escape scenarios: crowd surges, slips on the polished wood, someone pushing past the rope. Every angle was filed, every path calculated.

Meanwhile, Samantha—alias Kylie—was in her element. She had three solo performances, no private dances that night. She could focus on the stage, on the audience, teasing them just enough to bring them back. I kept my head on a swivel, noting the crowd's reactions, measuring distances, noting exits and barriers, tracking the staff's movement patterns. Every twitch, every glance mattered.

Kylie's first two performances were hypnotic. She moved like a breeze over flowers, her feet gliding, her body fluid and confident. There was fire in her gaze and freedom in her stance. Every arch of her brow, every sly curl of her serpentine smile, drew the audience in. I had to remind myself to breathe. Focus, York. Protect, observe, don't get lost in her magic.

Jill took her place at the edge of the stage, cheering like a queen at court. The chemistry between the two girls was intense, drawing tips from patrons, some even aimed at Jill. I filed it away as another variable in the human equation: chemistry can be weaponized, especially on the floor. My attention never strayed far from the crowd. I mapped the men who leaned too close, hands twitching, potential aggressors.

As Kylie's final performance approached, I wondered what information Samantha had gathered backstage, from the dancers or staff. Every whispered word, every glance, could crack this case wide open. I noted which entrances staff favored, which dancers had unsupervised moments, every small detail that might be useful later.

The DJ's voice cut through the club: "Give it up for Kitten Sheena!" Applause roared, and I extended my hand, helping her down the stairs. Then the DJ hyped the next act—Kylie's final performance of the night. Jill screamed ecstatically, feeding the club's energy. My job: keep her safe. Keep her in one piece. I ran the staircase in my mind: which step could trip her, where a fall could be fatal, how fast I could intercept if a guy lunged.

Samantha approached, hand out. I took it, steadying her as she ascended. My inner voice whispered: watch her, every move, every gesture. Lovely. Treacherous. Mine.

"Gorgeous," I whispered, my voice rough even to myself.

Samantha looked straight at me, lashes fluttering like butterflies, and the way she locked on made my chest ache. Neon light danced across her face, highlighting the freckles that dotted the bridge of her nose like stars. She drew a slow hit from her vape, the soft hum and gentle whoosh syncing with the pulse in my chest. Her breasts swelled against the tiger outfit, a subtle promise of the woman beneath.

Then she exhaled, white smoke curling, lips parting into that serpentine smile. "I love you," she whispered, drowned slightly by the din of the club.

She adjusted her tiger ears, winked, and said, "Showtime." Arching her back, tossing her hair, stepping into the spotlight. The crowd roared. My pulse spiked. My eyes scanned again—guys leaning too close, hands in pockets, anyone making a move. I planned intercepts, and mentally rehearsed evacuation routes.

She was in the light, I was in the shadows, but the whole place lay open in my mind, every corner accounted for.

Samantha left her mark on the club, and I stayed vigilant, taking in the electricity, cataloging the variables, ready for anything. Beautiful, dangerous, untouchable—tonight, she danced, and I ran the perimeter in silence, heart racing with pride and protective instinct in equal measure.

PART TWO

CHAPTER
THIRTY-SEVEN

The night pressed down, thick and heavy, when Frank barreled toward me, his footsteps cracking sharp against the asphalt. He looked like a man running from his own shadow.

"I've searched the entire club," he said, his voice low and urgent, the kind of rumble that carried bad news. "No sign of Jill. Angie saw her leave with an Asian woman, and she looked out of it."

The words hit like a sucker punch. My breath snagged in my throat, caught on a barbed hook. We'd been chasing the wrong ghost. All this time hunting for a man, and maybe the one pulling the strings wore a silk smile and sharper claws.

Samantha closed in, her face etched with worry lines that didn't belong on someone that beautiful. "Tiger, what's wrong? You don't look well." Her voice trembled, brittle with fear.

It nearly killed me to say it out loud. "Oh, baby... we think they may have taken Jill."

Her eyes brimmed, not from the cold night but from the hammer blow of my words. Frank's voice cut through, tight with stress: "Ty, what do you want to do?"

That was when the fire lit in Samantha. I saw it flare in her whole stance—the fear still there, but shoved aside by something harder, hotter.

"I'll tell you what we're fucking going to do," she said, her voice rising like a knife against the dark. "We're going to get her back. I don't care who they are, or what it takes—they don't know who they're messing with."

For a second, the night held its breath. I looked at her and thought: here's this woman, standing in heels in a goddamn parking lot, shaking off fear like rain off her shoulders, daring the world to push back. Part of me wanted to pull her close and protect her, shield her from the storm we were about to walk into. The other part knew better—Samantha didn't need a shield. She was the storm.

Behind the club, Jill stumbled forward, her limbs like rubber, while Jayde guided her through the dimly lit alley. Jayde's eyes swept the shadows, scanning for any sign of witnesses.

Jayde tightened her grip on Jill, grunting, "You're heavier than you look." Regretting the strong dose she'd given Jill, Jayde pressed on. She had about fifty feet to go before reaching the observation room, where Marty would help secure their new subject.

The sound of heavy footsteps thundered from behind them, and Jayde's senses heightened. She swept her gaze around, her eyes catching a figure emerging from the shadows—a tall man in a suit. The badge around his neck sparkled in the dim light, and his gun was drawn and pointed squarely at Jayde.

"Let her go!" His voice rang out, clipped and controlled. "I'm Detective Hammett of the CPD. Release the woman, and nobody gets hurt."

Jayde smirked. "Ah, a hero cop. Out of your depth. I'll keep the bitch, and you can keep your life. Deal?"

Hammett's jaw tightened. He'd seen standoffs like this before, but this one was different—Jill was too close, her life hinging on the smallest twitch of his finger. His training screamed: don't fire unless you're sure. He kept the muzzle leveled, breathing steady, forcing the seconds to stretch so he could talk.

"Release her now," he said, voice low but firm. "We can end this without anyone getting hurt."

For a second, he thought it worked. Jayde eased Jill to the ground. Relief washed through him—then her boot snapped across his wrist.

Pain flared. The Glock spun into the trash with a metallic clatter.

Hammett's heart slammed against his ribs. Shit. Empty hands now. His academy training kicked in: stay mobile, protect the body, control distance—survive until backup arrives. He raised his fists, feet shifting automatically into a defensive stance.

Jayde came at him fast. Too fast. She wasn't some street brawler—her strikes were surgical, fluid. Hammett blocked the first, took the second on his forearm, the shock numbing his hand. He tried to clinch, to tie her up long enough to wrestle her down—standard cop tactic. She slipped free like smoke, twisting his arm, sending a bolt of pain up his shoulder.

"You're good, Detective," she taunted, circling. "But you're no match for me."

Hammett grunted, jaw tight. "I've taken down worse than you." He drove forward, body weight behind a tackle, aiming to pin her against the wall. For a heartbeat, he had her—until her knee speared into his gut. Air blasted out of his lungs.

He staggered, fought to reset. Training drilled into him: survive the first thirty seconds, keep moving, wait for backup. His knuckles cracked against her ribs—a solid hit. She hissed in pain, clutching her side.

"Fuck!" Jayde spat. Then she smiled through the grimace. "Lucky shot."

Hammett's chest heaved, sweat stinging his eyes. "Won't need luck to put you in cuffs." He circled, hands up, mind screaming for an opening.

She pressed him, relentless. Every strike was faster, sharper than his. He blocked what he could, absorbed what he couldn't, gritting through the punishment. He wasn't winning—but he wasn't quitting either.

Then came the sound he needed: footsteps pounding pavement. Backup.

Jayde's eyes flicked toward the alley mouth. For the first time, hesitation.

Hammett seized it. His hand closed around a discarded pipe near his boot. He swung hard, connecting with her ribs. The crack echoed, and she reeled, staggering back.

He lunged, fist smashing into her jaw. She stumbled, dazed—but not broken.

Her gaze darted to Jill, then back to him. No words this time. Just the cold, precise choice in her eyes. She spun and bolted, disappearing into the night just as his backup rounded the corner.

Hammett dropped the pipe, chest heaving. His body ached from every strike, his lungs burned, but he forced himself down to Jill's side. Two fingers pressed her neck—pulse, steady enough.

"You're safe now," he muttered, voice ragged but sure. Even if he didn't fully believe it.

Ty, Sammy, and Frank ran up to Hammett, their faces stamped with worry and confusion. "Hammett, what happened? Is Jill okay?" Ty asked.

Hammett nodded, his voice calm but tinged with fatigue. "Someone drugged her, but physically, she appears to be unharmed. We need to get her to a safe place, then a hospital."

Samantha kneeled beside Jill, gently shaking her friend's shoulder. "Jill, can you hear me? It's Sammy." Jill's eyes fluttered open, her gaze unfocused as she tried to make sense of her surroundings. "Wha... what happened?" she murmured weakly.

Frank kneeled down next to Samantha. "We found you in the alley, Jill. Do you remember anything? Who did this to you?" Jill shook her head, "I... I don't know. It's all a blur. There was a woman, she was helping me... and then the detective and she fought... I don't understand."

Hammett intervened, his voice steady as he addressed Jill's friends. "We'll sort this out. Right now, we need to get Jill to safety. We'll take her to the hospital for a thorough examination."

Together, they carefully helped Jill to her feet, supporting her as they made their way out of the alley. They exchanged concerned glances, questions about the mysterious woman, the fight, and the danger that had befallen their friend.

As they reached Hammett's car, Samantha turned to the detective, "Hammett, who was that woman? Why did she want Jill? The other kidnapped girls were younger. Jill's a mom. The target was supposed to be me."

Hammett hesitated for a moment, choosing his words carefully. "I'm not sure, Sam. But I promise you, I'll do everything in my power to find out who she is and what she wants."

Frank added, "We won't rest until we get to the bottom of this. Whoever hurt Jill will pay for what they've done."

With Jill settled in the back seat, Hammett cast one last look at the alley, its secrets hanging in the dark like a promise of more to come. The fight had left scars, but answers waited ahead. As the car pulled away, a white panel Chevy minivan eased into the street and followed.

CHAPTER
THIRTY-EIGHT

Jill's eyes fluttered open, her gaze unfocused as she fought through the haze of the sedative. The sharp tang of rubbing alcohol and bleach lingered in the air, mingling with the sterile scent of latex and plastic. It was the unmistakable smell of a hospital—clean, cold, and impersonal. A middle-aged physician with a kind face and a calm demeanor entered, his white coat crisp as he flipped through her chart and checked her vitals.

"Jillian, my name is Dr. Delgado. We're going to run a few tests just to ensure everything is okay," he explained in a soothing voice. "Can you tell me how you're feeling now?"

Jill took a deep breath, her voice weak but steady, like a small flame flickering in the darkness. "I'm feeling better, Doctor. Still a bit groggy, but the dizziness is fading."

Detective Hammett stood by the bed, his brow furrowed with worry, his face filled with a deep concern. "Jill, do you remember anything about what happened at the club? Anything that could help us understand what led to this?"

Jill tilted her head, her brow drawn in thought as she tried to recall the fragmented memories from that night. "I... I was having a good time at the club. Watching Sam. But something must have been in my drink. I felt strange, disoriented. That's when a woman approached me. She said she needed my help, and she led me out of the club."

Dr. Delgado nodded, making notes on his chart. "It's not uncommon for individuals to slip drugs into drinks at crowded venues. We'll need to run toxicology tests to identify the substance, but it appears you were fortunate and only given a mild sedative."

The sound of beeping monitors intensified as a nurse entered the room, ready to collect blood samples and administer further tests. Dr. Delgado spoke with the nurse in hushed tones, discussing the necessary procedures.

Hammett leaned closer to Jill, his warm hand touching hers, his fingers wrapping around her wrist like a gentle vice. "We'll do everything we can to track down the person responsible for this, Jill. Your safety is my top priority."

"Thank you, Detective. I appreciate your help." Their gaze lingered, then Hammett squeezed her hand. Jill asked, "Where's my gang?"

Ty, Samantha, and Frank waited tensely in the hospital's crowded waiting room, the atmosphere heavy with worry. The fluorescent lights cast a peculiar radiance over the anxious faces. Ty checked his phone, hoping for updates.

Samantha leaned in closer to Frank, her voice a hushed whisper, like a secret shared between old friends. "I can't believe someone would do this to Jill. It's just... it's unfathomable."

Frank nodded, "We'll get to the bottom of this. Jill is like family to us, and we won't rest until we find out who's behind it."

As the trio continued their vigil, the hospital's atmosphere buzzed with activity, medical professionals tending to the needs of their patients. They were part of a larger tapestry, a community dedicated to healing and preserving lives.

Back in Jill's room, Hammett paced. "Jill, are you sure this woman said she wanted your help?"

Jill nodded, a lingering apprehension in her expression. "Yes."

Dr. Delgado returned with a smile on his face. "Jillian, I have good news. After the nurse takes a blood sample, I think we'll release you from the hospital. But I would encourage you to stay with family or a friend who can monitor your condition. We'll forward the test results to your primary care doctor, and you can follow up with them."

A wave of relief washed over Jill, and she looked at Hammett with gratitude. "Thank you for everything, Doctor and Detective."

"No problem, and call me Luke, please. Can I give you a lift home? Is there someone there who can monitor you in case you need anything?"

"No, my mom took the kids. I'll stay with Sammy and Ty. I'm sure they'll fuss over me."

"They're right outside. Put up a bit of a scene because they couldn't come in here. Rules are rules, as they say." Hammett smiled with a bit of unease. "Take care of yourself, Jill. If you remember anything else, no matter how small, please let me know. It could be crucial in our investigation."

With that, Jill was discharged from the hospital, the bright fluorescent lights giving way to the warm sunlight of the outside world, like a breath of fresh air. As she stepped through the doors, a bright smile spread across Samantha's face, her eyes shimmering with tears of relief and joy.

"Sammy!" Jill called out, with enthusiasm. The two friends' gazes met, and Samantha rushed forward, wrapping Jill in a warm and tight embrace. Tears streamed down Samantha's cheeks as she held Jill tightly.

Ty and Samantha linked their arms with Jill's, guiding her toward the exit. Their faces beamed with smiles, excited to have Jill back by their side. Frank, who had been waiting patiently, made his way over to join them.

Just as they were about to head toward their car, Frank's phone buzzed with a new message. He glanced down and saw a text from Hammett. *Let's meet tomorrow at your office.* Frank quickly replied with a proposed morning time. Almost immediately, his phone buzzed again, this time with a message from Quinn. *I'll call you this evening about what we found.*

By the late hour, Chicago had quieted into uneasy silence. Shadows stretched long across the deserted streets, cast by the high-rise condo that loomed like a sentinel. A lone streetlight flickered, spilling a jittery glow over its sleek exterior, while the city's pulse slowed to a measured, ominous beat.

Inside the condo, Frank paced the length of the carpet in his apartment, every step grinding into the silence. He was waiting on Quinn, waiting on answers. The pills sat heavy on his mind, their implications gnawing at him.

The phone rang. He snatched it up.

"Quinn, what did you find?"

Her voice came low, serious. "Frank, those pills... they're bad. A benzodiazepine derivative, like Rohypnol—but stronger. One dose shuts a person down. They go numb, unresponsive. Their will just... slips away."

Frank's grip tightened on the phone. "You mean they can be controlled?"

"Exactly. The drug wipes higher function. Victims become pliable—puppets. They'll follow commands without resistance."

A hot surge of fear and anger welled in Frank's chest. "We can't let this hit the street. We need to find whoever's behind it and shut them down. Lives are at stake. We almost lost one of our own tonight."

"Frank..." Her voice softened, then sharpened again. "Where did you get these pills?"

He hesitated. "We found them in a missing person's apartment."

Silence stretched, then Quinn exhaled. "You need to tread carefully. Whoever created this isn't small-time—they've engineered a weapon for the mind. Don't put your team in their crosshairs. That's what we were taught, wasn't it?"

Frank's jaw worked, but he forced his voice steady. "I hear you, Quinn. But we can't ignore this. Innocent people are at risk. We can't sit back and wait for someone else to clean it up."

Another pause. Frank felt his words had struck true—she had no quick comeback.

Finally, her voice tight with emotion, she said, "You're a civilian now. Protecting the public—that's my responsibility, not yours."

Her tone dropped, almost reluctant. "There's something I haven't told you. I've been reassigned. I'm no longer with the NAS. I'm now in the NCRD, the National Covert Response Division—handler role, in their ODNI division."

Frank straightened. ODNI—the Office of the Director of National Intelligence. The nerve center that coordinated America's sixteen intel agencies. If Quinn was under that umbrella, she wasn't just moving up—she was vanishing into the black.

"Wait," he said carefully. "NCRD? That's black-level territory. They only bring in top-tier."

Quinn hesitated. "It's a surgical unit. Small. High clearance. Specific targets."

Frank's gut tightened. He'd heard whispers before—rumors passed in smoky back rooms, operations redacted in classified reports. Kill squads.

"Not that unit..." His voice dropped. "You're not talking about the Raven Squad, are you?"

The silence confirmed it.

"Shit." He dragged a hand down his face. "I thought that was rumor. Ghost team. Quiet work. High body count."

"Then you know exactly what it means," she said flatly. "We have the manpower and the mandate. So please—stay out of it."

"That's a hell of a promotion," Frank said, though the words felt brittle in his mouth. "Sounds like you're where they need you. You'll have to tell me about it over a beer... someday."

But his tone hardened. "Don't expect me to walk away. You know more than you're saying. What's really going on here?"

Silence.

"We can help," he pressed. "You know we can."

Still nothing.

And that's when it hit him. The evasions. The clipped answers. The weight in her voice.

"Quinn..." he said slowly, like the words might trip a wire, "are you directly involved in this?"

She drew in a breath. When she answered, it wasn't a plea—it was an order.

"Back the fuck off, Frank. I've got agents in deep cover. Push any harder and you'll compromise the operation. You'll put lives at risk—including your own. And if that happens... I won't be able to protect you."

Frank sat in stunned silence, the warning settling like ice in his gut.

"For as long as I've known you, Quinn," he said quietly, "this is the first time you've scared me. And it's not what you're telling me that does it—it's what you're not."

CHAPTER
THIRTY-NINE

The silence in the office wasn't peace. It was punishment. It pressed down on me, harder than any fist, forcing me to replay the night in sickening detail: Jill, her eyes glassy, her body limp. And me—too slow, too blind to stop it.

Frank stepped in, the door creaking softly behind him. His expression softened when he saw me lost in thought. "What is it, Ty?"

I forced the words out, my voice rough. "I almost orphaned two kids the other night. Nearly got Jill killed. What have I done, Frank?"

His hand found my shoulder, steady and grounding. "It's not all on you. The info we had shaped our choices. We didn't see this coming. But we'll learn, adjust. Be more cautious next time."

Adjust. I can barely breathe without thinking of what could have gone wrong.

"Frank, I don't know if I can do this anymore. I'm putting everyone at risk. I should've known better."

He held my gaze. "We're a team. Risks come with the job. We protect each other. What happened to Jill was terrible, but fear can't stop us. We can do better, and we will."

Better. I hope better is enough.

The office door opened again. Hammett entered, his presence a reminder of what we'd survived.

"Did anyone at the station ask about your injuries?" I asked.

"I told them I broke up a bar fight," he said, his tone flat. "How's Jill?"

"She was back to herself by the time we got home. Samantha stayed with her in the guest bedroom. When I left this morning, they were peaceful."

Peaceful. For now. But nothing lasts.

Frank filled Hammett in on the alley, on Quinn's call. The mention of the drug—a mind-altering, obedience-inducing chemical—made Hammett's eyes harden. This is bigger than any of us imagined.

"I think we should get a warrant and search the club," Hammett said. "If we find evidence, it sends a message."

Every word felt like a weight on my chest. Each step from here could tip everything.

We traced the connections—the mysterious Asian woman, the scattered hints. My pulse picked up. This isn't theory. It's real. And I can't afford to misread a single move.

"That's it," I said, standing. The words tasted like iron in my mouth. "York Investigations steps back. Someone hired us to find Ava. She's dead. Hammett, you have all our intel. Our participation ends here."

Frank's persistence cut through my resolve. "Ty, let's meet later. Walk through it. Discuss possibilities. How can you say no?"

I gripped the edges of the chair, trying to anchor myself. I can't. I have to hold the line. For them, for Jill, for Ava.

"My name is on the door," I said, voice steady but heavy. "I get final say."

Silence stretched, thick as smoke. The room seemed smaller, the stakes closer, almost tangible. One mistake... one misstep... and it all comes crashing down. Every heartbeat felt like a countdown. The investigation, our people, the fragile lives hanging in the balance—everything depended on what we chose next.

CHAPTER
FORTY

Samantha leaned against the doorjamb of our bedroom, watching me like she could read the worry etched into my shoulders. She wore my dress shirt, the fabric draping softly over her curves, buttons undone just enough to hint at skin.

"We all need a break," she said, voice low and steady. "I know you're feeling guilty about the club, but we can't let it consume us."

I nodded, letting the words settle, a thin shield against the gnawing guilt. Jill's night hadn't been her fault—or ours—but that didn't make it easier to swallow. I should have seen it coming. I should have done more.

Jill had gone home and was recovering, Samantha said. She'd been shaken but was finding her balance again. Dinner at La Lumière de Paris later would include Samantha's sister Tiffany, visiting from Florida. Normalcy. That's what we need—even for a few hours.

I stayed in the office most of the day, juggling calls from contractors working on the office building. The project was nearly finished, a rare win in a string of messy days. Classical music hummed softly from my playlist, a thin veil over the churning thoughts in my head. Every ring of the phone feels like a test. Every notification, a reminder we're not done.

I also drafted a job posting for a receptionist, knowing Jill needed relief from her endless juggling act. Samantha and Jill would handle applicants—they had the eye for it, and frankly, I didn't. I'm good at breaking things. Let them fix the small stuff.

Finally, I called Robert Fields. Executive assistant to the governor, a man accustomed to decisions that rattled bones and shook worlds. I figured he'd have perspective—or at least a sanity check.

"Ty! How the heck are you?" His voice crackled with energy, bouncing off the walls of my anxiety.

We traded pleasantries, but I steered quickly toward the serious. Condensed the case, asked if York Investigations should step back.

"That's a tough one, my friend," he said after a pause. "I'm sure Frank's ready to go full throttle and bust some heads. But you're doing right—taking a step back, assessing."

"Thanks, Robert. I know you've got a lot on your plate."

"Before you go," he said, his voice lowering, the weight behind it impossible to miss. "Ted's not running for governor next election. He's pledged to support me."

Shit. That's a game changer. "Wow. You know I've got your back and my vote. Congrats, man."

"Appreciate it. Not public yet, but tell Frank."

I hung up. Talking to Robert helped. And the news? Shocking—but if anyone could pull it off, it was him. Someone actually navigating chaos. Unlike me, spiraling here.

I refocused on work. My phone buzzed. Randolph.

"How can I help you?" I answered, trying to keep the tremor out of my voice.

"Hey, Ty! How's it going? Thanks for the report—we won the case! Celebrating tonight, everyone's invited."

I imagined the chaos: laughter, glasses clinking, music pounding. Not now. Not in my head. Focus. "Not sure we can make it. We'll see."

"Outstanding! Hey, tomorrow we need a fourth for pickleball. Indoor courts, and the bar girls... Whoa! They wear next to nothing. It's gonna be great," he said, laughter like jagged glass in my calm.

I bristled, forcing politeness. Ignore him, Ty. Focus. "Randolph, I don't play pickleball. I'll pass."

"We'll teach you. Just come for the scenery," he chuckled. "Might have a couple of jobs for you next week."

"Great. Send them over."

A few hours later, Samantha poked her head into the office, soft smile holding back the worry I knew she carried. "Time to get ready, sweetie," she said. Relief washed over me. Finally. A pause. A breath. A moment of normal before the next storm.

The facade of La Lumière de Paris stood poised in the dying light, rustic stone and wrought iron softened by a bright awning, the French flag above flapping in a faint breeze. Inside, the room breathed with character—soft French music, the scent of fresh baguettes, murmurs in lilting accents. It felt like stepping onto a cobblestone street in Paris, and yet the tension under my skin reminded me we were still in Chicago.

The host led us to a small banquet room tucked away from the restaurant's hum. Samantha draped her jacket over a chair, her movements precise, calm, but there was a weight behind her eyes I couldn't read. She knows I'm still on edge. She can smell it, probably feels it radiating off me like smoke.

"I'm surprised we have a room to ourselves," I said.

"Can get loud in the main area," she offered, her voice low. "This way's quieter, and we can move if we need to. So, where did you and Jill sit for lunch that day?"

Memory snapped sharp. Jill and I had come here a while back, when Samantha was out of town. Turned out, it was a test—one she and Jill had set up. Nothing had happened, but the guilt still lingered, even now. I'd stayed loyal to Samantha, and in the end, things worked out.

"That table over there," I said. Samantha raised an eyebrow, a slight teasing curve of her lips. She touched my cheek, leaned in, kissed me. Short, sweet, a tether to sanity—but the moment broke as Jill entered, Hammett behind her.

"Oh, come on. Can't you two keep your hands off one another?" Jill teased. Her tone playful, but I sensed the tension under the surface. Hammett shadowed her, professional, polite.

Samantha motioned for Jill to sit. Hammett took the jacket from her, draped it neatly over the chair. Jill's smile was soft, warm. Samantha's eyes met mine, eyebrows lifted. Confusion flickered between us. What's going on here? Did I miss a memo?

Jill hugged me. Samantha received a kiss on the cheek. Small gestures, but every one of them screamed subtle cues of alliance, affection, hidden layers. Hammett's presence wasn't just courtesy—it was a statement.

"Hammett, good to see you," I said, hand out.

"York, Sam, how are you?" His tone bridged the awkwardness. Smooth. Calm. Calculated. Exactly how I'd expect him to walk into a room like this.

Jill broke the tension. "I invited Luke as a thank-you. He took a few punches for me last night. Dinner seemed appropriate."

Relieved, I nodded. "Of course. Always welcome."

Baguettes arrived, wine followed, and we tried to settle. Conversation skimmed across sports, easy banter, but I wasn't listening. I watched. Samantha and Jill laughed between themselves. Hammett laughed louder, sharper. He edged close to Jill without even knowing it—or maybe he knew exactly what he was doing.

Samantha leaned close. "Tiger, are you playing nice with the detective?" She didn't wait for my answer. "Tiff's on her way. Hopefully alone."

And then she appeared—Tiffany. Samantha's sister.

Samantha all but floated to her, smile bright but edged, a grin that didn't quite reach her eyes. Hugs, laughter, Jill slipping in to greet her.

And she was alone.

Relief loosened the knot in my chest. No entourage. No baggage. No new drama.

"Tiffany, this is my Tiger—Ty. Ty, my sister, Tiffany."

"Finally. Nice to meet you," I said—polite, steady, watching her eyes, reading the micro-expressions as we shook hands.

"Nice to meet you." She shot a look at Samantha. "Not bad, Sammy," Tiffany said playfully.

With the introductions complete, Samantha turned to her sister. "Tiff, red or white?"

"White," Tiffany replied.

Samantha took her sister's arm and departed, leaving Jill standing beside me.

"How are you, Ty?"

"Fine," I said, hiding the tension coiling in my chest.

"No, you're not. Let go of last night," Jill said.

"You could have died. Are you on a date with him?" I blurted, protective instinct blazing.

"Ty, he helped. I owed him. Don't know if it's a date. Kids, business, Samantha, you—they're priorities. Let's get through tonight." Her hand on my arm grounded me, but my mind raced. Every detail matters. Every expression, every pause, every half-smile—it's a puzzle I need to solve before the night detonates.

Jill left to join Tiffany. Unease settled like a stone in my stomach. I reached for my phone to text Frank, but he stepped into the room first.

"Frank! What are you doing here?" Tiffany's voice rang out, disbelief cracking the air.

I froze. Sparks of shock and alarm coiled tight. Frank and Tiffany. No. No way. Not possible. I've been blind. My pulse hammered. Samantha's eyes widened. Jill's gaze darted, confusion etched deep.

Frank looked at me—a flash of caution, and then a grin, too easy, too comfortable. Tiffany approached him, arms wrapping tight around him. Lips met in a kiss that wasn't casual—it was intimate, claiming.

Samantha stiffened. Fury radiated off her. Jill's face fell, disappointment carving itself deep. Goddamn it. This changes everything. Everything.

Time stretched. I tracked every flick of their eyes, every brush of a hand, every subtle inflection in tone. Sparks, tension, anger, confusion—all compressed into the small banquet room. Frank and Tiffany weren't hiding it. They were owning it. And the rest of us? Spectators to a revelation that would crack the table, crack the night, and maybe crack something in us too.

I clenched my fists under the table. My chest burned, my mind raced. This is more than a shock. This is a grenade. And I'm sitting in the blast zone.

CHAPTER
FORTY-ONE

Samantha's pupils narrowed, lips pressing into a thin line. Tiffany shifted under her sister's gaze, skin slick with unease. Samantha's probably stewing because she hoped Frank would end up with Jill, not Tiffany. And now? Chaos. Jill maybe leaning toward Hammett, Frank locked in with Tiffany, and me, stuck in the middle, trying to read the room without tripping over my own thoughts.

Without a word, Samantha hooked Tiffany's arm and steered her toward a quieter corner.

When Frank started to follow, I lifted a hand—halt. Instinct, not thought. Some things had to settle before a single word was spoken.

"Just give them a minute, Frank," I said. He nodded, the tight lines on his face softening slightly. "Let's grab a drink."

The bar was a refuge from the whirlwind. I requested high proof bourbon, dark and biting, the kind that left a trail in your chest and reminded you were alive. The bartender, a solid man with a thick beard, poured two generous shots and slid them across the polished wood. Ice clinked against glass, a tiny percussion to match the rhythm of my pulse.

Frank leaned in, voice quieter now, more reflective. "I had no idea Tiffany was Samantha's sister. Met her at the Incognito Bar. Amazing woman. I knew it was short term—she was heading home in a few days."

I nodded, swallowing a sip that scorched my throat. "I get it, Frank. No need to justify. But I want to apologize—for snapping about the case, for pulling rank like that. Didn't belong there, and I don't want it lingering between us."

Frank's eyes met mine, steady and unflinching. "Old friend, that's not going to get between us. Let it go. You have every right to pull rank. That's how we built this team."

Shoulders loosening, I let a small exhale escape. "So... we're good?"

"Yes." Frank clapped me on the back. "Now, tell me how to navigate talking to Sam about me slipping it to her sister without detonating a bomb."

The bourbon worked its way through us, burning and warming in equal measure, and when we returned to the table, the tension hadn't vanished, but it had softened. Hammett intercepted us at the door, shaking Frank's hand while launching into a debate about the Bulls' latest game. Samantha's gaze met mine, a small, knowing smile passing between us. We've weathered storms before. We'll survive this one too, if we remember to listen, to be honest, and to stay a little loose when everything's tightening around us.

We moved into the room, aware of the shifts in energy, the glances, the unspoken calculations at each table corner. Loyalty, patience, and restraint—the tools of survival at a table full of emotions. The night was far from over, but for now, there was a fragile truce, held together by bourbon, familiarity, and the quiet knowledge that some things could be managed, if only carefully.

Jill's eyes sparkled with mischief. "What a night, huh?" she said. "I thought I'd be the one with the big surprise when I walked in with Luke." She gestured toward Hammett.

I chuckled, trying to lighten the mood. "Yours was just the appetizer. Frank and Tiffany? That was the main course."

Her expression softened, concern threading through her eyes. "Feeling better?"

I shook my head. "Not really. It all just seemed to fall apart," I murmured. Her hand brushed my arm, warm and reassuring.

"Here's an idea," Jill said, her voice gentle. "Take a few days, go to the cabin. Sammy will be busy with her sister. Office construction will be done soon. We'll come see you in a few days. Tiffany wants to see the cabin. I'll bring the kiddos—they'd love it. A day trip. Then when you come back, it'll feel like a fresh start. I'll keep the place running, keep everyone in line—including our girl. And I promise not to get kidnapped."

I let the thought sink in. Pine-scented air, crisp and clean, the quiet hum of nature surrounding the cabin—solitude sounded like salvation. "Maybe Samantha needs me here," I said, hesitant. "I don't want her thinking I'm running away."

"Trust me, Ty. Samantha understands. She worries about you too. This could be your chance to recharge and get some clarity."

Her words lingered, a small beacon cutting through the chaos. Jill's suggestion was tempting—an escape from the whirlwind, a chance to breathe.

Jill caught Samantha's attention and outlined the plan, then went to find Hammett.

"Tiger, that's a great idea," she said, her voice softening with concern. "Honestly, I'm a little worried about you. Tiffany's going to want to do all kinds of things you probably won't, and you'd just be moping around the house and office anyway. Go. Relax."

"You won't feel like I'm abandoning you? Are you okay with Tiffany and Frank?" I asked, searching her face.

"Not at all," she said, leaning close. "Tiff and I can drive out there in a few days. And don't worry—I'll be all worked up and ready to play." A serpentine smile slid across her face. "Tiff is an adult. She can fuck who she wants. I'm over it."

The evening drew to a close. I relayed the plan to Frank, who nodded in understanding and agreement. He would take Samantha home, then Tiffany back to the Remington for her last night there. Hammett offered to escort Jill safely home.

Coffee in hand, I stepped out into the cool night air, the city lights casting long shadows. For the first time in days, I felt the pull of solitude, the promise of clarity, and the fragile hope that a few days away might help me face whatever came next.

CHAPTER
FORTY-TWO

I drove through the countryside as night settled in, the back roads winding like black veins through the fields. The silence pressed in too heavy, too close. Out here, there should have been peace, but I couldn't find any. Every mile gave me more room to think, and thinking was the last thing I needed.

My headlights carved narrow tunnels of light through the twisty roads. The fields on either side were freshly plowed into raw rows—stark, bare, stripped to the bone. The land was honest, but its honesty cut deep. It reminded me of last night—everything ripped open, nothing left to hide behind.

Samantha's wreck drifted back into my mind. Twisted metal, her body battered, her fire refusing to go out. She liked to joke that our "real" first meeting was in the cabin, right after she split my lip with a left hook. Truth was, I kept replaying that night on the road instead. If I'd been slower, even by a heartbeat, I wouldn't have her now. That thought stayed with me like a stone in my shoe—always there, always grinding.

The case gnawed at me, too. The Kinky Kitten Club wasn't just sleaze and shadows—it was poison. Drugs crawling into the streets, rot spreading no matter how far I drove from the city. I could smell it even out here in the clean air.

And then there was dinner. Frank and Tiffany. Jill's face when she realized. Samantha blindsided, her anger simmering just beneath the surface. Every expression at that table replayed like a broken reel, looping until I wanted to drive straight into the dark just to make it stop. We were tangled now, knotted together, and I was dead center, pulling the rope tighter.

I thought of Samantha again. She was my anchor, but even anchors slip if the current's strong enough. Trust holds—until it doesn't. I told myself we'd weathered storms before, that we'd weather this too. But even that lie sounded hollow in the car.

By the time I reached the cabin, the dark felt thicker than usual, the silence less forgiving. I texted Samantha that I'd made it safe, though the word "safe" didn't mean much anymore. I poured bourbon, heavy-handed, and sank into the armchair. Soft jazz floated in the background, a low hum that smoothed the edges just enough.

For the first time all day, I let myself breathe. The fields and roads hadn't calmed me, but here, in the cabin, the walls held the quiet steady. Not peace exactly, but something close enough to pretend for a while.

I started the day with a purpose. First came the yard, making sure it didn't look like a hermit lived here. Armed with clippers and a rake, I trimmed back the overgrown bushes, cleared the flower beds, and hauled away the debris the wind had coughed up over the weeks.

By the time the sun had tilted past noon, I'd moved on to chopping wood. The ax bit clean through the logs, each strike rattling up through my shoulders. The smell of sap and bark clung to me, sharp and grounding, the kind of honesty the city didn't know anymore. By mid-afternoon, the pile was high enough to earn me a quiet nod of satisfaction.

When hunger crept in, I thought about dinner. A mental list, then the drive into town—fields giving way to hills, the countryside stretching wide and bare. For a moment, I let the silence work on me. Even caught sight of the Donavan Pharmaceuticals building in the distance, standing there like a scar across the landscape. Couldn't escape it, not really. I loaded up groceries and headed back, convincing myself I was ready to play chef.

The call I'd been waiting for came just as I settled in. I answered with a smile in my voice. "Hi, baby, how are things?"

"Hi, Tiger. What have you been up to? Nothing bad, I hope," Samantha purred. That low, intimate tone of hers could stop a man mid-stride.

"Just fixing up the cabin. Getting it ready for you and Tiffany. Let her know she can stay the night. Bring a bag—no rush to head back."

"We might come out tomorrow. Jill's coming the day after with the rug rats. Have you seen Dash yet?"

Dash—the great horned owl that claimed the oak out front like a sentry. "Not yet, but I heard him when I pulled in last night."

Her tone shifted. "I talked to Tiffany about Frank."

I braced, knowing where this was headed. Frank and Tiffany weren't my business, but they were hers, which meant they were mine by proxy. She spilled everything—their first meeting, where it was heading, where it wasn't. Even the details I didn't want. I let her unload, dropped in the occasional reassurance, tried to steady the ground under her feet.

Then my phone buzzed. A new message. I glanced down—pictures. Samantha. One shot, then another. Lingerie, then nothing at all. My heart gave a jump.

"Not that I don't appreciate the show, but... why?" I asked.

"Oh shoot," she said, flat as a board. "I sent those to the wrong guy."

The floor dropped out from under me. "What? Who?"

A beat of silence—then laughter. It started soft and rolled until it filled the line. "Got you, Tiger. You know you're the only one. Those pictures are for you. For later."

"Later?"

"Well, Tiffany's out with Frank. I'm going to hook up with Jill. When the kids are down for the night—well, you know. So when you're missing me, needing to... relieve some pressure, you'll have something to look at. Like I'm right there with you." Her laugh curled through the line, wicked and playful.

I shook my head, half exasperated, half stirred. "You're thoughtful, all right."

We talked another half hour, then hung up. The cabin felt quiet again, but not the same kind of quiet.

When the moon climbed over the trees, throwing a pale glow across the clearing, I sat down to the dinner I'd made. Raised my glass in a private toast. To what, I wasn't sure—peace, survival, or just the lie of both.

The phone buzzed on the table. My pulse picked up. Maybe Samantha again—another photo, another tease to keep the night warm. But the number wasn't hers. Unknown. I let it drop to voicemail.

A minute later, it rang again. Same number. Not a telemarketer. I answered. "Hello?"

The voice was cool and deliberate, with a Parisian edge that cut sharp.

"Bonjour, Monsieur York. This is Élodi D'aubert. I have information on Donavan Pharmaceuticals. Can we meet?"

Her name slid into the room like a shadow under the door. Whatever quiet I thought I'd found in these woods bled out in an instant.

CHAPTER
FORTY-THREE

The rain pounded the roof of the abandoned church like a relentless drumbeat. Jayde stepped inside, her boots echoing on the cracked stone floor as she pushed the door shut behind her. The air was damp and cold, laced with the sharp tang of mold. A single bulb hung from the ceiling, its filament sputtering, casting a faint and unsteady glow across the decaying room. Shadows stretched along the walls like twisted fingers clawing for what little light was left.

Her trench coat clung to her body, soaked through, heavy as a shroud. Jayde ran her fingers through her dripping hair, shaking the strands loose from her face. The chilly draft slithered through them, raising gooseflesh along the back of her neck. Water glittered like tiny shards of glass in the weak light as it ran down her hands.

She drew in a long, steadying breath. It didn't help. Her heart thudded hard in her chest, the adrenaline twisting tight. Waiting wasn't something she excelled at.

"Raven."

Jayde spun on her heel, muscles tensed, ready. Quinn emerged from the shadows at the back of the room, tall and still, like she'd been there all along. She moved without sound, without hurry, as if the storm outside hadn't touched her.

"You're fucking late," Jayde said, her voice flat. "I don't have time for late."

"Easy, Raven," Quinn replied, calm and unreadable, the words floating out without urgency.

Jayde's frustration sparked hotter. "We can't afford to waste time. I should be in Canada already, retrieving the drugs myself."

Quinn shook her head, like a teacher indulging a stubborn child. "If the cartel finds out you're government, it's game over. We can't risk exposing you. You're too important to the squad." A pause. "Besides, we don't need Canada anymore."

Jayde turned away, pacing beneath the rusted overhang of the church's half-collapsed balcony. Her boots scraped against wet concrete, the sound sharp and brittle. "We needed that slut from the club last night," she said, anger tightening her voice. "But that cop crashed the party. What are the motherfucking odds? She would've been perfect."

"She was part of that investigations team," Quinn said, her voice a little colder now. "So I doubt it."

Jayde froze mid-step. "How do you know?"

"Classified," Quinn answered, cold and final.

Jayde didn't push. She'd been in this game long enough to recognize the tone. It wasn't just stonewalling. It was shielding. Whatever Quinn wasn't saying went beyond operational detail—there was something personal behind it.

"They'll back off now," Quinn added.

"Maybe," Jayde muttered, though the doubt simmered in her voice. She brushed her fingertips against the tender bruise hidden under her coat. "But one of them left a mark. I don't like being touched."

Quinn didn't respond.

The silence between them thickened, settling in like the mist clinging to the church walls. Jayde knew how this worked. Raven Squad operated outside the lines, buried deep within the National Covert Response Division, off the books with full deniability. Real names weren't used—identities were compartmentalized, need-to-know. Jayde didn't even know if Quinn was a first or last name. They were the government's invisible scalpel, sent in where diplomacy failed and conventional warfare was too loud.

And she wasn't just another agent. She was Raven One—the apex predator. A free asset with unrestricted authority and a kill count no one at the Pentagon would ever acknowledge. But even predators could feel the leash when it tightened. Right now, that leash had Quinn's hand on it.

"You're protecting them," Jayde said quietly.

"I'm protecting the mission," Quinn replied—too quickly.

Jayde clocked it. Quinn was lying, or at least bending the truth. Someone in that investigative team mattered, and Jayde could feel the unspoken line being drawn around them.

The rain finally eased, leaving only the whisper of water dripping from the broken roof. The biting cold glided through the gaps in the walls, nipping at Jayde's skin. She barely felt it. The pressure in her chest was heavier.

"You're hesitating, Quinn," she said, her voice sharp. "We've got the drug. The test results. Hell, even deniability. Why are we sitting on this? We're done with Donavan Pharmaceuticals."

"Because we're not ready," Quinn said, measured and steady as ever. "You know the rules. We move when Raven's Eye approves."

The wind howled through the jagged holes in the stained glass behind them. The sound carried like a warning. Inside the skeletal remains of the church, their voices were low, deliberate, carrying the weight of a confession.

They reviewed the situation in cold detail—supply lines, known players, secondary targets. Jayde's mind processed it all with surgical precision, but her frustration pulsed beneath the surface. Every delay, every approval she didn't control—it scraped at her like barbed wire.

"I'll contact you once I know," Quinn said at last, her voice final.

Jayde hesitated, her jaw tightening. She didn't like being leashed—not even by someone she mostly trusted. She gave a curt nod. No argument. Not now.

Quinn turned toward the cracked doors at the front of the church. Her silhouette dissolved into shadow as she reached the threshold.

"What about the doctor?" Jayde called after her, the words echoing off damp stone. "Did you relay my message to Raven's Eye?"

Quinn paused. For a heartbeat, the handler didn't move. Then she looked back, the barest hint of a smile ghosting across her lips. Jayde hated that expression. It told her nothing.

"Contain him for now," Quinn said. "Go back to Kickapoo. Marty is monitoring the situation here. I'll notify you when I get the go-ahead — no sooner, Jayde. We can't afford any mistakes. We transferred over to form this new squad; we can't fuck this up."

Jayde gave a short nod. She said nothing, letting the silence do the work. Her expression was blank, but her pulse thudded like a war drum.

She exhaled, the tension draining from her limbs like smoke.

"In shadows, we find the truth," she murmured.

Quinn's retort drifted softly back through the open doorway. "And in the light, we burn."

CHAPTER
FORTY-FOUR

I hesitated, turning the name over in my head. Élodi. The receptionist at Donavan Pharma. Pretty, if memory served. I'd given her my number, told her to call if she had anything useful. Now, it seemed, she did. Or claimed to.

"Yes, Élodi. What information do you have?" My voice came out guarded, flat as glass.

Her words tumbled in a frantic rush. "Monsieur York, I believe it would be better to meet face-to-face, not over ze phone. Please."

The fear in her voice pulled at me. "It's late. Would you rather do this tomorrow morning? I could swing by your place, or that diner on Main Street, if that's more convenient." I checked the clock—pushing past eleven. Too late for small talk, too early for trust.

"No, not my place or in town. I fear I may be seen. And I prefer to talk now, tonight. Do you know zat old, abandoned service station off Route 71?" Her voice cracked, trembling.

Frank's old garage. Isolated, no prying eyes. Also a perfect spot for a setup.

"I know the place." I said, working to keep my tone neutral.

"S'il vous plaît, Monsieur York. Please, I believe time is running out." She was pleading now, breathless. "You gave me your card, and I don't feel ze police will help me."

"Élodi, if this is serious, then you should call the police."

"Zey may revoke my visa. I don't want zat." Her voice shook, her French accent thickening with every word.

I let out a long breath. Part of me wanted to hang up and forget I'd ever answered, but I knew better. She was in something deep, and whether or not it was bait, I had to find out.

"Meet me at the garage. Thirty minutes past midnight."

"Merci, Monsieur York. I will be zere."

The line went dead. I sat back in the chair, staring at nothing. I could have ignored it, should have ignored it. But something in her voice wouldn't let me. A nerve I didn't know I had was still humming.

I stood, crossed to the safe, and spun the dial. The Beretta gleamed under the dim light, cold and ready. I loaded two clips, slid into the shoulder rig, and adjusted the weight until it felt like part of me again.

The bourbon sat there, dead in the glass. The room pressed in, silence cutting like wire. I'd stared down trouble before, more than my share. But this—this reeked different. Élodi's fear crawled under my skin, and no iron on my hip could smoke it out.

Jill's children, Preston and Caprice, slept soundly, like a gentle embrace. In Preston's room, the walls exploded with color and energy, posters of superheroes and planets plastered on the walls like a riotous celebration of adventure. His chest rose and fell rhythmically as he lay curled under a blanket, clutching a worn and faded teddy bear with a wonky eye. The bear seemed to gaze up at him with a fierce loyalty, as if guarding him from the dangers of the night.

Preston's desk was a mess of colorful chaos, scraps of paper and crayons scattered everywhere, a half-finished drawing of a rocket ship blasting off into the sky.

Across the hallway, Caprice's room was a haven of softness and warmth, fairy lights twinkling like fireflies around the space, bathing it in a mild radiance over the plush stuffed animals arranged just so on her bed. Her chestnut hair splayed across the pillow like a rich, dark waterfall, and her lips curved into a gentle smile, as if she were dreaming of magical tales.

Caprice's bedside table, on the other hand, was a neat and orderly space, books stacked like soldiers, each one a cherished friend in her imaginative world.

The night wrapped around the house like a lullaby—leaves whispering against the window, distant engines humming in rhythm with the children's breath

I mapped the place in my head—escape routes, blind corners, cover I could duck behind if things went bad. Every plan came with a worse ending than the last. I'd park behind the shop, come in on foot, stay low in the shadows. Eyes open, ears sharper. If the night went sour, I'd need an out.

The closer I got, the harder the adrenaline clawed at me. The rain had quit, but the air was still thick, heavy with nerves. Then it rose up in front of me—the service station. A tired shell of a building, sagging under neglect. Frank never kept it up to begin with. Paint peeling to rust, streaked with grime. A door hanging loose on one hinge, crying in the breeze. Windows cracked and dark, watching like hollow eyes.

And then the past hit me like a gut punch. Samantha—wild-eyed, fearless—erupting from behind that very shop. Uzi bucking in her hands, muzzle flash tearing holes in the dark. The sound of brass raining to the pavement, the stink of burning rubber, the smoke, the screams. She'd saved our skins that night. Saved me. God, I missed her. Was she asleep now? Or lying awake same as me, twisting with the same ghosts?

I blinked hard, dragged myself back to the now, and swept the shadows. Something was off. Too quiet. Too still. My thumb slid over the Beretta's safety. No second chances if this turned.

A creak. Close.

I froze.

Every sound was a hammer in my skull. My breath stopped short. Muscles wired, heart thudding, the silence itself felt alive—crouched, waiting to spring.

This was no meeting spot. It was too neat, too easy. A stage dressed in ruin. Élodi had sounded terrified on the line. But terror could be faked, rehearsed. I'd seen setups from the inside, and this had all the flavor.

The stink of mildew burned my nose. Doubt crawled my spine with every step. Still, I pressed forward.

If this was a trap, I'd walk straight into it—eyes open, finger on the trigger, ready to burn my way back out.

A silvery moonlight glow filled Jill's bedroom, illuminating the space with an ethereal light. In the background, soft jazz played, its smooth, sultry sounds creating a sensual haze that seemed to wrap around the room. Jill locked her bedroom door and approached the foot of her bed, her fingers moving with deliberate slowness as she unwound the tie from her robe. The soft fibers slipped from her skin like a lover's caress, leaving her exposed. Her eyes feasted on the enticing sight lying naked on her mattress.

As Sammy lifted the vape pen to her lips, the faint LED traced the curve of her face like a secret spotlight. Her mouth was shaped for sin, the top lip rising in a delicate bow that didn't need lipstick to draw attention. The pungent, earthy haze of marijuana curled through the air, mingling with the sultry trail of her perfume and the gentle mechanical purr of the vape. Her inhale drew a soft rise from her breasts—the movement slow, unhurried, like she wanted the world to watch but not touch—then fell with a long, deliberate exhale. Smoke curled from her mouth, a lazy tendril that danced upward before vanishing. Her lashes rested against her cheeks, and for a moment, she looked suspended in a trance—each breath she took whispering trouble in the dark, like every pull could make you forget your name.

"Up," came Jill's velvet command.

Sammy's lashes fluttered open, and she giggled, stretching like something feline before sliding off the bed. They stood bare before each other, skin lit by the low, pulsing amber of the bedside lamp.

Sammy passed the vape, fingers brushing Jill's with a spark that lingered. "Jill," Sammy murmured, her voice soft and playful, "the curtains are open."

Jill glanced at the window, a small smile playing on her lips. "Leave them," she said, her tone gentle yet firm. "*Que la nuit veille sur nous.*"

Sammy nodded. "Let the night watch over us. I like that." With a mischievous glint in her eyes, she turned back to Jill, the moment between them charged with anticipation and a hint of danger.

Jill inhaled deep, eyes locked to Sammy's with an intensity that didn't blink. Then, without breaking their stare, she leaned forward and pressed her mouth to Sammy's. The exhale flowed between them—warm, smoky, laced with something forbidden— until Sammy breathed it in like a secret only they shared. The contact lingered, not quite a kiss, more an initiation.

Jill's fingertip followed the curve of Sammy's jaw, light but certain. A trail of chills bloomed in its wake. Sammy shivered, though the room was warm.

Jill's body edged closer—heat radiating between them—as her hand slid over Sammy's shoulder and down the swell of her hip. Then pinned her to the wall with quiet authority, breath mingling, pulse quickening.

Sammy's knees weakened, a slow ache pooling in her center as Jill's energy wrapped around her like silk and smoke. She craved the pressure, the power, the way Jill looked at her like she already belonged to her. Sammy's nipples hardened like diamonds.

Then Jill's lips found hers—hungry, commanding, threaded with purpose. It wasn't tender. It didn't need to be. The kiss consumed, tasted, demanded. Sammy's heart hammered in her chest, her hands braced against the wall for balance, her moan swallowed by Jill's mouth.

Their bodies molded together, friction igniting skin against skin. Jill's hand explored, claiming without hesitation, leaving a trail of heat over the planes of Sammy's stomach.

Sammy gasped as a low growl escaped her throat, unfiltered and raw.

"I've been wanting to do this," Jill murmured, her voice dark velvet.

A flush climbed Sammy's throat. She didn't hesitate. "Then do it."

Jill's hand slipped down her thigh, fingernails grazing lightly, igniting nerves like sparks on dry tinder. The room fell away. Time unraveled. All that remained was breath, touch, and the collision of want they could no longer hold back.

Headlights slashed through the dark and ripped me out of my head. A car barreled into the lot—fast, reckless, tires howling on gravel. I didn't know what Élodi drove, but I pleaded it was her and not something worse.

The car skidded to a stop, nose angled sharp, dust curling around the beams. Élodi jumped out before the engine even settled. Panic clung to her like perfume, strong enough to sting my nose.

I kept my palm on the holster, thumb brushing the snap. "Élodi," I said, voice flat, measured. "What's going on? Why are you so scared?"

Her eyes darted everywhere—corners, shadows, places men could hide with rifles and bad intentions. She looked less like a woman with information and more like a rabbit flushed from cover.

"Zere is a place... not where you searched," she said, words tumbling fast, thick with her accent. "It is near ze labs, but apart. And bad zings 'appen zere."

Her panic might've been real. Or it might've been bait. My gut couldn't tell the difference, and that was worse than knowing.

"Where exactly?" I pressed, scanning the dark while she talked. My mind ticked through traps, crossfires, how easy it would be to stage a dead investigator here and call it an accident. "And what happens there? Is that where they cook the zombie drugs?"

"Non, Monsieur. Somezing worse." Her voice shook like glass about to break.

I felt my jaw tighten. "What?"

She spilled it fast, like the words burned her tongue. "Zere is a building, just off County Road Sixty-Two. Owned by Donavan.

I 'ad to do maintenance orders for ze place, and I would 'ear whispers. Zey called it ze apartments. Odd name for a lab, oui? When I asked, no one knew. Or pretended not to. One day, my computer failed, so I used a doctor's. I saw ze emails—photos of young women, my age. Zey call zem runners. Drugged, sent across borders to smuggle pills—small amounts, hard to trace. Donavan deconstructs ze pills, rebuilds zem, stronger. Zey control you, make you... compliant. Zat building is where zey keep ze runners."

Her words painted the picture clean—too clean. Like she'd rehearsed every syllable. Still, the hair on my neck rose. If half of it was true, Donavan wasn't just crooked—they were rotting from the inside out.

"Do they know you told me?" I asked, eyes never leaving the black corners around us.

"I don't sink so. But I fear zey will kidnap me, revoke my visa, deport me. Please, Monsieur York. I want to stay. Please 'elp."

Fear poured out of her, but fear was the easiest card to play. I weighed the odds, came up snake eyes. Still, I told her, "Follow me to my cabin." My mind spun through angles, plays, wondering if I was already be three steps behind.

Inside the cabin, her nerves sharpened — it felt like the walls were closing in. "Monsieur, I beg you—don't go alone," she said, tears brimming. "Ze Asian woman, Jayde. Jayde Kato. She is ze devil's warrior."

Her name hit like a fist to the gut. I'd crossed paths with Jayde Kato before. Cold steel wrapped in silk. A killer who smiled while she cut.

"I've run into her," I said, steady, though my pulse spiked. "I can handle her."

"I don't sink so, Monsieur."

Her words crawled cold under my skin, sharp as a razor. Maybe she was terrified. Maybe she was setting the hook. Either way, Jayde's shadow had just walked back into my life, and the air in that cabin was already choking tight.

Jill's warm breath skimmed over Sammy's skin as her lips traced the slope of her neck. "You taste incredible," she whispered, pressing tender kisses down to the hollow of Sammy's chest. Each touch lingered, leaving behind a shimmer of heat. Sammy's breath caught, her chest rising and falling against Jill's mouth, every whispered word of affection melting into her skin.

Jill's tongue teased over Sammy's sensitive peak, drawing a shiver that rippled through her body. Sammy arched in response against the wall, her breath breaking into a ragged gasp as Jill's mouth coaxed pleasure from her with patient, deliberate care.

A smile curved against Jill's lips as she looked up at Sammy's flushed face. She shifted her attention with equal devotion, covering her other breast in soft, reverent kisses. Sammy's fingers threaded through Jill's thick, dark hair, holding her close, unwilling to let her drift away.

Jill finally pulled back, kissing her way upward before sliding her knee between Sammy's thighs. The gentle pressure sent a tremor through Sammy, their bodies fitting together with unspoken urgency. Jill moved slowly at first, setting a rhythm with her knee that was more tender than hurried, every shift of her thigh drawing another shuddering breath from Sammy.

Their bodies pressed closer, movements building in intensity as they chased a shared rhythm. Sammy clung to her, her body strung tight with anticipation, every nerve alive, every sensation gathering into a wave about to crest.

"Jill," Sammy breathed, her voice trembling with need.

With a knowing smile, Jill murmured, "I've got you, petit chaton."

Jill's movements quickened, the rhythm carrying her higher and higher. "I'm close," Sammy gasped, her words sharp with urgency. Her whole body quivered, caught in the rush, until finally her cry filled the room, raw and triumphant.

Jill held her through it, watching the release wash over her like a storm breaking. Sammy's body trembled against her, face flushed, lips parted on a breathless gasp. Her eyes fluttered closed as the wave passed, leaving her limp between Jill's embrace and the wall, a picture of rapture and fierce, vulnerable beauty.

As I closed in on the building off Route Sixty-Two, Élodi's words wouldn't let go. *Apartments, not labs.* From the outside, she wasn't wrong. The place looked more like a low-rent housing block than a pharmaceutical wing—dim lights scattered, just enough to say someone was home, but not enough to feel it.

A massive oak loomed nearby, branches stretching like skeletal fingers, clawing at the night sky. Its shadow swallowed me whole. A good place to watch. A better place to hide.

The building itself was a slab of gray, dull as ash, sucking up what little light the moon gave. Windows thin and vertical, fortress slits. No welcome here. I pulled out my phone, zoomed across the angles—front, back, sides. No cameras. For a corporation like Donavan, that wasn't an oversight. That was intent. A place scrubbed clean to keep secrets dirty.

I vaulted the fence and dropped into a crouch, breath tight, knees bent. Luck smiled crooked—an unlocked window. My first break of the night. Or maybe bait, laid out for fools.

I peered inside: dark, empty. Small room. No movement. My gut warned me, but I slid the window up and slipped in, landing soft. The air smelled stale, shut-in. The walls were washed-out yellow, peeling at the corners. Furniture mismatched, hand-me-down junk. Like someone moved in to disappear.

I thumbed on my penlight. Its weak cone cut through the gloom, showing more of the same—sink and stove to the right, two doors off to the side. Bathroom. Closet. The place felt wrong, like a stage set abandoned mid-scene.

Something on the floor caught my eye. A crumpled scrap. I picked it up—paper gone soft from sweat. The handwriting was jagged, desperate. *Be careful, don't trust anyone – AC.*

Ava. Had she been here? Dropping breadcrumbs for whoever stumbled in after her?

The note clenched cold around my ribs. This wasn't theory anymore. I was stepping into her footprints, and whatever chased her might still be close.

I checked the bathroom—ordinary. Too ordinary. The closet held more—clothes, belongings, signs of life. Someone had used this place. Maybe still did.

My nerves stretched taut, violin strings ready to snap.

Then—footsteps.

Faint. Careful. Someone trying not to be heard. Coming from the hallway, closer with each beat.

I snapped off the penlight. Darkness folded around me. My hand found the Beretta, grip tight. Heart knocking hard, loud enough I thought they'd hear it through the walls.

The silence leaned in close, daring me to breathe. Whoever was out there wasn't a stranger passing by. They were coming here.

And I was waiting.

When Jill had first met Sammy at the WAR law firm, she'd known instantly there was something different about her. That first touch on her arm in Ty's office had been like a lightning bolt, awakening old desires Jill thought she'd left behind. Memories of Paris and Madame Dupont flickered in her mind—lessons in passion, control, and surrender. Now, Jill found herself offering Sammy the same slow initiation, guiding her with care.

Jill reveled in the rush of closeness and the subtle power that came with leading Sammy into uncharted territory. Watching her yield with trust—eyes searching Jill's, eager for the next step—was a heady kind of joy. Jill had never tired of that balance, the delicate dance she had once perfected abroad.

She could see Sammy learning to release her fears, to lean fully into desire. Each moment together brought her further out of her shell, more willing to test boundaries and discover her own strength. Jill wanted to show her the heights of intimacy, the thrill of passion that blurred the line between vulnerability and control.

There was no denying Sammy's allure. Whether draped in a sleek cocktail dress or curled up in jeans and a sweatshirt, she radiated a sensual magnetism that turned heads without effort. Her sharp wit, her husky voice, her serpentine smile—each piece of her was a promise, a temptation. It was no wonder Ty had risked everything more than once for her. Sammy carried an irresistible blend of fire, charm, and fragility that pulled people in like gravity.

Still catching her breath, Sammy whispered softly, "What are you thinking about? Where did you go just now?"

Jill's gaze sharpened back to her, a small, tender smile curving her lips. "Nowhere, baby. I'm right here."

She brushed a stray lock from Sammy's face, then took her by the hand, guiding her toward the bed. The edge met the back of Sammy's legs, and she sank down, breath trembling. Jill followed, slow and deliberate, climbing over her, bracing one hand beside Sammy's shoulder while the other traced her jaw. Their eyes met—warmth, trust, and something deeper sparking between them—before Jill closed the distance, capturing her lips in a kiss that deepened until their tongues tangled in a slow, teasing rhythm.

Her fingers drifted over Sammy's body with feather-light care, exploring as though each curve and contour was sacred. Sammy's breath quickened as Jill's hand brushed lower. Jill's voice, firm but gentle, cut through the haze. "Open."

Sammy obeyed. She spread her legs, knees rising in a quiet invitation, trusting Jill completely as she opened herself to her once more.

My grip on the Beretta clamped down like a vice, sweat slicking the metal. The footsteps had stopped. The silence pressed its ear to the door.

Slowly, I cracked it open.

A narrow slice of the hallway—enough to see a woman's back. Arms raised in a stance that wasn't surrender. In front of her, a man's legs kicked weakly, his strangled voice pleading through the chokehold.

I shoved the door wider and stepped out. "Let him go."

She did—dropping him like garbage. He crumpled to the floor, gasping. Then she turned, unhurried, as if she'd been waiting.

Jayde Kato. Jet-black hair bound tight, cheekbones sharp enough to cut, eyes like pits of tar. That smile—thin, cold, carved with cruelty—slid across her face.

"Well, well," she growled, voice like gravel. "Didn't expect you here, York. But I'm glad. Saves me the trouble of hunting you down."

The man wheezed, trying to crawl backward. I angled the Beretta at her chest. "Behind me, buddy," I barked.

Jayde's laugh slithered down the corridor. "He's not worth saving. He's the reason for all this shit."

I ignored her, pulling the man up by the collar. His eyes were glassy with panic, his breath sour with fear. I shoved him behind me and squared on Jayde. The hallway pressed in—walls narrowing, ceiling lowering, the stink of mold thick enough to choke.

"We're leaving," I said. My voice sounded steadier than I felt.

Her laugh deepened into a purr. "I can't let you do that. Tell you what—hand him over, and I'll let you crawl back to your little sugar-tits girlfriend. The one with the cat ears."

My teeth clenched. "Stay the hell away from her. Why'd you take Jill?"

Jayde's head cocked, feigned confusion sliding into amusement. "Who's Jill?"

"At the Kinky Kitten," I snapped.

Her grin widened, showing teeth. "She's more my type."

The man staggered as we backed toward the end of the corridor, every step tighter, heavier. The air reeked of dust and rot, pressing the life out of the place. I reached the door—locked. The man's whisper cut like a knife.

"Won't open."

Jayde's smile stretched wicked. "Trap sprung. Time's up, sweetheart."

I raised the Beretta, arm shaking but steady enough.

Jayde's eyes gleamed, hungry. "Looks like your big friend isn't here tonight. Just you. And me."

The walls seemed to lean closer, the hall shrinking down to a coffin. My finger found the trigger, but in that split second I knew—whatever move I made, there was no clean way out.

Jill's touch moved lower, with teasing and deliberate fingers, tracing through soft curls to the warm wet folds beneath, where a tremor ran up Sammy's spine. She lingered there, exploring with a feather-light rhythm that made Sammy gasp and arch toward her hand, her pulse quickening with the rush of sensation.

Sammy's breath hitched as Jill's body pressed closer, warm skin brushing hers. The scrape of Jill's hardened, pierced nipples across her chest drew a groan from deep in her throat, the mingled textures dizzying. Jill flowed gracefully onto the mattress, slipping between Sammy's thighs, close enough for Sammy to feel her heat and the whisper of her breath.

Sammy's lids fluttered, her fingers twisting the cool sheets as she surrendered to the moment. The air itself seemed charged, each ragged breath blending with the crackle of her own racing heartbeat. Beneath the desire, though, was gratitude—a rare, fragile certainty. Ty, with his rough edges and tender soul, knew how to steady and ignite her. And Jill—Jill was something else entirely. A siren, a guide, a force of beauty who coaxed her deeper into herself. Sammy loved the way Jill commanded her, yes, but also the way she made her feel safe inside the fire.

Anticipation coiled tight inside her. Jill was moving slowly, deliberately, and Sammy cherished it even as hunger clawed at her. She wanted more. She wanted everything Jill had to give. Between the two of them—Ty's storm and Jill's flame—she felt seen, desired, cherished.

Her thoughts shattered when Jill's warm breath brushed across the sensitive skin of her inner thigh, setting every nerve alight. Jill's touch hovered, deliberate, building the tension higher, until Sammy's body trembled with the exquisite torture of waiting.

I faced Jayde Kato, assassin, sadist, and predator in a human shell. My Beretta shook in my grip, the barrel steady only because I forced it to be.

"Back against the wall. Hands high. Move, and I put you down."

Her smirk curved thin and mean. "God, I love a man who plays tough." Venom in velvet.

I tried edging the man past her, but Jayde blurred into motion. One second she was grounded, the next she was sprinting sideways along the wall, a phantom. Her boot smashed into my ribs. The air blew out of me, the gun jarred from my hand. We crashed through a rickety table, wood exploding like shrapnel.

The Beretta clattered across the floor—gone.

"Bad move," she hissed.

I grabbed a jagged table leg, swinging wild. She slipped it easy, her kick catching my thigh, dropping me hard. Pain roared up my leg like fire racing a fuse.

The man tried to help. Jayde dropped him with a sweep of her leg, his skull thudding against plaster. Useless.

We stumbled into another room, my hand snatching a chair, shoving it between us like a lion tamer's whip.

Jayde prowled, eyes alight. "Looking for a lamp, old man?"

"Get out!" I barked at the man. "Call for help!"

Jayde lunged to intercept, but I slammed her back, just enough for him to stagger free.

Her finger jabbed at me. "You let Ava's killer go."

My voice shredded the air. "You killed Ava. Brent. Sophie. God knows who else."

Jayde's sneer faltered into something colder. "You really don't have a clue. That bastard killed Ava, fucked her corpse, shot Brent in an alley, and dosed Sophie till she flatlined. I don't need to lie."

The words rattled me, but the knife in her hand stole my focus. Serrated. Military issue. The kind of blade that wasn't for cutting—only tearing.

"Let's dance," she purred. "If you win, I'll let you watch your girlfriend and me lick each other."

"And if you win?" My voice sounded far away.

Her grin split wider. "I carve your asshole open with this."

The chair rattled in my hands as I blocked her flurry. Every strike sent shocks down my arms. Then steel kissed wood, and the blade bit through a leg like paper. The chair collapsed. Me with it.

White fire tore across my ribs as her knife found me—just a slash, not deep, but enough. I howled, hot blood soaking my shirt, the stink of iron filling my nose.

Jayde's laughter was merciless. "Got you, York. Payback, bitch."

I clutched the wound, staggering upright, lungs burning. The room tilted, my heartbeat hammering against broken rhythm.

She came again, knife flashing. I caught her wrist, twisted, skin slick with sweat and blood. For one second, the knife was mine. Then she spun, her judo grip snapping my wrist back. The blade clattered away.

We tore at each other—fists, knees, teeth. Each breath was glass in my lungs, each punch a sledgehammer. Blood spattered the walls, floor slick beneath our boots.

At some point, I didn't know if the blood was hers or mine. Didn't matter.

Jayde wiped her mouth with the back of her hand, grinning through the red. "I'm done playing, York. Last chance—fly or die."

My vision tunneled, black closing in. Muscles screamed. But somewhere deep, the old anger flared—the kind that kept me breathing when I should've stayed down.

I roared and threw myself at her with everything I had left.

Jill exhaled, her breath feathering over Sammy's heated wet skin, a spark racing through her body so sharp it made her toes curl. Sammy's face tightened, caught between need and restraint, her hips aching to thrust her pelvis in Jill's face. "Oh, Jill... please," she gasped, her voice breaking with desperation. "I... I can't wait."

Jill's smile was slow, indulgent, her eyes gleaming with control. She pressed Sammy's thighs open a little wider. "Beg, petit chaton," she murmured.

Sammy swallowed, her chest rising and falling in frantic rhythm. "Please, baby," she whispered, raw and trembling. "I need your mouth... now."

Jill answered with soft licks against tender flesh, sending a cry tumbling from Sammy's lips. The touch was gentle, teasing, but enough to set her body up from the bed. Jill held her steady, hands warm against her thighs, anchoring her through the storm.

Her tongue was skillful yet patient, each movement measured, each flick of her tongue designed to draw out the ache inside Sammy. Sammy's fingers tangled in Jill's dark hair, her body quivering under the mounting pressure. She rocked against the rhythm, helpless to the rising surge, every nerve alight.

A rivulet of liquid trickled down Sammy's inner thigh. She felt Jill's tongue catch it and trace it back to its origin. When Sammy's breath began to shatter, Jill suddenly pulled back, sliding upward until she hovered over her lover's face. Her chin glistened faintly with Sammy's essence, her expression both tender and commanding. She lowered her lips to Sammy's, their mouths meeting in a deep, consuming kiss. Sammy tasted herself on Jill's tongue, the intimacy as shocking as it was intoxicating, binding them closer than words ever could.

My eyelids creaked open like rusted hinges, every blink grinding against pain. The world seeped back in through a red haze—blood in my mouth, ribs screaming, breath shallow. Memory hit in jagged flashes: Jayde's fists, the copper taste of iron, the raw fact that I was still alive when maybe I shouldn't be. I quickly reached around to my backside, relief sinking in—my asshole still intact.

Through the fog, Samantha came to me. Not flesh—just memory. Her cognac eyes caught the light, her smile softer than mercy. I reached for her, trembling, desperate to feel the silk of her hair between my fingers, to believe she'd pulled me out of the wreck.

But the vision slipped. I was alone. Alone, broken, but still breathing. My throat clawed for water, my chest for air. I closed my eyes and summoned her back, her voice wrapping around me like a blanket in a storm.

And then—like a miracle—she was there.

"Tiger, it's me. Sammy."

The sound broke me open. I clutched her like a drowning man. "How—how did you find me? Are you okay?" The words rasped out like sandpaper.

Her answer flowed over me, steady, warm. Real or not, I let it stitch me together.

"I'm not alone," I growled, dragging myself upright on legs that wanted to quit. Every step was agony, but the fire inside burned hotter. Jayde hadn't won. Not yet.

Then a hand clamped my shoulder, spun me around.

"Samantha—?"

The name cracked in my throat.

It wasn't her.

It was Jayde. Eyes like stone. A grin sharp enough to cut glass.

I swung—weak, pitiful—but she caught me. Held me.

"Stay down, fuckface," she commanded.

The world tilted, dimmed. Her face was the last thing I saw, her smile the last knife she drove into me.

Then darkness swallowed me whole.

Every inch of Sammy was over-sensitized as she lay boneless on the bed. Jill traced a finger down her neck, then between the valley of her breasts.

"Do you know how beautiful you are?" Jill asked.

"Hmm..." was all Sammy could muster, still basking in the afterglow of their sex.

"God, I could eat you up," Jill said, looking at her with hunger and want.

"I think you already have." Sammy giggled.

Jill's finger traveled past Sammy's stomach once again to the soft patch of damp hair between her legs.

"What are you doing?" Sammy asked, quizzically.

"I'm gonna finish you off," Jill said.

"Oh, fuck me." Sammy rolled her eyes, closed them. She reached above her head, braced herself against the headboard. Her breathing grew ragged again.

"Exactly." The tip of Jill's finger probed Sammy's hot, wet opening. She circled gently, teasing, then slid inside. A soft groan slipped from Sammy's lips. The penetration filled but didn't stretch—gentle, controlled. Sammy whimpered, tightening her grip. Jill withdrew, then thrust deep and fast. Sammy's eyes opened, her serpentine smile spreading across her face.

"There's my girl," Jill whispered, smiling down at her.

Sammy raised her hips to meet Jill's thrusts. Jill worked steadily, moving deeper. With her eyes half-open, Sammy spoke in rhythm with the strokes. "Add...another...finger." Jill obliged, sliding another digit inside. A jolt of energy ran through Sammy's body. She whimpered, her heels digging into the mattress, hands reaching for leverage as Jill's fingers moved in and out, slow and deliberate. With each stroke coating Jill's hand with slickness, the wet sound filled the room.

Sammy's chest rose and fell quickly. She locked eyes with Jill, her gaze fierce. "Please, Jill," she begged. "Make me come." Jill quickened her pace, thrusting faster and deeper until Sammy cried out, spreading her legs as wide as they would go, desperate to be taken. The final thrust sent her spiraling, curving her back as pleasure ripped through her. She wailed, incoherent words tumbling free as her body shook.

Her thighs trembled, her abs tightened. She clung to the sheets, riding the crashing waves as long as she could—until she finally pushed Jill's hand away with shaking fingers. "Okay, okay," she gasped.

In the quiet aftershock, they clung to each other, breath uneven, their bond deepening with every heartbeat.

CHAPTER
FORTY-FIVE

"This is it," she said, her foot easing off the gas pedal as she pointed to a spot on the roadside. "Right here is where Tiger and I first crossed paths." Tiffany's eyes widened in surprise, and Sammy smiled, remembering the story of how Ty had rescued her from her car accident.

The sun's early rays filtered through the leaves, dappling the windshield with spots of luminous white. Sammy and Tiffany had embarked on their journey to the Kickapoo cabin with the dawn. She understood his need for solitude, the necessity of finding solace away from the recent turmoil. She still felt the hollow ache of his absence, longing for the moments they once shared—music, books, and television shows. The memory of lounging on the couch, legs draped over his lap as a silent plea for a foot massage, brought a hint of a smile to her lips.

"Your car was hanging over the edge?" Tiffany's voice held a mix of astonishment and concern, her hand brushing her cheek as if to physically react to the gravity of the situation.

"Yeah, and Tiger came to the rescue. He got me out and got me to the hospital." Sammy accelerated, navigating through a stretch of road colloquially known as the roller coaster among locals.

"I'm so glad he was there for you." Tiffany's smile radiated genuine warmth as her gaze fixed on her sister. "So, you like him? Despite the age difference?"

Tiffany's approving demeanor meant the world to her—it was validation of the connection she shared with Ty. The initial skepticism from family members regarding their relationship had been evident, but as people got to know Ty, the authenticity of their bond became undeniable. Sammy treasured the moments revealing Ty's true nature, and she rejoiced in her sister's acceptance of him.

As Sammy and Tiffany cruised down the winding road that led them through the heart of the small town, a vibrant tableau of autumn unfolded before their eyes. The sun played hide-and-seek through the boughs of tall oaks and maples, scattering speckled shadows over the road. With their windows down, the air was crisp, carrying the scent of fallen leaves and the promise of the harvest season. A gentle breeze whispered secrets through the leaves, causing them to rustle and sway in a synchronized ballet.

As they turned onto Main Street, the town's quaint charm unfolded before them. Brick and wood buildings bore the soft wear of time, flower boxes spilling with marigolds and chrysanthemums in fiery reds, oranges, and yellows. A breeze scattered crisp leaves across the pavement like confetti.

The town square buzzed with early morning life. A farmers' market was coming alive—wooden stalls brimming with pumpkins, apples, and gourds of every shape. Jars of honey glistened in the sun, and bushels of rainbow carrots and beets added to the harvest palette.

Sammy slowed the car, giving Tiffany a chance to take it all in. At a sidewalk café, patrons sipped steaming pumpkin spice lattes and nibbled fresh pastries. The sun glanced off vintage windows, casting prismatic reflections on the street. The clock tower, trimmed in autumn wreaths, chimed softly above it all.

With every turn, the town revealed its charm—less a place than a living postcard stitched together by nature, tradition, and the turning season. It was a moment neither sister would forget.

Sammy expertly maneuvered the car into the side driveway of the cabin. As they pulled up, a conspicuous absence caught her attention immediately—the lack of any other vehicles. Normally, Ty's trusty pickup truck would be parked here. She frowned slightly, her brow furrowing in perplexity. With a practiced hand, she located the garage remote and pressed the button, the door responding with a gradual ascent to reveal the interior. The sight of the truck parked safely inside only deepened her sense of bewilderment. Not to mention the addition of a car Samantha had never seen before next to the truck.

"That's strange," Sammy murmured, the lines of her forehead accentuating her concern. "Why would he have the truck in the garage at this hour? He usually uses it when he's here and leaves his car in the garage. And whose car is this?"

Tiffany offered a lighthearted suggestion, a playful twist to break the tension. "Maybe he decided to go on a quest for a pumpkin latte?"

Sammy chuckled, the sound a mixture of amusement and incredulity. "Tiger and pumpkin spice? Not a chance. He's more of a straight-up coffee guy. He'd have brewed up a couple of pots by now." A sudden realization struck her, her expression widening like full moons as the pieces fell into place. "I think I've cracked the case. He's sneaked out for breakfast with one of his buddies here. He promised me he was going to cut down on those big morning meals."

Tiffany chimed in with a dose of reason, attempting to balance out the unfolding theory. "Come on, Sammy. He's a guy, after all. A hearty breakfast every now and then..."

Sammy sighed, her disappointment clear in her tone. "Ugh, he was making progress," she grumbled, expressing a mixture of playfulness and genuine exasperation. The duo left the garage behind and strolled down the familiar path to the front door. An instinctual glance upward at the oak tree's branches revealed no sign of Dash, and a sense of mild disappointment swept over her. Today, something disrupted the routine.

At the front door, Sammy retrieved her keys and unlocked the cabin with practiced ease. She pushed inside—and froze.

A woman was curled on the couch, her wide eyes startled, mirroring the shock on Sammy's and Tiffany's faces.

Sammy's stomach dropped. For a beat, her mind spun: another woman, in Ty's place? A jagged thought cut through her—had he betrayed her, with Tiffany right here to see it? Heat surged through her chest, anger biting at her throat.

"Who are you?" Sammy's voice cracked the silence, sharper than she meant.

Tiffany gasped, clutching her sister's arm. "Sam—wait." She pointed toward the stranger's trembling hands, the way her body shivered. Fear, not seduction. Tiffany softened her voice. "She's terrified."

The woman spoke at last, her French accent trembling on every word. "Monsieur York is not here." Tear tracks shone on her cheeks.

Sammy's suspicion flared again. She stormed across the room, checking corners, eyes darting for signs of Ty. "Why are you here? Is anyone else in the cabin? What kind of trouble is Ty in?"

Élodi began to share her story, halting and afraid. Tiffany slipped into caretaker mode, busying herself with making tea, coaxing the woman into comfort. Sammy stayed planted, arms crossed, questions sharp, unwilling to let her guard down.

"Zat's all I know. I'm scared. Ze Asian woman, Jayde—she is dangereuse," Élodi concluded, her voice quivering as she took a sip of the tea.

Then she produced a folded note. Sammy snatched it, scanning the words. Ty's style, Ty's hand. Real. She passed it to Tiffany.

"Is that Ty's handwriting?" Tiffany asked.

The truth settled in Sammy's gut—Ty was in danger.

For a moment, the room tilted. Fear clawed at her ribs, the image of Ty hurt—or worse—flashing through her mind. Her throat tightened, chest burning. Then anger surged in, scorching away the panic. Nobody was going to take him from her. Not Jayde. Not anyone.

"Tiff, call Frank. Tell him what's going on. Ask how fast he can get here. I need to get ready," Sammy ordered.

"Ready for what?" Tiffany asked, even as she pulled out her phone.

Sammy didn't answer. She was already moving.

In the bedroom, she yanked a black backpack from the closet and unzipped a hidden compartment. "Hello, my friend," she whispered. The firearms training Ty and Frank had drilled into her kicked in. Loaded. Checked. Ready. A knife followed, slim enough to vanish into her pocket. Off came her blouse, replaced by a black T-shirt and leather jacket—armor, not fashion. By the time she slung the pack over her shoulder, her resolve was steel.

Back in the living room, Tiffany's eyes brimmed with worry. "Frank's on his way. He might be able to get a helicopter. I should come with you."

Sammy gripped her sister's shoulder. "No. Stay here with Élodi, in case Ty comes back. I need you to do this for me."

Tears welled, but Tiffany nodded. "You be careful."

The sisters hugged hard, the kind you don't want to let go of. Then Sammy strode out to her car, determination etched in every line of her face.

She was going after Ty. Whatever it took.

CHAPTER
FORTY-SIX

Sammy's car kicked up a rooster tail of fine dust as she veered off Route 62 onto a narrow gravel road.

The fall morning air was crisp, and the sun—still low in the sky—cast long golden beams through the thinning treetops. The gravel cracked and spat under her tires as she wound through the rugged stretch, jostled by ruts and dips in the terrain. A single crow flapped from a nearby tree, startled by her approach.

Her grip tightened on the steering wheel. Every second felt like a slow grind, each bump magnifying the anxiety swelling in her chest.

Then—around a sharp bend—the secluded building appeared, worn and silent under the pale sun. But it wasn't the building that made her foot slam the brake.

It was the car. Ty's car.

Parked slightly off-center, its body lightly dusted and dew-speckled from the night before, the driver's window partially cracked open. The engine was cold now—but it hadn't been cold long. He'd been here. Recently.

Sammy's heart slammed against her ribs. She pulled up beside it and killed the engine. For a moment, she sat still, breath fogging faintly in the morning chill, unsure if she should scream his name or brace for the worst.

She grabbed her backpack and stepped out, boots crunching the gravel. Fall leaves fluttered around her ankles as she approached Ty's car.

A fresh coffee cup sat in the cupholder—still upright, now empty, the lid askew. A candy wrapper lay crumpled on the passenger seat. No sign of struggle. Just... abandonment.

Dust streaks ran across the car doors, and faint boot prints—Ty's, she was sure—led away from the vehicle toward the building, then disappeared into the overgrown grass.

But there were other prints too. Wider. Heavier. Maybe someone else had been with him.

She opened the driver's side door and peeked inside. The familiar smell of his cologne clung faintly to the upholstery.

In the backseat, his jacket—half-folded, like it was tossed carelessly. The kind he wore when he knew trouble might be close.

On the passenger seat, his notepad. Pages bent, filled with quick, messy scrawl: names, numbers, and a hand-drawn arrow pointing to a word underlined twice—*apartments*.

Sammy's pulse quickened. That had to mean this place.

The trail of crushed grass and muddied footprints led to the side of the building. She followed, stepping lightly. The morning sun cast warped shadows through the high weeds. Her eyes darted. Nothing moved—yet something felt off.

She reached the door and tried the knob. Locked. She knocked softly, waited. Nothing. She circled toward a window, slightly ajar.

With care, she hugged the siding and peered in.

The inside was dim—lit only by pale morning light bleeding through grimy panes. It looked... empty. No Ty. No movement. But she didn't trust it.

She boosted herself through the window, landing in a crouch inside. Dust motes swirled in the beam of sunlight behind her. The air was stale but not ancient. The kind of stillness that came after someone just left.

She scanned the room. A metal folding chair sat beside an overturned cup. A boot print smudged on the floor near the back door. Ty's?

Then she spotted it—a scrape by the doorframe. Fresh. Someone had dragged something. Or someone.

Sammy's heart pounded louder now. Her voice whispered in her head: He was here. You're close.

Each step complained beneath her weight, the old boards whispering her presence. A faint, rusty sheen caught the light near the far wall. She crouched, fingertips hovering just above the mark before pressing gently to the floor. The surface was tacky, the color dark and brown at the edges. She lifted her hand—two fingers stained crimson.

Her breath hitched. The smell was faint but metallic, unmistakable. For a moment, she just stared, the room narrowing to that spot, to the blood clinging to her skin. Then she straightened slowly, eyes scanning the shadows, pulse hammering in her ears.

"Oh Tiger, what have you gotten into?" Her voice cracked the stillness, brittle with fear. The darkness gave no response, her words fading into the gloom.

Her hands trembled as she reached into her backpack and pulled out the cold weight of the weapon she'd brought. She inhaled slow. Focus.

She moved deeper inside. Curtains swayed with the breeze, casting restless movements across the walls. The stillness was stifling—like the room itself was holding its breath.

Something violent had taken place. She could feel it in her bones.

Sammy noticed a trail of blood leading out into the hallway. She followed with caution. The darkened doorways lined the corridor, their frames yawning open like mouths.

She tracked the trail, each step heavier than the last. The blood snaked and looped, a crimson breadcrumb path into the unknown.

It led her outside to a cracked path, where sunlight filtered through the trees, casting fractured shadows at her feet. In the distance, a weathered barn leaned against the horizon.

Her pulse quickened. She crept closer, ducking behind a tree. A woman emerged from behind the barn, mid-phone call, her voice sharp and charged. Sammy's skin prickled. Asian. There was no doubt—this had to be Jayde.

The call ended. Jayde drew a gun from her jacket and loaded it with chilling calm. With a fluid motion, she turned and entered the barn's mysterious depths. Sammy's breath hitched. Fear surged—but so did urgency. Ty was still out there. She was running out of time.

She inhaled, steadied herself. No backing down.

As she approached the barn, the world narrowed to sound and breath. The atmosphere grew dense, thick with tension—as if nature itself was bracing.

Then it hit.

A gunshot shattered the silence.

The barn erupted. Wings exploded from the treetops. Birds screamed skyward. The blast thundered through Sammy's chest, rooting her in place.

She couldn't breathe. Couldn't move.

Frozen.

Helpless.

Ty was out there—and she couldn't reach him.

She was too late.

CHAPTER
FORTY-SEVEN

I staggered in the dim barn, ribs screaming, every step a fight against blacking out. Movement stirred near the shadows—panic licked at my nerves, a phantom of the last fight replaying in my head. I braced for Jayde, but it was the man I'd tried to save in the apartment.

"Easy," he croaked, his voice a rasp. "You're alive. I'm a doctor—I work here."

Doctor. Murderer. Pawn. My thoughts tangled. Why had Jayde spared him? Why accuse him of Ava's death, then walk away? None of it tracked.

"We need out," I said, steadying myself against a beam. "Before she comes back."

He nodded, eyes darting to the barn door. "She could be watching."

My chest tightened as I approached the door to test the lock. Locked. My hopes deflated.

I found a discarded shovel and jammed it under the latch, trying to pry the door open. The wood groaned in protest. Then—footsteps. Fast.

"Someone's coming," I whispered.

The doctor snatched up a rusty tool, knuckles white. "I'll help," he said.

I nodded, setting the plan. "I'll distract her. You hit her when she passes."

The lock clunked. The door swung wide, light flooding the barn like a flash grenade.

Jayde slipped past my desperate lunge, her shoulder grazing my knife wound. Pain ripped through me—white, sharp, blinding.

The doctor dropped the tool, hesitation flickering across his face. Something in his eyes froze me. The air felt wrong—too still.

"Why didn't you attack her? What's this about?" My voice came out raw.

"Sorry," he said quietly. "I'm on her side."

"No. You're not." Jayde's voice cut through the light—cool, detached.

My rage spiked, but she didn't flinch. "I wasn't going to kill your friend, and I'm not going to kill you now," she said. "Your team... they all put up a hell of a fight."

Her hand barely moved. The gun came up, steady, deliberate.

"He killed them," she said—almost bored. "Ava. Brent. Sophie. I don't kill without orders. And I have them now."

My pulse hammered. The world tilted, her words slamming into me like static. Lies—layered on lies. "I don't believe you."

"I don't care."

The shot cracked through the barn.

The doctor's chest burst open, red blooming fast across his shirt. He jerked once, twice—eyes wide, mouth working soundlessly—

then folded into the barn straw. Blood spread beneath him, thick and dark.

I just stared, hollow. Another ghost added to the pile.

Jayde grabbed me and dragged me into the daylight. My body hit the dirt; pain detonated through me. She loomed above, a smirk curling, lazy and dangerous.

"I thought you don't kill without orders?" I blurted.

No emotion crossed Jayde's face. "I just got the call—the go-ahead. You're free, Mister York," she purred. "But breathe a word of this, and your government will ruin you. Or I'll come back myself. We'll have... another talk."

My chest heaved, each breath a knife. I would've agreed to anything if it meant seeing Samantha again.

Then—like lightning splitting the storm—I heard her voice.

"Hey, cunt."

Samantha stepped from the tree line, eyes alight with that serpentine grin, an Uzi in her hands. "Mister fucking Uzi sends his love."

Jayde and I locked eyes, same thought blazing between us.

"Run," I said.

CHAPTER
FORTY-EIGHT

Samantha grimaced, finger clamped on the trigger, and the Uzi roared to life. Bullets shredded air and timber alike, the barnyard erupting in chaos. I dropped flat, dirt grinding into my cheek, praying she didn't cut me down along with Jayde.

Jayde dove into the grass, rolling behind rusted oil drums. The rounds sparked against corroded metal, ricocheting wild. Samantha's hands shook with every burst—her aim lost in the storm. The gun clicked empty. Silence, except for her ragged breath.

She tore at her backpack for a fresh clip. Too slow. Too exposed.

"Samantha, stop!" My ribs burned as I forced myself upright, waving her down. "Please, baby, it's okay!"

"Ty, get behind me!" Her voice cracked, equal parts fury and fear.

I stumbled forward, grabbed the Uzi, and dropped it into the dirt. "Jayde isn't here to kill us. Not today. She's working for the government."

Jayde rose from cover, palms up, a smirk tugging at her mouth. "Damn, girl. Wild as a shotgun wedding."

"Fuck off," Samantha snapped, eyes wet and fierce.

I stumbled toward her, legs shaky, adrenaline still burning through me. I grabbed her face in my hands and kissed her—hard, desperate, grateful.

"You came for me," I breathed against her lips. "You shouldn't have risked your life for me."

Her touch lingered against my face, trembling just a little. "We're a team," she said softly. "We protect each other."

I kissed her again, slower this time—less about fear, more about everything I couldn't say.

"Can I get in on this?" Jayde's voice broke the moment like a bottle on concrete, snapping us back to reality.

I turned, swallowing hard, blood still pounding in my ears. "So all the deaths—Ava, Brent, Sophie?"

Jayde's smirk faded. "Again, that wasn't me," she said. "It was the doctor. He... made mistakes. I'm here to fix them."

"Donavan Pharma?" I demanded. "Working for the government?"

She nodded, wiping dirt from her cheek. "Yes. Developing a drug—military-grade, neuro-suppressive. But Donavan got sloppy. Slower than the competition. Another company beat him to the punch."

Samantha's eyes narrowed. "You expect us to believe that?"

"I didn't have a choice," Jayde admitted, her voice dropping. "Orders were orders. Don't like it? Too bad. Now you know."

Then came the thrum—distant, growing. Rotor blades chewing the sky. A Black Hawk dipped into the clearing, grass whipping in its downdraft.

From its belly stepped a woman—composed, deliberate, steel wrapped in poise. Jayde gave a small nod. The woman answered with clipped authority. "Get in, Jayde."

Jayde smirked at me. "York—you hit harder than you look. We'll tangle again. Maybe next time I won't be under orders." Then, to Samantha, a wink like a knife. "Save me a dance, tiger ears required."

The woman stepped closer, extending a hand. "I'm Quinn," she said, voice low, commanding. "Senior strategist. Raven Squad. Jayde's handler."

Samantha spat. "She nearly killed him!"

"And yet you're both alive," Quinn said, calm. "That was never her order."

I narrowed my eyes. "Then why?"

"To assess. Contain. Cut Donovan loose when he overstepped."

Samantha's fists clenched. "Innocent people were experimented on!"

Quinn's gaze flickered, but her voice stayed flat. "Unauthorized trials. That's why we shut him down. But he wasn't the only one. Others had the formula first. Bigger pockets. Fewer scruples."

I pressed. "So you let the bodies pile up?"

"We don't answer to paper." Her eyes hardened.

I leaned closer. "Who do you answer to?"

"Above your pay grade," Quinn said. A pause, a razor-thin smile. "No borders. No badges. Just results."

"Reassuring," Samantha grunted.

Quinn's eyes softened, just a flicker. "Not here to reassure. To make you understand why you're alive, and why you walked into hell and came out breathing. You've got instincts, York. Your team—tactical, resourceful. Surprised me. Impressed me."

"Recruitment pitch?" I asked.

"Not yet," she said, turning toward the chopper. "When the unseen rises, we'll call. And I expect you to answer. Tell Frank I said hello."

She boarded the chopper.

The rotors swallowed her, leaving silence behind.

I looked at Samantha. "Either we made a powerful ally—or painted a new target on our backs."

"Either way," she said, eyes narrowing, "the shadows just got a little deeper."

CHAPTER
FORTY-NINE

Two weeks had passed since the chaos at the barn, but inside the cabin, peace had finally settled. The fire crackled softly, casting golden light that danced across the walls and wrapped the room in a quiet hush.

Ty and Samantha sat on the floor, tucked beneath a plush blanket, bodies close. His arm rested over her shoulders, anchoring her in the calm they'd both longed for. The flames painted their faces, highlighting a connection that needed no words.

"Here we are again," Ty said, the pop and snap of the firewood punctuating his remark.

Samantha nestled closer. "Hmm, yes. No place I'd rather be."

"Did Tiffany make it home?" Ty asked, keeping the tone light.

"She texted me. Flight was fine, and she's back home. Misses us already. Tomorrow she'll be back at the office, getting Dad's campaign started."

"I hope her next visit is calmer—less drama," Ty mused.

Samantha broke the silence, eyes on the fire. "Jill called while you were out chopping wood. Had dinner with Hammett. Nothing serious—he got called into work halfway through and left her with an Uber ride home. Jerk." She gave a dry laugh, but it didn't hold.

"Someone better will come along. It'll piss me off, but…" Her voice softened, almost swallowed by the crackle of the logs. "For her—and for the kids—I'll have to let her go when that happens. And the whole Frank–Tiffany thing… what a mess."

Ty nodded, the weight of Jill between them grounding him. Samantha didn't look away.

"She said Hammett got enough evidence to lock Donavan up." She paused, letting the words hang in the air. "And shut the company down. I wonder if Quinn had something to do with Hammett getting the evidence?"

Ty exhaled slowly, feeling the tension ease a fraction.

"And the doctor—the one behind Ava… and the others," she continued, voice dropping, "finally named for what he was."

"It won't bring her back," she said, her fingers brushing against his arm, "but at least the truth is out."

A pause. She looked at him, eyes softening, resolute. "Quinn came through."

A long moment of silence followed, the fire crackling between them.

The ache rose in Ty's chest, sharp and fleeting. He tightened his arm around Samantha, steadying the moment before it broke.

"Frank wants a decision on bringing in someone new," Ty said, steering the talk elsewhere. "Reception, mostly. Free Jill up for more of the computer work—and to give her more time with the kids."

"We could check with the university and see if they have a student available for an internship until we find someone permanent." She didn't wait for an answer. "I'll call them tomorrow."

Samantha leaned into him, her body settling with his. He pressed a kiss to her hair, grateful for the quiet, for the fire, for the fragile peace in her shoulders.

Outside, the great horned owl lifted from its perch, wings stretching wide. It cut across the fading light, silent as a shadow. The last trace of day slipped away with it, leaving only the dark—and the things that moved within it.

CHAPTER
FIFTY

Bill Thompson's office in Chicago's Old Town neighborhood mirrored his chaotic way of life. Papers teetered in unstable piles on his desk, and the wastebasket spilled over with crumpled notes and empty coffee cups. The stale scent of cigarettes mixed with the acrid bite of burned coffee, hanging heavy in the room. Overhead, a few flickering fluorescent bulbs cast a sickly light, catching dust motes as they drifted through the stagnant air.

Bill's eyes fixed on the computer screen as the progress bar filled, signaling that the photos had finished downloading onto his flash drive. The light on the drive blinked rapidly, then stopped, and Bill ejected it with a satisfying click. He smiled to himself as he slid the drive into a tan envelope.

He picked up the phone, his fingers drumming a staccato beat on the desk as he waited for the call to connect. "Hello, Bill Thompson here. From Thompson Private Investigations. Is Mister Sanders there, please?" His voice was smooth and practiced, but a hint of anticipation crept in.

The person on the other end put him on hold, and Bill's gaze wandered to the envelope, his fingers tracing the edge of the seal. Ten seconds ticked by, then the line clicked back to life. "Bill, what do you have for me?" Mister Sanders's voice was urgent, expectant.

Bill's smile widened as he launched into his report. "I have about 500 photos, a few videos, and some audio that I think will help in your case." He paused, letting the weight of his words sink in.

Mister Sanders's response was immediate. "Excellent. Give me the rundown."

Bill leaned back in his chair, eyes glinting with satisfaction. "I have some good dirt here. And with the right lawyer, I think your odds are pretty good. Everything is on a flash drive, just as you requested. Nothing is on the internet or sent by email."

"Excellent. That's what I wanted to hear. I can't wait to see what you collected. Can you come over now so I can get you paid?"

The conversation wrapped up, and Bill hung up the phone, his mind already turning to the next step. He grabbed his sport coat, the worn fabric a witness to his years of service. The straw hat, his trusty companion, sat atop his head, its brim worn and faded.

As he descended the stairs to the street, the sounds of the city filtered in—car horns, chatter, the wail of sirens in the distance. Bill's eyes scanned the crowded sidewalk, lingering on the passersby. He wondered, not for the first time, if he was crossing some unspoken line by investigating another private investigator's service. But the thought was fleeting, dismissed by his pragmatic nature. All's fair in the investigative world, he told himself.

He opened the creaky door to his white Chevy panel van, the hinges protesting with a metallic groan. The interior was a mess, papers and fast-food wrappers scattered across the floor. Bill slid into the driver's seat, the worn vinyl creaking beneath him. He cranked the engine, the motor roaring to life, and pulled out into the crowded streets of Chicago. The city was a jungle, and Bill Thompson was just one of its many predators. York Investigations was in his crosshairs, set to crumble under the mountain of proof he'd spent weeks carefully collecting.

ACKNOWLEDGMENTS

To you, the reader, my deepest thanks. I'm grateful you chose to spend time in the world I've created. I hope this book gave you a few hours of escape, suspense, and enjoyment.

My sincere gratitude goes to Scribendi for their expert editing, which helped shape this story into the best version of itself. Any remaining errors—grammar, timeline, or otherwise—are entirely my responsibility.

To Miblart, for once again bringing my vision to life through incredible formatting and cover design. Your talent and creativity made this book shine.

To my wife, Debi, who not only fills my life with love and joy but also served as my proofreader, beta reader, and toughest critique partner. Your insight, patience, and honesty made this book stronger, and I couldn't have done it without you.

To my family and friends, your encouragement, support, and faith in my writing have been invaluable. Thank you for always believing in me and walking this journey alongside me.

And finally, to my granddaughter Cece—the smartest, sassiest, most unstoppable force I know. Sorry, kiddo, this book is strictly a twenty-one-and-up affair. I know, I know... you'll just have to wait... and imagine the chaos, the danger, and the drama until then. Consider it a long, tantalizing teaser.

ABOUT THE AUTHOR

Andrew Kenning is a storyteller at heart, crafting suspenseful thrillers that pull readers into the world of Tanner York and his crew. Born and raised near Chicago, he retired after 30 years in research and development and now writes from North Carolina.

Enter the Raven is the second book in his Tanner York Thriller Series. Andrew's wife, Debi, serves as his trusted proofreader and beta reader, helping shape the stories you love. When he's not writing, Andrew enjoys wildlife photography, keeping up with Chicago sports, and time with friends and family.

Discover more at DYKPub.com.

**TANNER YORK
AND THE
CREW WILL RETURN.**